ALONG *FOR THE* RIDE

ALONG *FOR THE* RIDE

RACHEL MEINKE

PENGUIN BOOKS

PENGUIN BOOKS

UK | USA | Canada | Ireland | Australia
India | New Zealand | South Africa

Penguin Books is part of the Penguin Random House group of companies
whose addresses can be found at global.penguinrandomhouse.com.

www.penguin.co.uk   www.puffin.co.uk   www.ladybird.co.uk

Published in Great Britain by Penguin Books in association
with Wattpad Books, a division of Wattpad Corp., 2021

001

www.wattpad.com

Printed and bound in Great Britain by Clays Ltd, Elcograf S.p.A.

The authorized representative in the EEA is Penguin Random House Ireland,
Morrison Chambers, 32 Nassau Street, Dublin D02 YH68

A CIP catalogue record for this book is available from the British Library

ISBN: 978–0–241–46064–1

All correspondence to:
Penguin Books, Penguin Random House Children's
One Embassy Gardens, 8 Viaduct Gardens
London SW11 7BW

For my Wattpad readers:
without you, none of this would be possible

LOS ANGELES, CA
CHAPTER 1

"Excuse me?" a voice asked behind me. I turned to see a young girl, a bright smile on her face. "Could you take our picture?"

Looking up, there was a life-sized cutout of Connor Jackson a foot away from me. He was wearing a white button-up and navy shorts, his brunette hair mussed to perfection. It looked like they'd added a little bit of sparkle to his brown eyes, his smile flashing a row of pearly white teeth. He sported the newest edition of Luxem shoes, which is why he'd been conveniently placed in the middle of the shoe store.

Standing next to the cutout was a group of teenage girls, all around the same age as me. And they were more than eager to pose next to the fake Connor Jackson.

"Of course," I said, taking her phone. I snapped a couple of pictures before handing it back to her.

"Thank you," she gushed, her eyes bright with excitement.

It was a very surreal experience to see a cardboard figure of my brother in a shoe store. It was even stranger to have a group of girls ask to take a photo with it.

"What's your favorite song?" I asked, unable to hide my smile.

"'Shades!'" she proudly exclaimed, and the other girls nodded in agreement.

Only the worst song that Connor had ever released. "Really?"

"Do you listen to Connor Jackson?"

"Only every day."

I felt a tug on my arm, and I turned to see my best friend, Jenica Terry, standing behind me. "We're going to be late!"

"It was nice meeting you!" I called over my shoulder, as Jenica all but dragged me toward the store exit.

Jenica's mom was waiting outside, keys in hand. "Come on, girls!"

I slid into the back of the minivan, followed closely by Jenica.

"Did you get something to eat?"

Jenica's mom was like a second mom to me. Due to my parents' busy schedule, Momma Terry was always the one to take me to soccer practice and games. We'd spent many long hours in the car, complaining about schoolwork and listening to Jenica gush about Connor while we laughed and rolled our eyes.

"Who were those girls?" Jenica asked.

"Connor Jackson fans."

Her eyes lit up. "Really?"

Momma Terry and I both let out a laugh.

"You girls are in need of a shower," Momma Terry said, with a shake of her head. "I can't imagine what state your uniforms must be in. That won't be a fun laundry load."

"We had a game this morning," Jenica said, laughing. "What did you expect us to smell like?"

"I didn't realize how terrible it was." She reached over and opened up the sunroof. "Luckily this is the last game of the tournament."

We pulled into the parking lot, the mall only a short distance from the soccer fields.

"I really hope we win," I said as the car came to a stop. "I can't handle making it to the championship game and then losing."

Jenica let out an annoyed huff. "And I can't handle being this incredibly sore for nothing."

We grabbed our soccer bags from the trunk before meeting up with the rest of the team.

"Where did you guys go?" Leslie asked, as we joined the rest of the team, who'd clearly hung around the fields between games.

I plopped down on the ground. "The mall."

Coach Jefferson laughed. "Did you finally get a pair of new cleats?"

I pulled my freshly duct-taped cleats out of my bag. "Absolutely not. A little duct tape and the soles are good as new."

"You missed the tournament tradition of Subway and gossip," Leslie said as we stretched, with a shake of her head. "Very disappointing."

"I'll make it up to you, I promise," I said, with a laugh.

"Captains, let's go," Coach Jefferson called out.

And that was my cue.

"Where's my midfield?" I called, as I backpedaled toward the goal.

I looked at Coach Jefferson, who flashed me a one. One minute left in this tournament. One minute before we'd claim victory.

Haley cleared the ball, landing it right at Jenica's feet.

"Come on, Jen!" I called out, using the bottom of my shirt to wipe the sweat off my forehead.

She dribbled around the stopper before passing it off to the outside left wing, sprinting up the field as the wing chipped it over the defense.

"Use your head!" I screamed.

Jenica jumped up, her head connecting with the ball and sending it into the corner of the goal.

I sprinted from my position as sweeper to the opposite side of the field. Jenica jumped into my arms, shrieking with joy. We took a moment of celebration before the ref ushered us back to our positions. This team was coming for us. As predicted, they sprinted down the right side of the field.

I backpedaled, "Contain!"

Monica stabbed at the ball, and the midfielder chipped it up to the forward.

That left it to a footrace, between me and Marci Adams, the star forward of the San Francisco Snakes.

I reached the ball half a step before she did, jumping up and headed the ball out. She collided with me in the air, sending us both into the dirt.

"You good?" Michelle asked, reaching out her goalie glove.

"Fine," I answered, gripping her hand and pulling myself up.

Marci stood up, glaring at me.

"Watch your back," she spat, storming back to her position right as the ref blew his whistle, signaling the end of the game.

Us: 2. Snakes: 1. That was a championship win.

"I would hug you," Jenica said, as I jogged off the field, "but you're covered in dirt."

I wrapped her up into a tight hug, letting out a squeal.

"You smell like BO!" she called, laughing as I squeezed her tighter.

Coach Jefferson reached over and offered up a high five. "Proud of you."

I joined the line of girls as we shook hands with the other team. Marci pulled back her hand as she reached me.

"Good game!" I called out to her, as we went our separate ways.

"Don't antagonize, Katelyn," Jenica said, steering me toward our bench.

I took off my shin guards, taking in the celebrations of our team as I stuffed everything back into my backpack. As Coach Jefferson congratulated us on winning the tournament, it finally hit. All of our hard work had paid off.

My grin widened throughout his speech, and I pulled everyone into a group hug as he finished.

"Katelyn!" Leslie screeched. "Jesus Christ."

"Get in here, Coach!" I called out. "A celebratory, mandatory, group hug!"

Amidst the groans and the complaints, I could feel the positive energy radiating from the girls as we cheered. And then suddenly I was at the bottom of a collapsed group hug.

"Get off!" I cried out. But I was unable to contain my laughter, the overall excitement of the weekend seeping through me.

"Medal ceremony!" Coach called out. "Come on, let's head over."

We traipsed to the medal tent, giggling and chatting about the game. Standing beneath the hot, non-air-conditioned tent, we were forced to listen to the tournament hosts drone on about the sponsors and how grateful they were. When you're hot and sticky and in close proximity to other hot and sticky people, the excitement dies down.

As we received our first-place medals, the picture-taking frenzy began. The most unflattering pictures always come from posttournament medal ceremonies, when you're all dirty, sweaty, and tired. But they're also the best ones.

The ceremony came to a close, and we began saying our good-byes. This was the last tournament of the season, with the upcoming summer focused on conditioning and team building before we started all over again. And I was going to be gone for all of it.

"You won't even be thinking about us," Leslie said. "You're going on the road trip of a lifetime."

"It's an overglorified bus tour," I corrected, "and I'd much rather be here with you guys."

"You're going to have fun," Monica argued. "Relax and actually let loose."

That *definitely* didn't sound like me. "I'll do my best."

"Is your dad on the way?" Jenica asked, as we walked back toward her car.

I checked my phone for the first time in hours, my dad having sent me a text nearly an hour ago that he was on his way from our home in Los Angeles to the tournament fields in Santa Monica.

"He should be here any minute," I said. "He's not really good at keeping me in the loop."

She folded her arms, her eyes flitting around the parking lot as we waited for my dad. "Are you watching the interview tonight?"

"It's apparently a family event," I said.

"I'm excited. Connor is so famous these days."

It was true. Connor had taken the country by storm after one of his YouTube covers went viral. People noticed his singing, and it wasn't long before he was in the studio, recording a demo track for which my parents fronted the money.

Before we knew it, Connor was sitting in a meeting room with Lightshine Records, his demo playing in the background. And now he was a walking, talking, pop star poster boy. It's been a whirlwind, to say the least. Everything about our lives changed: my parents quit their nine-to-five jobs to manage his career, my brother's songs are on the radio, his video for "Shades" has been viewed over two hundred million times and he's guest-starred in sitcoms and even appeared in movies. And now we're all going on a cross-country tour with Mackenzie Lewis, an up-and-coming pop superstar, and Skyline, my favorite band.

Out of the corner of my eye, I saw my dad's Lexus pull into the parking lot.

"He'll be proud of you," Jenica said.

"I bet you ten bucks he won't even ask how my tournament went."

"I'm sure that's not true," she said, unconvincingly.

"Yeah right, I've got to go."

"I'll call you tonight after the interview."

I flashed a thumbs-up before heading over to my dad's car.

"No, no, no," Dad said into his Bluetooth. "That's not the jacket we ordered."

I plugged my headphones into my iPhone, putting the right one in my ear and leaving the left ear open in case my dad decided to start a conversation with me. Closing my eyes, I let the Skyline song play as I leaned my head against the window. I'd seen Skyline via livestream when they played to a venue of thirty people in Beaufort, South Carolina, which was their hometown. They were four brothers who quickly rose up the pop charts after my brother promoted their album on his social media, which I may or may not have had a hand in.

"Why does he need to come in for another fitting?" Dad argued. "We already came in for a fitting and the wrong leather jacket was ordered."

My tournament went great, Dad. We won first place. Thanks for asking and engaging with me.

"Okay, okay," my dad muttered. "Let's get it done right this time."

Me? I'm okay. Tired and pretty sore. But it was all worth it, ya know? Since we won first place and all.

My dad hung up the phone, silence filled the car.

"Everything went well?" my dad asked. "You know, with the soccer and all."

A bubble of excitement sparked. It was more than I'd expected him to ask. "It actually went really well," I said. "We won—"

My dad held up a finger in the air as his phone rang. "This is Lorie; I have to go over schedules with her. Hold this conversation."

Closing my eyes, I let Zach Matthews's voice soothe my wounded ego. The hour-long drive was excruciating, and I couldn't get out of the car fast enough once we pulled up to the house.

"Katelyn?" my mom's voice called from the kitchen.

Ignoring her, I headed up to the second floor and locked my bedroom door. I ripped off my uniform, throwing it across my room. The only time he bothered to ask me about the tournament, it was interrupted by Connor's needs. Everything was about my brother these days. Connor's schedule. Connor's tour. Today, Connor's leather jacket fitting.

Connor freaking Jackson.

It was like my parents forgot that I exist too. I have hobbies and interests and do things that are outside of the Connor Jackson realm. Lately, though, nothing seemed to exist outside of the Connor Jackson realm.

I threw off my sweat-soaked bra and underwear and grabbed a quick shower. Then I lay down on my bed with a towel wrapped around my hair.

"Katelyn?" my mom's voice called through the door. "Are you going to join us for dinner?"

I hopped up off my bed, walking across my wood floor to crack the door open. "No."

She came into my room and sat on the edge of the bed. "I never got a text update after the last game."

"You actually want to hear about it?" I asked, as I eased myself down next to her.

"Of course, my love. Every detail."

"You don't even understand the game," I teased.

"Just the offsides stuff," she said, with a wave of her hand. "And, you know, the card system. And maybe the rules on hands."

My body melted into hers, like it did when I was a kid and upset.

"Your brother's interview is going to be on in a few minutes," she said. "Are you going to come and watch?"

As much as the Connor Jackson hype got to me, he was still my brother. And I was pretty damn proud. "Yeah, I'm coming."

"I kept a plate of lasagna warm for you," she said, nudging my shoulder. "And cooked a fresh batch of garlic bread right before you got here."

"For me?"

"Who else can eat an entire loaf of garlic bread by themselves?"

Mom led me downstairs to where my plate of lasagna and heaping pile of garlic bread waited. When I got to the couch, my dad was already seated, the TV on.

"Connor, grab your sister a TV tray," my mom said as she cleared a spot for me.

He glanced up from his phone. "Huh?"

"TV tray for your sister."

"Are her legs broken?"

Dad reached behind the couch, handing me a TV tray with a pointed look. "The interview will be on in a minute. Save the arguments."

I hadn't said a word.

"Connor Jackson," the reporter announced as my brother's face lit up the screen, and the live recording audience applauded.

"Did they have signs?" I asked. "You know, making sure people cheered for you?"

Connor flipped me off without looking away from the television. My dad gave me another pointed look. I deserved that one.

The reporter gushed over Connor and his accomplishments. "So tell me," the reporter said, leaning into him. "How does it feel to be headlining your own tour?"

"It's an honor. I'm so excited to share my new music with my fans."

"I've heard rumors of a worldwide tour on the horizon. Any comment?"

I choked back a laugh. This is the first headlining tour in his career, and there are already rumors of a worldwide tour?

"I'm taking it one tour a time," he said, with a laugh as well. "Let's start with the United States and see where it goes from there." He cleared his throat. "But a worldwide tour is definitely something I'd be interested in later on my career path."

The real-time Connor let out a groan. "That sounded so *scripted*."

"I didn't think so," Mom said. "I thought it sounded genuine!"

"It was scripted though, wasn't it?" I pointed out.

"It's not supposed to *sound* like it."

The interview continued for another ten long, excruciating minutes.

"After the commercial break, we'll hear 'Shades,' Connor's hit song!" the reporter said.

Of course it's "Shades."

"For your first national interview, I thought it went exceptionally well," Dad said. "Smooth talking, easy smiles, you really charmed them."

"I guess."

My mom looked over at me. "Katelyn? What did you think?"

"About the interview?"

"What *else*?" Connor asked.

I felt the bubble of anger stir within my chest, and I took a bite of the lasagna to help push it back down.

"I thought it was fine," I said. "Standard. Wasn't great, wasn't bad. Average."

Connor's lips pursed together, and for a moment I felt guilty.

"If you don't have anything constructive to contribute, Katelyn, then next time keep it to yourself," Dad said.

With that, any ounce of guilt I had washed away.

"I'll do my best."

"Here's Connor Jackson performing his hit single, 'Shades!'" the reporter announced. The camera swung over to the stage where

Connor was standing. It went off without a hitch. His voice was smooth; his dance moves were on point.

To me, it was your average pop song: repetitive and without substance. He sang "Shades" because that's what people asked of him, because that's all people wanted to hear these days. But his heart wasn't in it.

Mom clapped at the end of the clip. "You did beautifully."

Dad stood up, his phone in hand. "As I said before, I thought it went very well. And I think it'll help open more doors in the future."

He left the room, followed swiftly by Mom, who promised she'd be right back. I reached over and grabbed my phone, an unread text waiting for me from Jenica.

"You weren't a fan," Connor stated, matter-of-factly.

"I don't have anything constructive to contribute," I shrugged.

"But?"

"But I wasn't impressed. You didn't even look like you were enjoying yourself half the time. You looked stiff and awkward and uncomfortable."

"Probably because I was."

Mom came back into the room, a smile on her face. "Okay, Katelyn, let me hear it." She sat down next to me. "As I said earlier, every detail. Tell me all about the offsides."

"About what?" Connor asked, leaning forward.

"Katelyn had a soccer tournament this weekend, remember?"

Connor didn't answer. Of course he didn't remember. Unlike his interview, my games weren't broadcast throughout the house. Nobody came to see me; my mom was the only one who even took the time to call. I didn't have a platinum-selling album. I didn't have a national tour that started in two weeks. I didn't have meet and greets to schedule and public appearances to attend.

I was just Katelyn Jackson. And lately that seemed to be more of a burden than a blessing.

LOS ANGELES, CA
CHAPTER 2

"You're not answering my texts." Jenica plopped down on my bed.

My phone was sitting facedown on my nightstand. "I'm trying to focus." I was standing in front of my closet, with piles of clothes around the room, trying to figure out what I could fit into a single large suitcase that would last me most of the summer.

"I didn't come over just to watch you pack," Jenica said. "The Limitless Showcase emails are supposed to come out today."

Shit. *How had I forgotten?* I bolted upright. "Have you gotten yours yet?"

She shook her head in response. "Still refreshing my email every sixty seconds."

I grabbed my phone, doing the same. Nothing. The Limitless Showcase was the most renowned soccer showcase of the year. All of the top-ranked Division One soccer coaches come to scout, and the U.S. Women's National Team notoriously chooses recruits from the Showcase. To be invited was an honor in itself.

"It's going to be a *long* day," Jenica said. "I texted Coach Jefferson and he said he hasn't heard anything yet either."

Before I could answer, there was a knock on my bedroom door.

"I'm packing!" I shouted. "Jenica is helping."

"I don't really care about that," Connor called back through my door. We had stayed away from each other since our sort-of fight after his interview yesterday.

"What do you want?" I called.

"To talk."

"I'm busy!"

There was a clicking noise, and then my door opened. Connor came in, shutting the door behind him.

"I have pizza," he said, holding up the plate for me to see. "It's my peace offering." He placed it on my bed, flashing Jenica a smile. "Hey, Jenny."

"You know I hate that nickname," she said.

"But it's cute," he teased.

"*I'm* cute," Jenica corrected. "Let's not get that mixed up."

"What do you want?" I asked, interrupting their flirtatious banter. I wasn't in the mood to be a third wheel in my own bedroom.

"To talk," he repeated. "Can we step outside for a sec?"

"I'll start sorting Kate's piles of clothes. You guys go on."

I pushed myself up off my bed with a groan, following Connor over to his room.

"I have more pizza in here, don't worry," he said, shutting the door behind him.

I took a slice as I sat down on the edge of his bed. "What's up, pop star?"

His face soured. "Don't call me that."

"You're *famous* now."

"Shut up," Connor said. "Are you going to come to rehearsals with me today?"

"Why should I?"

I didn't know anything about the show. I didn't even know the setlist. Dad micromanaged all of that.

"There's a closing number that I want a second pair of eyes on," he said. "It's the encore written for the show, and Mackenzie, Skyline, and I all perform it together. And you're the only one I trust to give an honest review."

"Why?"

Connor hadn't asked for my opinion on anything since his very first live performance, when he wanted to know which song he should go with. Since then, it's always been him, Mom, and Dad. And I've been the bystander to the Connor Jackson show.

"You're my target audience," he said.

Oh. It was all a strategy.

"I've got a lot of stuff to finish before the tour," I said. "Jenica's helping me pack, but I still have a science project to do and—"

"It'll only be one afternoon," Connor interrupted. "Please, Katelyn? I really need your help."

Connor must really be desperate if he was willing to beg.

"Um, okay," I said. "If you think I can help."

"Thanks, Kate. It means a lot."

I stood up as I finished off my slice of pizza. "I've got to get back to it."

"Okay, cool. I'll let you know when we're ready to go. Maybe, like, thirty minutes before?"

"Sounds good."

Silence lapsed between us, and I cleared my throat to break it. "Okay, see you then."

Jenica was sitting on the floor with my clothes when I came back into my room.

"What did he want?" she asked, without glancing up from what she was doing.

"My help, I guess."

That caused her to look up, raising an eyebrow in question. "With what?"

"I'm not really sure. Something about the closing number for the show."

"That's awesome, Kate," she said. "Maybe you'll get to finally meet Zach Matthews."

"Shut up."

"Don't roll your eyes, you never know!" she sang. "Tell me about the Matthews brothers again? Which one would be perfect for me?"

Jenica knew how to get me talking. I was the biggest Skyline fangirl there was.

I flopped back on my bed. "Jesse is the oldest at twenty-two. He has brown hair and these dark, dark chocolate-colored eyes. He's the more serious and broodier one, the bad boy almost. He plays bass. And then there's Aaron, the keyboardist—he's twenty. He has sandy blond hair and light brown eyes. He's the quiet one that I think holds the band together. He's not nearly as serious as Jesse, but not as much of a goofball as Ross. He's a perfect middleman."

"And who's Ross?" Jenica asked.

"Ross is the third oldest, he's eighteen, the drummer. He has dirty-blond hair and bright brown eyes. He's the class-clown type, always cracking jokes and making light of situations."

Jenica leaned in with a teasing smile. "And the fourth brother?"

"You know it's Zach. He's sixteen, nearly seventeen. Lead singer. Songwriter. Lead guitarist. Basically perfect all-around. He has caramel eyes that stare into your soul, and brown hair that is always the perfect amount of messy. He's the lone wolf, always in the background of his brothers. But when he sings . . . it melts your heart."

"And I wonder which one is your favorite."

I turned to glare at her. "Don't call me out!"

Jenica giggled as she held up a pair of lacy underwear. "Oh, you're definitely packing these."

Connor's driver pulled up in front of the house, rolling down his window as I stepped up. Connor was already at the rehearsal space, and he'd sent his driver to pick me up.

"Hey, Richard," I said as I slid into the backseat.

"How was the tournament this weekend?" Leave it to Richard to be the only person to actually care about me and my accomplishments.

"We came in first."

"Of course you did. You're Katelyn Jackson!"

"Thanks, Richard. Thanks for caring."

"Play hard?"

"Win hard." That had been our saying for as long as I could remember. Richard flipped to Bluetooth radio, my phone connecting.

"Are we listening to Skyline today?" Richard asked, with a teasing smile.

"Always."

The ride to the rehearsal space was short, and Connor's bodyguard, Eddie, was waiting outside once we arrived.

"Afternoon," Eddie said, before opening the door for me.

"Thanks, Eddie."

He led me upstairs and I could hear "Shades" before I even went in. Connor and his choreographer, Christopher Kline, were blocking it. Connor smiled and waved at me, and then managed to fall off the chair he was standing on.

"Sorry, Chris," I said.

"Just in time. Can you press play, Kate?"

"Sure." The dance was flawless, Connor actually managing to pull off the choreography. Chris cheered at the end, reaching over to high-five Connor.

"At least we know it'll work," Connor said, hopping down off the chair.

"We need to do that consistently," Chris said.

I helped Chris clean up the studio space while Connor gathered up his stuff.

"See you in twenty for group rehearsal," Chris called out after us.

I followed Connor up to a room with his name taped on the door. Inside the small space was a single chair and a garment bag hanging from the ceiling. Connor sat down in his chair and let his head fall back, closing his eyes. "I'm already taxed."

The door opened and, Lorie, Connor's publicist, stepped inside. She handled everything from assisting in scheduling Connor's interviews to handling his social media accounts.

"Lana wants to speak with you," Lorie said. "Before your Q&A session this evening."

Lana Regas, Connor's ex-girlfriend. Connor and Lana had met at a red carpet event, and the two of them had immediately hit it off. And things had been great between them . . . for a while. And after one drunken night of confessions between the two of them, NDAs were signed and the relationship abruptly ended.

Lana was a Greek goddess. She stood tall, at five foot nine, and often walked the runway for luxury brand names as a lead model. But most of all, she was a massive bitch. And everybody knew it. When she wanted something, she got it. Not always in the right way.

"I have no interest in talking to her today," Connor said. "Tell her whatever it is, we can talk about it next week."

"You know how Lana gets . . ."

"I'm midrehearsal for a tour that starts in two weeks," Connor said. "I don't care what she threatens to do. I don't have time to deal with her bullshit today."

"Noted," Lorie said, writing in her planner. "The rest of today is pretty light media-wise. We'll continue dropping teasers about the music video on your social profiles, and you have the fan Q&A at seven tonight."

Connor nodded.

Lorie glanced toward me. "Hi, Katelyn."

"Hi."

"Can I get you anything?"

I shook my head. "I'm okay for now."

She wrote something else down in her planner before leaving, shutting the door behind her.

"Is this your every day?" I asked.

Connor opened both eyes this time. "What?"

"People drop in and tell you what your daily schedule is, and you just have to go with it?"

"Pretty much."

"That sounds awful."

And then, as if on cue, my dad came through the door, iPad in hand. "You need to be dressed and ready."

"Skyline is never here on time," Connor whined. "I'm not getting dressed in that leather suit until the absolute last minute."

Connor had specifically requested Skyline as an opening act, and I'd screamed when I heard they'd accepted. Not only would I get to hear them perform at every tour stop, but I'd actually get to meet them in person. Sometimes being a Jackson had its perks.

"Ten minutes," my dad said icily. "I'll see you in the rehearsal studio." And with that he was gone again. Connor didn't seem bothered by the encounter, instead taking to his phone with an impassive expression. This life wasn't something I envied. My dad and I could hardly have a two-minute conversation. There's no way I could handle having him bark orders at me. My career would've been over before it started.

"You can't fangirl," Connor said without looking up from his phone.

"Fangirl?" I asked.

"Over Skyline, when they get here. You can't fangirl."

"Who says I'm a fan?"

"Are you for real? The giant poster of their lead singer on your wall, for starters. The fact that you basically begged me to help promote them ... the fact that you play their songs all the time."

All valid points. "I can play it cool," I shrugged. "Watch, I bet I won't even bat an eye."

"Fat. Fucking. Chance."

"I'm cool as a cucumber, you just watch."

We cracked up.

"Who's the kid you have a poster of again?" Connor asked. "Is it Zach?"

"Yes. Are you best friends with him yet?"

"I'm pretty sure they think I'm an egotistical douche," he said.

"Why would they think that?"

Connor was silent a few moments. "I'm not really good with the whole *friend* thing."

"I guess I'll have to get the scoop," I said.

"I bet you will." He stood up, letting out a yawn. "I've only met Zach once."

They'd been rehearsing for weeks. "Really?"

"He doesn't really come to group rehearsals often; we usually use a stand-in for him."

"What do you mean he doesn't come to group rehearsals?"

If Mackenzie, Skyline, and Connor all came together for the last song, how would Zach know his cues if he didn't show up to rehearsals?

"He's got that condition," Connor said, his eyes flickering shut. "God, I'm so tired. What's it called?"

"Epilepsy," I filled in.

Being a Skyline fangirl meant that I'd fallen into a deep Reddit thread about the ins and outs of Skyline. And an even deeper rabbit hole about epilepsy.

When Skyline began gaining notoriety, they appeared in multiple interviews. But Zach was always noticeably missing. At first he was labeled as a diva by the industry, but eventually he announced that he suffers from epilepsy, and that rehearsals, interviews, and tour would be too much for him when he had a scheduled routine to follow with his doctor. He never did any late-night or early-morning interviews, as he'd said that sleep was a key factor in managing the disorder. Sometimes he'd come around throughout the day, dropping in for a few minutes to say hello. But the other three brothers usually took care of the press releases.

"Yeah, we have a training session on that before the tour starts," Connor said.

"For epilepsy?"

"For what to do in case of a seizure. It was requested by their management . . . which is essentially Jesse."

And it made sense. The last thing Skyline would want to happen was for their lead singer, their brother, to get hurt.

"I'm going to get dressed," Connor said, checking the time. "I'll see you in a sec."

That's my cue to leave. "Same rehearsal room?"

"Yup."

I headed back to the space. "Hello again," Chris said.

I waved in response before taking a seat at the front of the room, my back against the mirror.

Mackenzie arrived next. Everyone in Hollywood knew Mackenzie Lawrence. She was notorious for late-night parties, one-night stands, and subpar pop music.

"Chris," she said, snapping her gum.

"Mack," he said.

Mackenzie's eyes landed on me. "Who is this?"

"Connor's sister," Chris answered. "She's going to watch the closing number."

She gave me a once-over. "If you think that will help." She took a seat in one of the chairs. "This outfit sucks. I can barely move."

She was dressed in a maroon leather jacket with matching pants. She was wearing a tight-fit, white T-shirt underneath and a pair of maroon pumps.

"That's why we'll be rehearsing in them for a week."

The answer clearly didn't satisfy her, but she didn't press the issue any further. "Who all is coming today? Connor?"

Chris nodded.

"And the Jonas Brothers?"

I couldn't help but laugh, Chris joining in.

"All four of them," Chris confirmed.

I pressed my lips together to keep from outwardly fangirling.

"Impressive," she said, with an arched eyebrow. "What's the little one's name again?"

"He's a hell of a lot taller than us."

She frowned, once again displeased with Chris's response. "Name."

"Zachary, but I think he told me he goes by Zach."

She waved her hand dismissively. "There are way too many of them for me to remember."

"Jesse, Aaron, Ross, and Zach," I said, more loudly than I thought.

"Cute," she commented, her face impassive.

I had no idea what to take from that. "Thanks?"

The door flew open, Connor coming into the rehearsal room.

"Whose idea was it for all-leather?" Connor asked, his hands immediately going to cover his crotch. "My dick is way too exposed."

"Wear a cup," Chris said. "You'll survive." He stood back to survey him. "And where's your jacket?"

"Still waiting," Connor said, with a slight frown. "From my meeting with Dad yesterday, I guess they ordered it in red instead of black. The right one should be in ASAP."

Connor took a seat in one of the folding chairs, next to Mackenzie. "Did I miss anything?"

"Other than me complaining about the leather monkey suits too?" Mackenzie asked. "Not much."

As Chris and Connor took to chatting, another ten minutes clicked by.

"They're always late," Mackenzie said, her gaze still focused on her phone. "How do they expect to go on a national tour if they can't even show up to rehearsals on time?"

"Relax," Chris said, with a slight laugh. "Everyone has their flaws. I can deal with them being late."

"We're lucky if *you* show up on time, so no shocker there," Mackenzie scoffed.

"I am surprised, actually, that you were here before all of us today," Connor said, leaning over to Chris.

Chris pointed to his head. "Beanie, sweats, and a T-shirt—I was out the door in less than five."

The door clicked open again. Two members of Skyline walked in. My eyes widened to see Ross and Aaron Matthews also dressed in leather.

"Look who finally decided to show up," Mackenzie snapped.

"I'd say this is record time for us," Aaron said, taking one of the seats.

Ross immediately glanced toward me. "Who's the newbie?"

As soon as his eyes landed on me, my cheeks immediately burned. It was all I could do to stare at him, trying to process the fact that Ross. Matthews. was actually talking to me.

"That's my sister," Connor said, answering for me. "Katelyn."

"Cool," Aaron said, flashing me a smile. "Are you coming on tour?"

I nodded. Not like I was really given a choice.

"Had to hunt down Zach's leather suit," Ross said. "He and Jess should be here momentarily."

"Do we need a lesson in how to tell time?" Mackenzie asked, sarcasm dripping from her voice.

"The first two numbers are the seconds, right?" Ross asked, flashing her a pearly white smile.

Mackenzie flipped him off in return as the door clicked open again. My heart felt like it was doing somersaults in my chest as Jesse walked in, followed closely by Zach. I stared at Zach in his white T-shirt, black leather jacket, and pants. His brown hair was swept off to the side in the messy style he usually wore. And his brown eyes looked unusually dark. His jacket was tight against his biceps, and I could see the ripple of muscles underneath the thin, white T-shirt. I couldn't take my eyes off the perfection that was Zach Matthews.

"Found your leather gear?" Chris asked.

Zach tugged on the jacket. "Is it supposed to be this tight?"

"Unfortunately," Connor said.

"This is Katelyn," Chris said, gesturing toward me. "She's going to be watching today, because Connor doesn't trust my opinion."

Heat pooled in my cheeks as all eyes turned toward me.

"Not true," Connor said. "I'd like a second pair of eyes before we actually go live in our skin-tight leather."

Ross flashed me a smile, and my heart pounded even harder in my chest. "If you want to suggest a costume change, I'd be all ears," he said.

"Music in five!" Chris called out. "Positions now."

Everyone shifted around the room, moving chairs and taking their places for the start of the song. My eyes immediately focused on Zach, although I tried to convince myself it was solely for research purposes and not because he's Zach. Matthews.

Mackenzie opened the song. Her voice was smooth, but her music wasn't for me. I enjoyed songs with a deeper meaning behind the lyrics. And she was nothing more than bubblegum pop music. The choreography was intricate, and involved a lot of balancing on chairs, which, by the looks of it, was really hard for Connor. And as predicted, Connor fell off the chair during his solo, which had Chris cackling.

Ross was the only one from Skyline who seemed to have any sort of rhythm. I could see Aaron glancing at Ross, trying to follow along. Jesse didn't even bother trying. And Zach gave up about a quarter of the way through the song, taking to tipping his chair back and forth as he sang. The ending was perfect though, with everybody hitting their marks.

"So?" Chris asked.

"I thought the ending was really good," I said.

The room busted out laughing, even Mackenzie.

"I think Mackenzie has the choreography down really well," I said. The look she gave me said she clearly agreed.

"Connor has no balance." I ignored the look he gave me. "Overall, I didn't think it was *bad*. It's just obviously not show-ready."

Ross raised his hand from where he was seated in one of the plastic folding chairs. "*We* don't get a rating?"

The heat rose in my cheeks again. "Ross has enough rhythm to follow along in the choreography."

Ross fist-pumped. "Let the record show that I'm the best dancer in Skyline."

"As if he didn't have a big enough head already," Aaron muttered.

"I don't need a rating," Zach said. "I know I sucked."

"Zach doesn't have dance skills," Ross said, reaching over to ruffle his hair.

His brother ducked away from him, "Leave me alone."

"Should we scrap it?" Chris asked.

"No," I said.

"Katelyn, I thought you were on *our* side," Ross whined.

I was trying really hard not to let my inner fangirl out, but I could feel the heat spread down the back of my neck as Ross said my name. *Ross Matthews knows my name.* It was hard not to be starstruck.

"Can we at least scrap the chairs?" Jesse asked.

"I like the chairs," Mackenzie argued.

"We have a little over a week to nail down the choreography," Chris said. "If we scrap the chairs, we have to reblock. And if we don't, then we have to learn to balance in that time."

Jesse let out a short laugh. "Both sound impossible."

Clearly choreography wasn't Skyline's thing.

Mackenzie groaned. "God, Negative Nancy, can you cool it?"

I could tell Jesse wanted to snap back, but Aaron gave him a quick shake of the head. They seemed to have a silent conversation.

"Let's run it again then?" Chris questioned.

"Great," Zach said, in a listless voice. "Can't wait."

The words slipped out before I could stop them. "I can tell."

His eyes slid toward mine, his lips pressed together and turned up into a smile. And now I was sure I was the color of an actual tomato.

"Okay, Katelyn, game plan," Chris said. "I'll be watching Connor, Aaron, and Ross. You've got eyes on Zach and Jesse."

Oh God. Connor looked up at the ceiling, clearly concealing his laughter from the rest of the group.

"Do I have to run the choreo again?" Mackenzie asked.

"Practice makes perfect," Chris quipped.

"Perfect?" Mackenzie panned. "I'll settle for mediocre."

My eyes zeroed in on Zach as he took his place. *I'm not con-centrating on how Zach's shirt rides up when he reaches up. I'm not concentrating on the blush in his cheeks whenever he missteps. I'm not concentrating on how his head turns to look at Jesse whenever he forgets the choreography. I'm only watching him under Chris's instruction.*

And maybe if I keep telling myself that, I'll eventually believe it.

After the second run-through, it was determined that a choreography refresher was needed.

"I'm going to run through the choreography, top to bottom, just with Skyline, since dancing isn't really their thing," Chris said to Connor. "You don't need to stay for this. And, yes, Mack, I was getting to you next—you don't need to make that face. You definitely don't need to stay for this. But you're essential to this number, and I *do* need you both back here in two hours."

She flashed a peace sign in the air as she walked out of the room. I followed Connor out, glancing over my shoulder one last time at the Skyline boys. What I wouldn't give to be a fly on the wall in that room.

"Want to grab dinner?" Connor asked, causing my attention to snap back to him.

"Sure, where?"

"Olive Garden?"

Olive Garden breadsticks were the surefire way to my heart.

"Deal. Let me just peel off this leather number first."

As I waited for Connor, I quickly refreshed my email to see if I'd heard anything from Limitless. No email. No text from Jenica. No text from Coach Jefferson.

We met Eddie out by the entrance, where he was standing with his back to the door, arms folded across his chest.

"Paps," Eddie said, with a nod toward the door. "We'll have to wait."

Paparazzi. Great. Connor let out a groan. "I'm *starving*."

"You'll survive."

Connor glanced toward me, raising an eyebrow in question.

"What?" I asked.

"Do you care about the paps?" Connor asked.

I'd never had to deal with a group of people shoving cameras and microphones into my face. "I don't know."

"Good enough for me. Come on, Eddie. We're going to Olive Garden."

"You don't want to wait and go out the back?" Eddie said.

"Nope."

"Of course not," he muttered.

"Keep your head low and don't make eye contact. Stick behind Eddie and you'll be fine." Connor said to me.

We followed Eddie out to the car, the paparazzi snapping pictures and shouting things left and right. I kept my head ducked low. Next time, I was definitely voting to go out the back. I hated the flashing of cameras coming at me from what felt like every angle, although, in reality, there were probably only four cameras in total.

Connor opened the door to Richard's car for me, letting me slide in first before plopping down next to me. Eddie wedged his giant body into the front seat.

"Why didn't you use the stage today?" I asked, as Richard began to back out of the parking space, trying not to hit any of the paparazzi.

"Scheduling conflicts. Getting Skyline, Mack, and myself there all with the sound and light crew was a scheduling disaster."

That didn't bode well for the upcoming tour.

"But we'll be rehearsing on stage for the next three days," Connor continued. "Clear schedules."

Richard came to a stop at a red light, and Connor rolled down his window for the teenagers in the car next to us trying to peek inside. He waved and flashed a smile for them.

"How long is the show expected to be?" I asked.

The light turned green and he rolled his window back up, before turning his attention back to me.

"Roughly about three hours—three and a half if need be."

We pulled into the Olive Garden, as it was less than a mile from the rehearsal studio.

"Dad texted and said we have a private area inside," he said, checking his work phone as he stepped out of the car.

The table was ready, and the hostess tried not to stare as she grabbed the menus. We were led to a back room, usually used for birthday parties, with a door that closed for extra privacy.

"Does that ever get old?" I asked, once she left.

"What?" he said, without looking up from the menu. It was no surprise that Connor didn't notice the fumbling hostess. He'd always been humble about his rising fame, stopping to take a picture with a fan, or to make a video with them, or whatever he could do to say thank you.

"The hostess obviously knew who you were."

Connor leaned back in his seat. "I know. I come here often."

The smell of pasta and breadsticks wafted through the air as we opened our menus.

"Did I mention I'm starving?" Connor asked after the waitress took our orders.

"Once or twice."

"All I had for lunch was McDonald's, if you count that as food."

"I don't."

The waiter brought over the first basket of breadsticks, which I immediately dug into.

Connor reached over, taking a sip of his water. "I'm impressed."

"With what?"

"That you didn't outwardly fangirl over Skyline."

"Told you I'd be cool as a cucumber."

"I saw you checking out Zach Matthews for the entirety of the rehearsal."

"That's not true! Chris asked me to keep an eye on him."

"And you did just that."

"You're the worst," I said.

Back before Connor had blown up on the *Billboard* charts, we spent a lot of time together. We didn't have a close extended family, and it'd always been the two of us growing up. We'd spend late nights gossiping about the *one day*. One day when Connor was famous. One day when I played soccer professionally. One day when we would get to do all of these things together.

Between our busy schedules, we hadn't had much time to sit down and talk like we used to. And being here in this secluded corner of Olive Garden felt like old times.

"I have to get back to choreography," Connor said as we finished eating. "Richard will drop me off and take you home, if that's okay?"

Exhaustion had started to creep through me, and I could feel my eyes growing heavy.

"Sure." A yawn escaped. "I don't know how you keep all this up."

"You get used to it. Not that there's much of a choice."

That answer didn't sound happy. "Are you okay, Connor?"

"Of course. Let's get out of here."

If you say so.

LOS ANGELES, CA
CHAPTER 3

A morning run was a staple of my morning routine. What wasn't a staple was coming home to Connor's voice reverberating off the walls.

"I read the script that your management wrote verbatim!" Connor's voice shouted. "You signed the fucking NDA, just like I did. If you want to sue for slander or defamation, that's on you. But don't come at me with the rest of *your* bullshit. I'm in the middle of rehearsals for a nationwide tour, and I don't have time to drop everything for this."

I could attest to Connor's packed schedule. There's no way he was going to have time to deal with a media storm if Lana opened up a lawsuit against him. Lana's voice carried through the hallway as she shouted through the phone, but I couldn't make out what she was saying.

"Then set up a conference call to have your manager call mine."

I heard her voice again, which was cut off by some colorful language by Connor.

A few seconds later, his phone collided with the wall. He stormed into the hallway where I was taking off my shoes, his eyes blazing.

"How did I ever think I was in love with her?" Connor blazed past me and shouted at top volume for our dad. This wasn't going to end well, and I didn't want to be around for it. Instead, I headed upstairs to take a long, hot shower to wash off the grime from the run.

"Good morning, honey," Mom said, coming into my room.

"Morning," I said, turning to face her.

She took a seat on the edge of my bed. "I talked to Coach Jefferson this morning to iron out some of the details of the tour."

I sat down next to her. "What do you mean?"

"To make sure that we have some teams you can guest-play on, to see the status of the Limitless Showcase—"

The Limitless Showcase! Nobody had received their emails yesterday, and I'd tossed and turned all night in anticipation.

"What did he say?" I asked.

"He's still waiting to hear too."

I tried to ignore the clenching of my chest. "Understood."

"I'll keep checking my email today, in case it comes through to me," she said. "You're important, too, Katelyn. And I'm sorry if we ever make it seem otherwise. With the tour and the album release, and everything happening with your brother, it doesn't make your accomplishments any less."

She wrapped her arms around me, and I leaned into her, resting my head on her shoulder. Quality time with my mom was easily one of the things that I missed the most in this new transition with Connor's career. And while I'd been trying to adjust to taking advantage of the moments we did get to spend together, it hadn't been easy.

"What did he say about the guest teams?" I asked.

Playing on guest teams for exhibition games took a lot of coordination. There were teams around the country that were willing to take on players from other competitive teams to play as a one-off guest. My coach had been working with my mom to schedule games where I could play while we were in different cities.

"We have a couple of games lined up," Mom said. "And then if the Limitless Showcase works out, that should be plenty to keep your soccer juices flowing."

"Never say those words again."

"I love you, Katie," Mom said.

She was the only person I'd tolerate calling me Katie.

"I love you, too, Mom."

She kissed the top of my head before standing up. "Now how about you deal with the piles of clothes all over the floor? That's not exactly packing, Katie."

I gave her a salute as she left.

As I picked up a handful of running shirts, my phone buzzed. A text from Jenica.

LIMITLESS EMAIL. TEXT ME ASAP.

I immediately went to my email, refreshing the page.

And there it was. My invitation to the Limitless Apparel Showcase. My stomach bubbled as the adrenaline rushed through me. Everything I'd worked for felt validated, and I let out an excited scream as I ran out of my room.

"Katelyn?" Mom's voice called.

I ran downstairs, practically plowing her over. "*Mom!*"

Her eyes were wide as she held me by my shoulders. "Katelyn, what in the—"

"I have my Limitless email! I got my invitation, Mom!"

"Oh, Katie!" she grabbed me in a bear hug. "I'm so, so very proud of you!"

My heels bounced as I tried to contain myself. "We need to get out of here. Let's go celebrate!"

Mom bit her lip. "I'm headed to the studio for the cast rehearsal, I'm sure I could—"

My excitement instantly deflated. "No, it's fine, Mom, don't worry about it," I said. "I'll go over to Jenica's, since she got the email too."

Despite what my mom said, Connor would always take front and center. And I'd forgotten that. For a moment, I thought that my accomplishments mattered too. And her hesitation felt worse than I could ever imagine.

"I'll see you later?"

I could see the conflicted look on my mom's face. "What if we go to dinner at your favorite restaurant?"

"Yeah. Maybe."

She kissed my forehead. "I'm so proud of you, Katie."

But not as proud as you are of Connor.

"Thanks, Mom."

She headed toward the door, glancing back at me one last time. She blew me a kiss before leaving.

There were times when I really thought that I was the main character in my story. And then times like these remind me that I'm just a background character in Connor's.

Despite what my mom had said, she never ended up taking me to dinner. And so the next day a few teammates and I spent the day together. After an afternoon of popcorn and Netflix, Jenica was the only one still here, and I wasn't quite ready to say good-bye to her yet.

"So this is really it?" Jenica asked, as I flipped on the TV.

"I guess so," I answered, flopping down on my bed.

"You're leaving me tomorrow?" she said, her eyes wide.

"I don't want to leave tomorrow."

She dug her spoon into the tub of ice cream. "This sucks."

"Agreed." We lay side by side, eating ice cream while watching an old episode of *Grey's Anatomy*, which we'd been binge-watching all day.

"Is this our good-bye moment?" Jenica asked.

"No."

She sat up, stretching her arms above her head. "I have practice tonight." She gestured toward the piles of clothes around my room. "And you definitely need to finish packing. Don't you leave at like four in the morning or something crazy?"

Jenica was right. It was getting close to the time her mom would pick her up, to whisk her away to soccer practice while I was doomed to packing all of the outfits I had laid out in preparation for my suitcase.

It felt as though there was a weight pressed against my chest as I stood up. "Lots of pictures?"

She nodded, standing up as well. "Text me every day."

"Promise."

I wrapped my arms around her, wishing I could switch places with her. I wanted to be the one to train this summer, to play in the summer three-on-three league, and to go to the team sleepovers.

"Love you," I said, as we pulled away.

"Love you more," Jenica said. "Make sure those guest teams realize they're stealing our best player, okay?"

"And make sure that Monica remembers she's *co*-captain—don't let her steal my place."

Jenica let out a fake gasp. "She could never."

We hugged one last time before Jenica's phone beeped with a text from Momma Terry to say she was in the driveway.

"Every. Day," Jenica said.

"Promise."

And then I was alone.

I knew with too much time to think, the sadness of leaving everything familiar would start to sink in. So I turned on my favorite indie music playlist and got to packing.

CHAPTER 4

The flight from L.A. to Seattle went by in a blur, filled with adrenaline and sleep deprivation.

I wasn't used to flying as a part of Connor's entourage; usually that duty was left to my dad, with my mom tagging along on occasion. And I definitely wasn't used to flying first class.

And now, sitting in the arena as the crew prepped for a full-cast rehearsal, I felt very out of my element. Connor stood in the center of the stage, microphone in hand, as various people scurried around him to prepare for rehearsals to begin. The lights were continuously changing, dimming and flickering through different-colored sequences. And I felt lost in the process.

"Hey, Connor's sister." Mackenzie stood behind me. She flashed a wide grin. "Do I have lipstick on my teeth?"

"No."

"Thank God. Where the hell is Skyline? I swear, if I have an eight a.m. call time, everybody else in this show better too." Mackenzie flipped her phone back into her pocket and turned on her heel. "Geraldine!"

"Run-through starts in five," my dad said as he walked toward me. "Where's Skyline?"

"I don't know. Mackenzie was—"

Dad pointed to his Bluetooth. "I'm standing in the arena, they aren't here."

He continued walking past me. *Oh. Of course he wasn't talking to me.* I stood still for a moment, watching the chaos continue to unfold around me.

"Katelyn?" Chris called out for me from the stage. "Come sit," he said, pointing to the front-row seats.

I made my way toward the front, Connor flashing me a smile as I took a seat.

"You looked a bit lost out there," Connor said.

"I'm okay," I said.

The chair squeaked beneath me as I sat. Being in this large arena felt surreal. Voices echoed off the walls, and a crew of people were shouting orders and making last-minute adjustments as they ran through light cues. I couldn't imagine what it would be like when the arena was full.

Mackenzie came out onto the stage. "Since Skyline isn't here, what's plan B?"

"We'll run 'Let's Get Crazy,'" Chris said. "Go and join Katelyn for a minute, Connor."

"I'm not sticking around for this," Connor said.

Mackenzie took to ordering the stagehands around, her hands on her hips. "Where are Alicia and Kelly?" Mackenzie asked. "*Geraldine!*"

"Her backup dancers," a male voice said behind me as a girl ran on stage. "And Geraldine is her very uptight, very annoying manager."

Aaron stood behind me. *Aaron Matthews had initiated a conversation with me.* He plopped down in the row behind me. "Ooh, did I get here in time to see a run-through of 'Let's Get Crazy'? Kill me now."

Mackenzie leaned over and kissed the girl on the cheek. "Thanks for being flexible, Alicia."

"Kell!" Alicia called out. "Let's go!"

The other girl, Kelly, came jogging on the stage. Half of her shoulder-length, red hair was in a top bun, with the other half resting around her shoulders. "I guess I'll poop later, it's fine."

"We're only running through choreo," Chris said. "We're using a soundtrack; I need Mack's voice ready to go for opening night."

The song began after Chris's countdown, and the girls ran through the choreography. While I may not be the biggest fan of Mackenzie's music, her dancing was on another level. She hit every beat, every move. She was in sync with her backup dancers throughout the entire song, nobody missing a step. Each movement was mesmerizing. So much so that I didn't notice the donut in front of me until it was being dropped in my lap.

"There are donuts in wardrobe," Ross said as he sat in the seat next to me. "Connor said you might want one."

Aaron leaned forward, his head between Ross and me. "What about me?"

"Jesse's still there," Ross said. "I could only carry so many."

The music had ended, Chris now talking to the girls up on the stage.

"Thanks, Ross," I said, as the heat rose on my cheeks.

Ross had thought of me. Well, Connor had thought of me. But *Ross Matthews brought me a donut.*

"Okay, group number! Starting positions!" Chris called over his shoulder. "Ross, Aaron, you'd better find those other two brothers of yours. We need to stick to the schedule this morning."

Ross stood up and saluted. "They're in wardrobe. I'll go check on them."

"I'll call them," Aaron said.

"Oh. Or that."

Ross headed up the stairs on the side of the stage as Aaron called Jesse.

"I can go check on them," I offered. "If that's easier."

"Sorry!" I heard Jesse's voice call out as he and Connor came into the arena, Zach following close behind.

Chris tapped his wrist. "Come on, boys. We have to do better than this."

"Sorry, sorry," Jesse repeated, as they approached the stage. "I would say it won't happen again, but . . ."

Chris lowered his gaze.

"I'll be more on top of it," Jesse said.

"Get up here. We have a rehearsal to run."

Skyline headed up the side stairs to the stage, joining Mackenzie, who was waiting with her hands on her hips.

"Sorry, Mack," Zach said. "My fault."

"Get a fucking alarm clock," she muttered.

Chris grabbed a microphone. "Backup dancers! Opening positions! Let's go." He scanned the audience, his eyes landing on me. "How's the opening look, Kate?"

I flashed him a thumbs-up.

He stepped off the stage. "Let's do a run-through then. I want you to sing this time instead of using the track."

As they chatted on stage, I turned to look at the expanse of the arena behind me. Soon this place would be jammed with screaming fans, all here to see my brother. And I didn't quite know what to think about that.

Chris's voice turned my attention back to the stage. "That's fine, Zach. Stumble through."

My eyes settled on Zach as Ross passed him a permanent marker. Zach began to scribble on his hand, clearly deep in concentration.

Once everyone was mic'd, Chris signaled the light booth. The lights in the entire arena went out, and my heart picked up a little.

Connor's drummer started off the song with a solid beat. A spotlight fell on Mackenzie, as she had the opening line to the song. The choreography ran a lot smoother, and it showed that Skyline had been practicing. It was also obvious that Zach was reading from the palm of his hand during his lines.

"Good run-through!" Chris called, hopping up on stage. "Take five and we'll run it again. Then after that we'll head back to choreography to touch up on some of the rough spots."

Stagehands brought water onto the stage, along with a couple of boxes of donuts. I signaled for Connor to toss me one, and he tossed me an entire box. My mom sat down next to me. "How'd the run-through go?"

Before I could answer, Connor's voice interrupted me, his mic still on.

"Hey, Mom!" Connor called out. "I'm not a huge fan of the donuts. Can you see if the fruit has been delivered yet?"

Everyone on tour had a rider, which outlined what exactly they were requesting of the venue. My requests had been tacked onto Connor's, and included fresh-cut watermelon, flavored water, and high-speed WiFi for FaceTiming friends when I was dead bored. Connor's part of the rider was much more extensive. I'd only glanced over it but had noticed his request for a variety of fresh fruit, aspirin, and a room with a lock on it. My mom stood up, never finishing our conversation, to head backstage and check on Connor's fruit. *Same story, different day.*

"Let's have everybody back on stage!" Chris called.

The epilepsy training was being held in the hotel conference room. A neurologist and his team, not one that had worked with Zach directly, had been hired on by his management. It was a mandatory training session and everyone that was going to be on the tour had to go. And of course I'd gone to the wrong meeting room.

" . . . about to start." It sounded like Aaron, but I couldn't see anyone.

"It's useless for me to sit in a meeting about epilepsy." That was definitely Zach. "I'm not going to be assisting anyone."

As I rounded the corner, the two boys were standing outside of the meeting room doors.

"So you're not going to come inside?" Aaron asked.

Both of them glanced toward me as I walked up.

"Sorry," Aaron said, moving off to the side. "They've already started but you should be able to slip inside."

Zach's gaze was fixed on the ceiling, his arms folded tightly across his chest.

"Got it, thanks," I said, as I stepped around them.

There was a woman standing at the front of the conference room, a PowerPoint presentation up behind her. I tried to discreetly slide into a seat next to Mackenzie in the back. She had her feet kicked up on the chair in front of her and her phone in hand.

"You're late."

"I realize."

The presentation went over the most common types of seizures and how to assist each one. It explained when to call for a medical emergency and what steps to take postseizure. It was overwhelming, and by the end of the training, I didn't feel ready to handle *any* sort of emergency situation. When the presentation finished, Mackenzie leaned over and whispered, "If someone has a seizure in front of me, I'm calling 911."

Then Jesse stood up. "Thanks for coming, everyone. We want to take an extra few minutes to go over Zach's specific condition. With Zach, we don't worry about grand mal seizures too much; he's only ever had one. Zach suffers mainly from partial seizures."

The presenter handed Jesse the remote, and he flipped back to the slides that went into seizure details.

"With a partial seizure, he doesn't lose consciousness or seize," Jesse explained. "It can happen at any time, but the first sign is that he seems spaced out. If you're unable to capture his attention, that's when you know something's wrong."

Leaning forward in my seat, I tried to study the text and memorize the details. I wanted to make sure I was as informed as I could be. Not that I anticipated ever being alone with Zach, but I don't want to be the person in the room and fail him.

"He may nod if you ask him a question, but it's more likely he'll just stare at you in confusion," Jesse continued. "Depending on how coherent he is, he might try to stand up. Make sure he always remains seated. But it's also important to stay hands off."

I pulled out my phone to take bullet point notes.

"He'll remain in this state—not speaking, staring straight ahead, for a few minutes. Just stay calm—that's *extremely* important. You'll know that he's coming around because he'll ask for water. He likes ice-cold water, says it helps clear his head. He usually still can't hold complete conversations at this point, but he'll be able to answer simple questions. That's when it's safe to get him somewhere that he can lie down, as he'll have a raging headache and will be very tired. He'll undoubtedly fall asleep afterward, but it's still not safe to leave him alone. By that time you should have been able to let one of us know, and we can handle the situation from there. But absolutely do not leave him alone, as he may wake up confused and incoherent and then we have a safety risk."

Mackenzie leaned over, glancing down at my notes. "Send those to me after?"

I nodded.

"Safety risks are always a big concern," Jesse continued. "During a partial seizure, don't let him get up and walk around. If he's doing any activities, make sure he stops. The most recent example I have is that Zach was doing the dishes, and during a partial seizure the dish dropped to the floor and shattered. So we had broken glass on the floor and couldn't really explain to Zach what was going on. Ross ended up getting glass in his foot. It wasn't ideal."

"An obvious solution would be to wear shoes around broken glass," Aaron said, causing a bit of laughter from around the room.

"It's a lot," Jesse said. "And we understand that. We'll always try to be there the moment we hear of the situation, which is why I'll be writing our phone numbers on the whiteboard. Please make sure you save them, and if you need anything at all don't hesitate to call."

Aaron stood up. "Jesse's the best person to call. Ross would be a last resort, as he tends to crack under pressure."

And suddenly I had three-quarters of the Matthews brothers' phone numbers.

"Too bad," Mackenzie said, flashing me a smile. "It's missing the one phone number you care about."

I'm going to kill Connor.

The next week of rehearsals was a whirlwind. The talent was trying to find their rhythm for the tour, and as opening night approached, it was still pretty messy. Between the early-morning call times and the late-night meetings, I'd hardly seen Connor, Mackenzie, or Skyline.

Aside from my morning runs, I hadn't really had time to explore the city. So on the morning of opening night, I decided to do so; after all, if I was going to be touring the United States, I wanted to actually get out and see it.

"Make sure you have your phone on you the entire time," Mom said as I loaded up my backpack. "And your location had better be turned on." She picked up her phone. "I'm checking right now."

"It's on." I stuffed a banana into the side pocket of my backpack. "I'm going for a walk and coming right back."

I gave my mom a quick kiss on the cheek before she could come up with an excuse for why I shouldn't go. "I'm getting cabin fever in this hotel room, Mom. I'll be back in time for the show, I promise."

Mom hugged me tightly. "Be safe, okay?"

"Always."

After throwing my backpack over my shoulder, I headed outside. Usually I'd do this kind of thing with Jenica, the two of us heading out on an adventure. But I didn't have a go-to friend on the tour, someone whom I could coerce into sightseeing with me. Today was a solo Katelyn day and I pushed away the lonely feeling as I headed outside.

In my traveling experiences, the best moments were the unplanned ones. So I let the connecting sidewalks lead me through Seattle without a destination in mind.

As I walked, I couldn't help but contrast Seattle to L.A. The overhanging clouds and drizzly weather were much different than the never-ending sunshine and drought back home. People were dressed in layers, but despite the overcast weather, nobody was carrying an umbrella.

Throughout the tour, I'd wanted something to be my *thing*, something I could look forward to in each city. I hadn't quite figured out what that was yet, and was running out of time to decide. My phone buzzed in my pocket as I jogged across another crosswalk, as the seconds were counting down to zero.

Are you being safe? Love you, Mom.

Only my mom would sign her texts.

I replied quickly before pulling up my location on my phone. According to the interactive map, I was pretty close to downtown Seattle. Close to the pier. Perfect. Downtown Seattle was bound to have something that would catch my eye.

The wind picked up as I started down the stretch of Broad Street, my hair whipping behind me as I walked. I let my head tip back, turning my face toward the sky to feel the air on my face.

And then there was downtown Seattle. I was suddenly self-conscious of my sweaty appearance as I slowed to a stop. The cool air-conditioning hit me as I stepped inside the first store, and a shudder went up my spine. Sweaty clothes and AC weren't a good mix.

My hands ran across the soft fabric of the tacky Seattle tourist sweatshirts. Maybe this could be my thing. A giggle escaped my lips as I weaved through the tourist stores filled with tacky T-shirts and bobbleheads. I ended up buying a long-sleeve shirt with the word *Seattle* written on it in different colors all across the front.

This was the perfect item to kick-start my tacky tourist collection.

As promised, I made it back in time for the show. My mom had been waiting in the hotel room, wanting to hear about my adventuring around Seattle. Dad and Connor were long gone.

"Did you have fun?" Mom asked as she was pleating my hair.

I hadn't told my mom about buying a tacky Seattle shirt, as I knew she wouldn't understand. And I liked having something for *me*. "It was a nice walk."

She finished, my hair now split into two Dutch braids.

"Thank you."

"You look so cute with the double braids," she said. "Like my little girl."

"I'm almost seventeen, Mom. Not a little girl," I said, teasingly.

In the bathroom, I freshened up. Face wash. Moisturizer. A little mascara to brighten up my eyes. Some chapstick to salvage my always dry, rough lips. And that was the extent of my makeup journey.

Thirty minutes before the start of the show, we finally left the room. The hotel was a couple of blocks away from the arena, and it was a nice night to get some fresh air.

"I want to make sure you don't get lost in the hustle and bustle backstage," Mom said, as we walked. "Text me when you're getting ready to come backstage and I'll come get you."

"Understood."

My All-Access pass hung around my neck as I followed my mom into the side entrance where the artists and tour staff had been instructed to enter. I wasn't used to being on the other side of the show, and it was a much different experience. As opposed to the bright lights and the screaming fans out front, behind the stage was much more muted. You could feel the vibration of the conversations out front, but backstage the chatter was much quieter and more direct, everybody moving about with a purpose.

"Ms. Jackson," the security guard said to my mom. "And younger Ms. Jackson."

We were escorted to the reserved All-Access seats.

"Are you watching the show?" I asked.

She shook her head no. "Your dad and I are going to make sure everything runs smoothly backstage."

I took my seat, alone again.

As I waited for the show to start, I glanced at the fans around me. Girls decked out in Connor Jackson shirts carrying handmade posters; others dressed in flashy outfits that they'd probably spent months planning, alongside reluctant parents who looked as though they'd rather be anywhere but here.

The lights dimmed, and the fans began to scream.

Per usual, Mackenzie's performance was flawless. Not a misstep. Not a missed note. Not even a missed lyric. She looked like she was born on stage. Adrenaline pumped through me as Mackenzie left the stage—Skyline was up next.

The transition took about twenty minutes, and when the house-lights dimmed, the four boys were on stage, and I couldn't help but scream along with the rest of the arena.

"Hi, I'm Jesse."

"I'm Ross."

"Aaron."

"And I'm Zach." He flashed an award-winning smile. "And we're Skyline!"

The screams were deafening, and I moved to the edge of my seat in anticipation as I waited for the first note. The first sound. And it didn't disappoint. My eyes never left Zach, his voice all-consuming.

Unlike Mackenzie, they did have missed notes and lyrics, which they managed to laugh through, and the crowd corrected. Their performance was just as special, bringing its own charm and personality. Screaming along with the other girls in the audience, I shouted every lyric, closing my eyes as their melodic voices filled the arena. There was no denying it: I was hopelessly in love with Skyline. As their set ended, the arena lights came up again. The girls screamed, knowing that Connor Jackson was up next.

And after what felt like an eternity, the lights went out again, and the screams grew louder. Connor's band was backlit, their silhouettes playing the opening beat of the song. The smoke machine turned on, and Connor came up from under the stage and arrived amidst the vapor, the spotlight illuminating him the moment the band hit the biggest note of the song.

It was remarkable.

Connor put on a spectacular performance, all the way up to "Shades." When the chair came flying out and Connor jumped onto it, he flipped it and fell. The audience gasped, and Connor stopped singing, but the band kept playing.

After a split second, Connor flipped the chair back over, hopped back up, and continued singing like it never happened, but he had a pained look on his face. Knowing my dad, he was already waiting in the wings to make sure that Connor was still up to performing. I leaned back in my chair, waiting for the end of the set. I had to see how the encore played out.

Connor disappeared, and the crowd began to scream, begging for an encore.

After a few minutes of loud clapping, screaming, and foot stomping, a spotlight came on, and Mackenzie stood alone in the middle of the stage. Skyline joined her, and a verse later, Connor jumped back into action, much to the audience's glee. But I noticed right away that whenever he danced, or snapped his fingers, his left hand remained as still as possible, and he would wince whenever it moved. And when it came to his and Jesse's guitar solo, he tried to play a few notes, but gave up, grimacing and shaking his head.

Other than Connor's obvious discomfort, the song went off relatively smoothly. A few missteps, a missed song lyric by Zach, but nothing too noticeable to someone who hadn't heard the song for the past few weeks. I slipped out of my seat and headed backstage to avoid the postconcert rush.

I strode down the hallway in what I thought was the direction of the stage, but it led to a dead end. *Where was I?* Despite having not spent much time backstage, I was fairly certain I could navigate my way around. I'd managed to get around Seattle by myself; it couldn't be that hard to find my way through a few halls. Backtracking to where I thought I'd started, I turned left. The hallway broke into multiple different directions, voices coming from every angle. Everybody looked like they had a mission, phones in hand, and orders being shouted.

Way out of my element, I ducked around the corner, pulling my phone out of my pocket to call my mom to come and rescue me, but there was no service. And I had no idea how to get back to where I started to try to find my mom, dad, or brother.

Take two on another solo Katelyn adventure.

When the backtracking technique didn't work, I followed some important-looking people who appeared to know where they were going. Everyone was splitting off down different hallways, heading to rooms I'd never seen before, and shouting for things I'd never heard of.

"Did you check the call board?"

"Last I saw they were coming down the escape stairs."

"Dark house tomorrow, need to get the clean-up crew in here."

Everyone was preoccupied. And nobody cared about the lost teenage girl standing bewildered in the middle of the hallway.

" . . . and there was a bathroom around this corner, I swear."

Ross Matthews came into my line of vision, followed by Jesse. Ross opened the door a few feet in front of me, revealing a small bathroom. "Ha! Told you it was here. You're welcome." Jesse dipped inside without a word, shutting the door behind him.

Ross turned and saw me, a quizzical look on his face. "Are you looking for the secret bathroom too?"

It took me a moment to work up the courage to speak. "I think I'm lost."

"It's pretty easy to get caught up in the postshow madness. We had a bathroom brawl over in our neck of the woods. You can follow us back."

His easygoing nature made it a little easier for me to relax. "You guys had a great set."

"You think? Zach was a little pissy after," he said.

Jesse stepped out of the bathroom. "We need to get back if we want—" He paused when he saw me. He took a step back, gesturing toward the bathroom. "Are you waiting?"

"She's lost," Ross said, before I had the chance to say anything. "Got caught up in the never-ending hallways."

As we followed Ross back to the dressing rooms, I tried to come up with a way to kick-start a conversation with the two boys. This was the whole reason I'd come backstage early in the first place. And now I couldn't think of a single thing to say that didn't sound like I was major fangirling. Which I most definitely was.

"Katelyn said she liked our set," Ross said, glancing over his shoulder toward Jesse and me. "I told her Zach disagreed."

Jesse's gaze flickered upward. "She's being nice."

"She actually really did like it," I finally found my voice. "And she thought that even though you guys stumbled a couple of times, it was still a great set."

"And she also apparently speaks in the third person," Ross added.

"Mistakes are part of it," I laughed. "You guys made them fun."

"Zach is convinced it's the worst show we've ever done," Ross said. "Maybe give him your five-star review."

I didn't think I'd be able to speak a full sentence in the presence of Zach Matthews. Not a coherent one anyway.

"Katelyn!" Mom came down the hallway ahead of us. "I've been worried about you! Where have you been?"

"And this is our cue to leave," Jesse said. "Have fun."

He and Ross slipped into their dressing room, the door quickly shutting behind them.

"I got lost," I mumbled, much to my mom's dismay.

"I told you to call me!"

"No service."

"I'm glad that you're okay," she huffed. "Next time you text me *before* you come backstage, and I'll meet you at the entrance."

"Where's Connor?" I fell in step with her.

"Doing meet and greets."

"How's his hand?"

"Not broken, maybe sprained," Mom said. "The chair is being removed from the choreography ASAP. And we're going to see what we need to do to make sure he's okay for the next show."

Chris wasn't going to be happy. "What does Connor say about all of this?"

"He won't have it." She checked her watch. "We should head back to the hotel to gather our things; we need to get on the road tonight after the excitement dies down. We'll talk more about this when your father and brother are done tonight."

The tour bus door opened, and Connor and Dad both came in. My brother had changed into a pair of sweatpants and a tour T-shirt, his hair wet from either sweat or a shower. I was really hoping for the latter.

Mom wrapped her arms around Connor, pulling him in tight. "Great show, honey!"

He gave her a brief hug before collapsing down next to me on the couch.

"How's the wrist?" I asked.

He held out his left arm, flexing his hand a few times. "Stiff. No swelling. No broken bones. I'll survive it."

"Without that chair," Mom added.

"Would you stop meddling with my choreography?" Connor groaned. "I'll get it figured out."

My eyes drooped shut during their argument, my body suddenly feeling heavy.

"What time is it?" I yawned.

Connor flashed me his watch, it was after midnight. "There's an after-party, I'm getting ready to change and head out. You coming?"

"I don't think that's really my scene."

He wiggled his eyebrows with a teasing smile. "What if Zach is there?"

"Every magazine article I've ever read about Skyline all concur that Zach doesn't do parties."

Connor's face fell. "So you're not coming?"

"Let's do a preshow party. Then it wouldn't be so late."

"Okay, Grandma."

Stretching my arms overhead with another yawn, I stood up. "Good night."

My mom kissed my temple. "Good night, dear."

There were two sets of bunk beds, each set three high. And, somehow, I'd ended up with the middle bunk. I climbed inside, letting my head fall back onto my pillow.

It was strange to think that once I woke up, we'd be in another city. Another state. My eyes slipped shut, but I was unable to block out the conversation happening in the other room, less than ten feet away. Not to mention the road noise that seemed to be amplified in my bunk. And the sound of the toilet flushing as my dad relieved himself.

This was definitely going to take some getting used to.

PORTLAND, OR
CHAPTER 6

I left a note on the counter of the tour bus's small kitchen, letting my mom know I was going on my morning run. Apparently, the drive had taken only a little over three hours. We were already parked at the next arena, the stage crew unloading the buses to get ready for tonight's show.

The sleep inside of the tour bus had been rough, to say the least—I tossed and turned most of the night, unable to get comfortable. It was a big transition from my custom mattress at home to the hard brick they called a mattress here. There was a break after the show tonight, and my mom had mentioned checking into a hotel and leaving for San Francisco in the morning. I would take a hotel bed over that bus bunk any day.

My phone's GPS led me on a run. We were staying in the Alberta Arts District of Portland, which had much more of an eccentric, hipster vibe. The streets were lined with hole-in-the-wall coffee shops, all seemingly brimming with life. Bright, colorful murals lined the walls.

Los Angeles had a reputation for being bright and filled with life. But the atmosphere in Portland was less Hollywood and more laid-back. And I loved it. My morning run helped wake my body up, and I felt more refreshed once I got back to the bus.

"Did you have a good run?" Mom asked as I stepped inside.

"Very refreshing." She passed me a bottle of water. "Is the shower open?"

"Dad went ahead and checked us into a hotel for tonight, which is bound to have more room and better water pressure."

"Excellent."

"Tomorrow night, on our off night? There's a team that wants you to guest-play with them. The San Francisco Vipers."

A smile stretched across my face. "Really?"

"The coach said her sweeper is going on vacation, whatever that means, and they'd love to have you play in her position."

"That sounds awesome!"

"You know what a sweeper is?"

While my mom always tried to be supportive, she wasn't really soccer savvy. "That's my position, Mom."

Her mouth formed an O shape. "Right!"

"That's okay, Mom. Thank you for setting it up for me."

"Of course, dear. I want you to succeed in your soccer playing as much as I want Connor to succeed with his singing. I love you both."

And for a moment, I allowed myself to believe that was true.

My dad had left a room key for me at the front desk, and I was able to take a long, hot shower. As I luxuriated on the comfortable bed, I jolted awake to my phone beeping.

Would you like to come to the arena with us? Connor should be getting up any minute. Love, Mom.

I made myself a cup of coffee, contemplating my options. Go to the arena with Connor or stay in the hotel room by myself. Aside from watching some YouTube videos and listening to music, there wasn't much for me here.

See you there.

I quickly pulled my hair up and got dressed.
My phone buzzed a few minutes later.

We're downstairs in the lobby getting some coffee for Connor. Meet me. Love, Mom.

"We need to get a move on," Mom said, as I joined her and Connor. "You have to sound check first."

"Why do I have to leave before Skyline?" Connor asked.

"You're the headliner," Mom explained for the millionth time. "You always sound check first."

"Well maybe this headliner could sound check a little later next time?" he grumbled.

"Real humble," I said.

Mom pushed open the back door to the arena, holding it open for the two of us.

Connor's band was starting the sound check on stage as we weaved through the back hallways. Inside Connor's dressing room, his outfits were already preset for tonight, and along the mirror was an assortment of hair products and a curling wand.

"And people think that's natural," I said, bouncing one of his curls.

"If they only knew," he teased.

A knock came on the door, and Dad walked in, followed by another man.

"Great," Connor said, setting down his coffee mug. "Is he here to tape me up?"

Dad nodded. "And then you've got to get to stage."

"Tape you up?" I asked, as the man pulled out a bag. "Like your wrist?"

"No, I like to wear tape around my head," Connor deadpanned. "It's the new fad I'm trying to start."

"You know, all your fans would start doing it if you did."

Connor chuckled, then winced as the tape clearly wound around a tender spot.

"Sorry," the medic apologized.

"It's fine," Connor said.

"He's dramatic," I added. "You get used to it."

Connor shot me a disapproving look. "Don't you have somewhere else to be?"

I stood up. "I'm going to go FaceTime Jenica."

"Tell her I say hi!" Connor called after me.

"Don't worry, I won't!" I called over my shoulder.

I sat in the hallway scrolling through my social media pages while I listened to Connor run through his sound check. I tried FaceTiming Jenica, but the signal was terrible, so I went to the arena side doors to try to get a better signal outside. As soon as I opened the door, I realized my mistake. There were a group of girls standing outside, decked out in Connor Jackson T-shirts and posters.

"OMG!" a voice screamed. "It's Katelyn Jackson!" They sprinted toward me, swarming me so I was unable to escape.

"You're, like, totally pretty in real life," one girl said, a smile on her face. "What's Connor like in person?"

"Like . . . a human?"

The girls giggled, and I tried to inch farther away.

"Excuse me, girls," a voice said.

"Oh my God, it's Zach Matthews!" one of the girls screamed.

Zach is here? Right now? I turned to see Zach stepping out of a taxi, his eyes connecting with mine.

"Uh, hey . . . Zach," I said, desperately trying—and failing—to sound casual.

He came over to the group, a teasing smile on his face. "I'm sorry, guys. But I'm going to have to steal Katelyn away to a meeting." He reached out and grabbed my arm. "Very important, time sensitive." *He knows my name he knows my name oh my God he knows my name.*

I'm sure my eyes were as wide as everyone else's as he lightly pulled me back to the door. "I hope you guys understand," he said, before opening the door and hurrying me inside.

A tingling sensation ran down into my hands as I tried to calm my nerves. I was standing next to Zach. Matthews. He was perfect in person. *Say something, Katelyn.*

"Thanks," I said. My voice was a pitch higher than normal.

He leaned against the inside of the door, that teasing smile still playing on his lips. "It's no problem. Those girls were next-level fans. Those are the ones I try to keep at an arm's length," he said.

The fans who'd been clamoring after him, desperate for his attention. Ridiculous. Not like my legs were currently turning to jelly as I tried to formulate complete sentences in his presence.

He was close enough to brush his arm against mine, close enough so that I could smell his Old Spice deodorant. Looking up at him at this proximity made my breath catch in my throat. Freckles spattered across his cheeks, and he was undeniably attractive. I felt as though I was going to melt in my shoes as his eyes met mine. I'd never imagined being this close to Zach Matthews.

He reached up and ran his fingers through his already messy hair.

I nearly reached up to smooth it back into place but caught myself just in time.

Stop staring, Katelyn. My eyes traveled down the hallway as I tried to think of something else to say.

"We should probably head toward the dressing rooms," Zach said. "Before my brothers send a search party for me. And I'm sure your mom is looking for you too."

Heat spread across my cheeks. "You heard her last night?"

Zach laughed, the sound filling the space around us. It was a deep, husky laugh that sent a warmth radiating across my chest.

"She cares about you," Zach said.

I heard a buzzing sound, and I quickly checked my phone. Nothing.

Zach's eyes slid down to his smart watch, his lips pulling into a slight frown as he checked the text coming through. As he lifted his hand to read the message, I couldn't help but notice the faded lyrics written on his hand.

"What song is that for?" I asked.

His gaze followed mine, and he flipped over his hand. "The second verse for 'Rhythm of the Night.'" His voice took on a bit of a gruff tone, leading me to believe that I'd hit a nerve.

"I *love* the drum solo in that song, Ross kills it every time."

"It'd be even better if I didn't screw up the lyrics every time. I practice every day and still feel like I can't get it right."

What he just described was something every athlete feels every day. *Oh my God I had just discovered common ground.*

"What do you do when you feel like you're forgetting the lyrics?" I asked.

For me, whenever I felt as though I wasn't playing to my full potential, I would hold up a hand toward Jenica. And she would mimic a high five. It was something silly, something we'd invented as kids playing on opposite sides of the field. But it always gave me a boost of confidence.

"Look at my hand," Zach said, "and hope I wrote the lyrics down."

Maybe Zach needed a ritual of his own.

"Do you have a marker?" I asked.

He reached into the pocket of his sweatpants, pulling out a permanent marker. "I'm always ready to sign some autographs. Where would you like it?"

I took the marker from him, pulling his hand toward me. "Trust me."

He did so without question. I traced a rest note right below his thumb. Small enough to be ignored, but large enough to notice if you tried.

"What's this?" he asked. His eyebrows furrowed together as he studied the rest note. "I don't get it."

"Whenever you think you're going to forget the lyrics, remember to pause and take a moment to think," I said. "And if you need some support, raise up your hand. Your audience knows your lyrics. They're there to support you."

Before I could explain any further, we were interrupted by another voice.

"Hey!" Jesse walked down the hallway, an unenthused look on his face. "You forget how to use a phone?"

"Chill," Zach said. "I'm coming now."

Jesse stopped short when he saw me. "Just . . . get to stage. We're late, as usual."

"Guess I'll see you later then?" Zach asked me.

Zach actually wanted to see me again. I wanted to scream. "Yeah, guess so."

He let Jesse pull him out to the stage, and I watched him go, the two of us grinning as he raced away.

Jesse immediately began to question him, but since he wasn't wearing a mic I couldn't hear what they were saying. The nosy fangirl in me definitely needed some time to calm back down.

But not before I told Jenica *everything*.

" . . . don't understand why."

I tried to tune out Connor's voice, tried to force myself back to sleep.

"Keep your voice down," Dad said. "Your mother is asleep, and I believe Katelyn is too."

So much for falling back asleep. I looked at the clock: three a.m. Maybe some cold water would help. My dad and Connor were both standing in the hotel suite kitchen as I ventured out of my room.

"Tomorrow is my day off," Connor said. "I don't want to be stuck on the bus all day." His arms were folded tightly across his chest, his jaw set. You could feel the tension in the room.

"Can I get some water?" I asked. He was standing in front of the refrigerator, blocking the pathway.

"Of course," Connor said, taking a step back. "Anything for Katelyn."

Connor's brusque attitude caught me off guard. "Um, thanks?"

My own spine stiffened as I grabbed a bottle of water, the tension in the room seeping into my skin.

"Is something wrong?" I asked.

Dad shook his head. "Nothing that can't be worked out."

"Please, enlighten me," Connor said, bracing his hands on the counter. "Why are we leaving at seven in the morning?"

"To head to San Francisco, I already explained this," Dad said with a heavy sigh.

What was supposed to be the catch here? The next tour stop was San Francisco, which was a ten-hour drive.

"It's my day off," Connor said. "Remind me why we're loading up *that* early."

I felt a knot in my stomach start to coil as I realized what he was getting at. "Is this about my game?"

"I don't get many days off, Katelyn," Connor said, in a clipped tone. "It would be nice to relax outside of a tour bus for a day."

"We just started this tour, Connor. We've only been on the road for like two days," I said.

"I'm sure we can work something out," my dad said. "To make everyone happy."

Now it was my jaw that was set. "Wait, are you serious right now, Connor? I gave up my entire summer to get on a tour bus. I gave up my team, my friends, my social life, *everything*. And you have the audacity to complain because Mom scheduled *one* game around your tour schedule?" My voice was rising, and as much as I tried to control it, my temper slipped away from me. "I don't want to crash on a tour bus, either, Connor. I don't want to be your summer groupie. But I don't get a choice in all of this!"

And then I laughed. Uncontrollably. My body felt like it was on fire, the heat of my anger taking control. My arms spread wide. "Welcome to the Connor Jackson Show, everyone! Where we're all the background support to Connor's success story."

"That's not fair—" Dad started, but I cut him off.

"When's the last time you saw me play, Dad?"

He didn't respond, which led to my anger bubbling over into laughter once again. "And you, Connor? Because I can tell you the last time I saw you perform was a few hours ago. When's the last time you took an interest in *anything* that I do?"

Connor didn't respond.

I snatched the water bottle from the counter. "Please, stay here tomorrow. Enjoy the sights. Enjoy your day off. I wouldn't want you to have to uproot your life for me, of course."

No response from either one of them. Not that I expected one.

My body was tense and my muscles quivering as I went back to my room. Portland was officially a bust. And I couldn't wait to get the hell out.

SAN FRANCISCO, CA
CHAPTER 7

Due to my lack of sleep the night before, falling asleep on the tour bus had never been easier. I didn't wake up until lunchtime, my body and mind feeling much more relaxed and at ease. Mom was sitting on the tiny couch, reading.

"There's coffee in the pot for you," she said, without glancing up from her book.

I poured myself a cup before taking a seat next to her. "How far out are we?"

"A couple of hours. We'll need to rush to get to the fields on time." She flashed me a smile. "But it shouldn't be an issue."

After last night's fiasco, my dad had agreed to stay back with Connor and fly in for the show tomorrow. And my mom had hopped on the tour bus with me so we could make it in time for my game. Connor, as usual, had gotten his way.

Silence lapsed between us as the drive stretched on. I pulled out my phone and flipped through my social media accounts, my follower count increasing with every show. My usual dad jokes and meme reviews seemed daunting to post with so much social media attention. I settled for a quick GIF to keep my account relevant.

And then I took to scanning through Zach's Twitter. He wasn't one to use social media much, but I checked for any updates just in case.

"He's a cutie, isn't he?"

I glanced over my shoulder to see Mom standing over me. "What are you doing?"

"I could ask you the same thing."

I'd been caught red-handed, and I didn't have a comeback for that. "Go read your book, Mom."

"I find *this* romance story to be much more intriguing."

My entire body felt warm, my discomfort growing. "I should've never gotten out of bed."

Mom continued to laugh. "I love you, my dear."

"Can't say the feeling is mutual."

As my mom predicted, we made it to the Vipers game just in time.

I was wearing my club team's uniform, but I knew they'd give me one of theirs to use for the game this evening. The other girls on the team were already warming up on the field. They glanced at me as I walked up, but they never stopped their warm-up.

"You must be Katelyn Jackson," a woman said when I got to the bench. "It's such a pleasure to meet you! I'm Coach Nicole." She didn't look any older than twenty-five, and she had an easygoing smile on her face.

"Nice to meet you," I said, shaking her hand.

She handed me a team backpack. "Inside is a jersey, shorts, and socks."

"Thank you."

Another girl came jogging over to meet us. She gave me a once-over, her lips pursed as she studied me. "This is her?"

"This is Katelyn Jackson," Coach Nicole said, with a bright smile. "Go ahead and get dressed; game time is only forty-five minutes out."

I went over behind the team bench to do a quick change. On my club team I was number two, but on this team I'd been given number twenty-six. Luckily, I'd worn my Limitless Apparel sliders under my shorts, which made the changing process much quicker. Pulling on the white socks over my shin guards, I shoved my feet into my Limitless Apparel custom cleats, the duct tape still wrapped around the sole.

"You've played this team before?" Coach Nicole asked, pointing to the Snakes.

"My home team played them in a tournament a couple of weeks ago," I redid my ponytail. "We beat them."

"Their star forward, Marci Adams, is fast."

"Like lightning," I agreed, handing her bag back.

"Keep it."

"Thanks." I placed it down next to mine. "But I have her beat so long as I don't have to go up against her repeatedly."

Coach Nicole nodded. My nerves were on edge as I joined in with warm-ups. I wasn't sure how I'd measure up to these girls. After a few minutes I felt myself settling into the routine. No matter where the game was played, at the end of the day it was still soccer. And that's the one thing I could wholeheartedly say I'm good at.

"So, you're Katelyn Jackson," the same girl from earlier said to me.

I nodded as I squirted some water into my mouth from my water bottle. "And you are?"

"Wendy."

"Nice to meet you."

I couldn't tell if she was sizing me up or being friendly, so I kept my tone light, waiting to see where she was going to take the conversation.

"What are you doing in town?" she asked.

"My family and I are here with my brother for his work."

Dropping Connor's name in conversation was something I hated doing, as the conversation would immediately take a sharp turn after. And as selfish as it seemed, I wanted these next few hours to be about me.

"You've got pretty good ball control. I don't think I've seen anyone do a lace trap as smoothly as you did out there."

She *was* sizing me up. "Thank you," I said. "So are you, you have a good shot."

"I know. Thanks."

I admired her confidence.

The refs cut off our conversation with a check-in. We patted our shin guards for the refs and showed them our cleats. They called us off one by one, checking our player cards. For me, they had to locate my guest player form.

"Ten minutes before game time," the ref said to Coach Nicole. "Let's get captains!"

"We got this side of the field," one of the captains announced, coming back to the bench. "They got kickoff."

"Those are some nice cleats," the goalie said to me, once I reached my position. "Even with the duct tape."

"Thanks," I said, with a smile.

"Here's the heads-up," Zelda said. "Jade doesn't play defense, and if she doesn't like the position she'll purposely suck at it until Nicole pulls her. Angela's good, but she has a problem with stabbing. Caroline's going to be your rock. She's got stopper down like the back of her hand."

"Goalie, you ready?" the ref called to Zelda.

Zelda gave him a thumbs-up.

The whistle blew, and I already knew the play. It was the same every time we went up against them. Their star forward was lightning fast, and they'd chip the ball out to her in hopes she'd outrun the defense and they'd start off the game with a quick score.

"They're coming for you, Jade!" I called.

As predicted, the opposing team sprinted down the left side of the field. And as Zelda said, Jade let them blow right past her. The left midfielder chipped the ball to the center of the field, but I had Marci beat to the ball by a half step, and I headed it out to the right side.

"Surprise seeing you here," Marci snarled.

"I like to keep you on your toes," I shot back.

"I don't lose twice," she spat before turning to head back to the halfway line.

As the defense pushed up to the halfway line, I took a moment to look at the parents' side of the field. There were rows of camping chairs, some the basic foldouts, other seasoned soccer parents having sun covers and footrests. And then there was my mom. We hadn't traveled with any sideline gear, so she'd taken one of Connor's tour merch hoodies and had spread it on the ground, sitting on top.

I waved at her, and she enthusiastically waved back.

The first half passed by uneventfully. We didn't score and neither did they.

"How does it feel to be back out on the field?" Coach Nicole asked me, as we broke for halftime.

"Great," I said, guzzling down some water. "Feels like home."

"They're a good match for us," Coach Nicole said to the team, once we had some water. "But we're better, even if we're not playing like it."

"That's so cliché," Jade said.

"We're playing hard out there," Quinn argued. "It's not connecting."

Coach Nicole held up her hand to stop the girls. "Playing the blame game is only going to make things worse. That's not team-work."

Quinn and Jade exchanged glances, obviously both pissed.

"Let's get back out there and kick ass," Coach Nicole ordered. "Because I'm tired of watching this lackluster performance."

We hit the field again for the second half as the refs blew the whistle. This time we had kickoff, so this half didn't start as intensely for us defenders. The ball bounced around in the offense for a few minutes before a bad pass gave it away to one of the opposite team's defenders. I immediately readied myself, and I saw Marci tense up as well. It was down to another footrace.

The ball was chipped over our heads, just in the right place. Marci and I took off, the two of us neck and neck. I cut in front of her at the last second, passing the ball out to the right before she collided with my back at full speed. We hit the ground, and I let out a groan, my back throbbing. A hand appeared above me, and I used it to hoist myself up.

"You good?" Jade asked.

"Yeah," I said. "I'm good."

Marci pushed herself up off the ground, absentmindedly rubbing her shoulder blade. She gave me a death stare before jogging back to the halfway line.

"You look like you're done," Coach Nicole said to me, as I came to the sideline for water.

My body felt like it had been put through the wringer.

"I can take her maybe one more time," I said.

"She's too fast," Angela said, shaking her head. "I've never seen anything like it."

"Trust me, I know."

The ref blew the whistle, and we hit the field for the last quarter.

"I'll try to help you out," Caroline said, as we headed back to our positions. "I'm not as fast as she is, but I might be able to trip her up a bit, enough to give you a little head start."

"That would be a huge help."

It was our throw-in over by the goalie box, and our striker took a shot on goal. It went straight to the goalie. My insides were churning as I anticipated what was coming next, with both Marci and me backpedaling. Caroline tracked the punt, battling Marci for it. Caroline won control and passed it off to Quinn. I was happy to have dodged the Marci bullet.

The ball bounced around for the majority of the quarter, nobody really taking clear control.

Then, with less than one minute left, a bad pass gave the ball to the opposite team's defense. Everybody knew the play. They chipped it over our heads, and Marci and I took off, once again side by side.

I knew what needed to be done, but it meant sacrificing my body. But if it kept Marci from scoring, from winning, I was willing to do it. Without the time to cut in front of her again, my sprinting slowed from exhaustion. Instead, we were both going to reach the ball at the same time.

At the last second, I went for the slide tackle, taking the ball before I took her out, which made the move legal. She rolled over me as Zelda came out to clear the ball. The refs blew the whistle, signaling the end of the game, nil–nil. I didn't want to move, and I wasn't really sure that I could. My entire body ached. Marci was also still down on the field. Zelda offered me a hand up.

Marci's team had already hit the sidelines, oblivious to her still lying on the field. As I thought back to the game, I realized that nobody ever took the time to help her up when she was down. I limped over to Marci, offering my hand.

She looked up at me and grimaced. Ignoring my hand, she pushed herself up off the ground.

"Good game," I said. It felt bitter on my tongue.

"I will get you back, Jackson," she spat.

"I'm not here to start anything."

We lined up to shake hands with the opposite team. Marci didn't shake a single person's hand, and she took the time to stare at me as she passed by in line. I waved in return.

"Good game, girls," Coach Nicole said, as we settled in. "You played hard. We have one round of sprints and then we'll head home. Practice on Monday."

With all of the adrenaline bouncing inside of me from the game, I couldn't quite subject myself to the quiet night in my mom was set on having inside the tour bus. After a few strong suggestions of simmering down, I found myself with an agility ladder, running through footwork drills outside the arena.

High knees. Sidestep. Crossover. Centipede. In and out.

"Am I interrupting something?"

I let out a startled yelp, my foot getting caught in the ladder as I ungracefully fell to the concrete floor. I looked up to see Zach standing behind me, an amused smile on his face. He was dressed in a pair of black sweatpants and a thin, white T-shirt. *I don't think I'll ever get used to seeing Zach Matthews.*

"What are you doing?" he asked, with genuine curiosity.

Am I sweaty? I tried to do a discreet smell test. "Agility training. Just burning off some excess energy."

He flashed his watch. "At midnight?"

"The best time."

He reached his hand down. "Sorry for scaring you. Need a hand?"

I felt frozen as I stared at his hand, unsure as to what I should do. Zach Matthews offering me his hand was never a situation I'd expected to be in.

"Katelyn?"

As I hoisted myself up, I tried not to think too much about the fact that I was holding Zach's hand. *His callused but gentle hand.*

As quickly as it started, it was over as Zach released his grip, letting our hands drop. "So what has caused the need to burn some excess energy in the middle of the night?"

"My mom is trying to have a peaceful night in. And I'm not quite ready to wind down yet."

He shoved his hands into his pockets. "I won't bother you then. Have a good night."

No way was I letting this opportunity slip by. "I'd be happy to burn some excess energy with you."

Oh shit. That didn't come out right. And by the amused look on Zach's face, he agreed.

"I mean . . . through conversation," I said, the words tumbling out before I could stop them. "You know, just talking. Hanging out. Or not. Whatever—"

"I'd be happy to," Zach said, interrupting my rambling. He gestured toward the arena wall. "Want to sit?"

I nodded, afraid that if I kept talking I'd embarrass myself even further.

"All of my brothers went night swimming," he said, as we took a seat. "I went downstairs to hang out for a bit, but I didn't really feel like joining in. So I decided to take a walk, get some fresh air."

"Night swimming? Is that something you guys do often?"

"It's a Skyline tradition; every city we stay in we swim in a hotel pool after dusk."

Having a family tradition was something I didn't know I was jealous of until now. "That's fun."

He extended his legs out in front of him, glancing over toward my agility ladder. "You play soccer?"

I nodded, surprised that he remembered that.

"Which position?"

"Sweeper."

His face went blank as he stared at me. "Riiiight."

"The last defender before the goalie."

"Oh! That makes more sense."

His phone went off, and he silenced it before sliding it back into his pocket.

"What do you do aside from singing?" I asked.

"Write songs?"

Such a musician answer.

"I find it relaxing," Zach continued, "which is ironic because everyone else I know finds it frustrating."

"Like going out and juggling a soccer ball," I mused.

"Juggling?" Zach asked. "You can juggle?"

How to explain this? I picked up the soccer ball, tossing it back and forth as I mulled over my explanation. "It's juggling . . . but with your feet."

"What?"

"Seriously? You've never heard of juggling a soccer ball?"

"No."

I shook my head. "You've been deprived."

"Sounds like it."

Jesse came rounding the corner, a towel draped over his bare shoulders. His hair was still dripping water, spilling into his eyes. "Oh, hey."

Zach offered up a wave. Once again, I felt frozen.

"I'm headed back to the tour bus," Jesse said, jabbing his thumb in that direction. "Wake me up if I'm asleep before you get back?"

"Will do," Zach said.

Jesse's eyes flickered over to me momentarily, and my heart thumped in my chest. A smirk spread across his face. "Don't get too crazy out here, you party animals."

"Go away," Zach ordered.

Jesse laughed as he continued walking past. And then Zach's phone went off again.

"I think someone is really trying to get in touch with you," I said.

"Yeah, I guess so." He slid his finger across the phone. "Hey, Mom."

I couldn't help but smile at his clear discomfort. "Yeah, Mom. I'll let him know." He cleared his throat. "I'll call you tomorrow, okay?" He shoved his phone back into his pocket. "Sorry, my mom is a little . . . overbearing sometimes."

"Does she tour with you?"

"She said she can't imagine following us around. She's that kind of person that always has to be doing something. And she had four kids, so she's used to always being busy. Plus, she can't imagine giving up her job as a nurse to try to manage us—that's definitely not her forte."

It seemed odd to me. My parents had dropped everything in their lives for Connor, and they managed his career to a T.

"Don't you have a manager then?" I asked.

"Right now it's Jesse, but we're looking into hiring somebody."

That seemed like a lot on Jesse's plate. "How does Jesse have the time to be in the band and to manage?"

"It's actually not that hard. But it can cause arguments between us, which is why we're looking into hiring somebody."

It sounded . . . nice in a way. To have a mom whose life wasn't consumed by the fame.

"What about your dad?" I asked.

Zach's smile fell a little. "Our dad left."

"Oh . . . I'm so sorry."

"It's not something we talk about much," Zach said. "It happened when I was young, so I don't really remember him. I guess after the fourth kid he decided it wasn't what he wanted after all, so he high-tailed it."

"Your mom must be one strong woman."

"She's a hell of a mom."

As he reached up to smooth back his hair, I noticed the faded rest sign below his thumb.

"Has it helped?" I asked, pointing toward the temporary tattoo.

He let his hand drop, his leg brushing against mine as he leaned back, his head tipping toward the sky.

I squeezed my eyes shut for a moment, forcing myself to keep calm. *It's just two legs touching. Chill out.* "My memory can be spotty at best," he said. "It gets a little frustrating."

The plan needed tweaking. "Still have that marker?" I asked.

He reached into his pocket, coming back empty-handed. "Somewhere?"

"I can draw one on my hand for moral support. But we'll need a marker beforehand."

"I'll see you before the show, then?"

The question was simple enough, but there was an underlying eagerness, desire almost.

"Maybe we could ... hang out?" I suggested.

He shifted so that he was facing me, leaning in a bit closer. "What did you have in mind?"

"I want to get out and see San Francisco while we're here. If you want, before mic check tomorrow, we could go out and explore?"

"I'd like that."

The air escaped from my lungs in a giant whoosh. "I'll do some research, see where the hot spots in town are."

"I'll whip up a disguise," Zach said. "And by that, I mean find a hat and some sunglasses."

"You do realize it would have to be an early morning?" I asked, leaning over to knock shoulders with him.

"You may have to drag me out of bed," Zach said, with a sheepish smile. "But I'll be there."

SAN FRANCISCO, CA
CHAPTER 8

The next morning, I knocked three times before taking a step back from Zach's door. I waved at Paul, Zach's bodyguard, who was standing outside of the door. A full minute passed by until Jesse opened the door. And it was clear I'd woken him up.

"Sorry," Jesse said, with a yawn. "We're not morning people. Zach's in the bathroom." He pushed the door open, flipping on the light. "Is that coffee for me?"

I took a sip of my to-go coffee and grinned. "No, but there's some downstairs."

When he came out of the bathroom, Zach was dressed in a button-up flannel shirt, dark jeans, and his shoes in hand. "Hey, Jess, have you seen my black—"

"Katelyn's here," Jesse interrupted. "And it's in your suitcase, front zipper."

Jesse ushered me inside. "Where are you two crazy kids off to today?"

"Don't you have somewhere to be?" Zach called over his shoulder.

"Don't have too much fun. Make sure you're back at one for sound check."

Zach stepped past me, and I was hit by a whiff of cologne. It was a musky smell, mixed with a hint of citrus. It was close to the Old Spice smell he'd been sporting yesterday, but somehow better. He opened the bedroom door. "Go back to bed," he said to Jesse. "Bye."

Jesse waved us out the door, flipping off the lights as we left.

"I really do need some coffee," Zach said. "Did you get that downstairs?"

I took another sip as we waited for the elevator. "There's a whole breakfast spread down there."

"Not a breakfast fan."

"Then you haven't had the right breakfast."

We stepped into the elevator. "Banana and I'm good to go."

"Have you ever had cold pizza for breakfast? It will change your life."

He laughed. "I don't think that's the answer."

The elevator came to a stop, and it felt like I left my stomach behind on the upper floors. We stopped by the breakfast bar, where Zach grabbed a banana and a coffee.

"What did you find in your research last night?" Zach asked, as we stepped outside.

I led us over to our taxi, the two of us sliding into the back-seat, along with Zach's bodyguard. And I somehow ended up in the middle. I tried not to think about the fact that Zach's thigh was *firmly* pressed against mine, his jeans rubbing against my bare leg. And I tried not to think too much about how much he smelled like cologne and a fresh shower, when all I really wanted to do was lean in and—

"Where are we headed?" Zach asked.

I grabbed my phone, trying to clear my thoughts as I pulled up the website. "We're going to Fisherman's Wharf." I handed him my phone, trying not to glance over his shoulder as he scrolled through.

"I see a Beans," he said, as he zoomed in on the map. "First stop is definitely a shot of espresso."

"You're definitely not a morning person."

Zach shook his head. "I'm a sleep-until-noon kind of person."

"My body is naturally up by eight a.m., I have no control."

"That sounds like literal hell to me."

The conversation came easy between the two of us on the drive. Never in my wildest dreams did I expect to be going on a day excursion in California with Zach Matthews. And the moment felt surreal.

The taxi driver dropped us off at Beans, per Zach's request, and picked up some Zach-approved coffee.

"Are we off to anywhere in particular?" Zach asked, as we started down the sidewalk. Zach's bodyguard stayed a couple of steps behind us.

I shrugged. "There's a lot to Fisherman's Wharf. But the Internet said we had to go here."

"You're the tour guide, so lead us."

We walked over to the water, glancing over at the fish down below.

"It kind of smells like bird poop," I said, looking over at Zach for confirmation.

He nodded. "Definite bird poop vibes."

We ended up falling off the main path, taking small, brick roads as we explored the different avenues.

"What's that?" Zach asked.

I tried to look in the same general direction he was looking in. "What?"

His fingers brushed the side of my face, and I felt the goosebumps run down my arms. He turned my head to the left. "That."

It looked like an abandoned building, but I could see lights inside. But I wasn't ready to admit that I saw it yet, Zach's fingers still brushing my face.

"Come on." His hand dropped, and I found myself wanting to grab it back.

But I shoved my hands in my pockets, following him to the hole in the wall. Inside was an old-fashioned arcade.

"Oh, we have to play," I said, stopping at the coin machine.

We spent over an hour feeding coins into the arcade-style games, going from an arm-wrestling challenge to spinning a wheel for a career choice.

"Schoolteacher?" I questioned, as the light came on. "I was rooting for nudist."

And then Zach found a strength test.

"How does this work?" I asked, as he inserted his coins.

"There are these two metal arms," he said, as he extended his arms to grab each one. "And then you push them together and pull them apart. And I guess it gets harder as you go until you max out."

"Okay tough guy, let's see it."

The machine lit up, and Zach pushed the two metal arms together. He shifted his stance, trying to complete the first round.

"Shit," Zach said, with a laugh. "This is a lot harder than it looks."

"Let me try," I said.

I managed to pry the two arms open but was unable to push them back together.

"Okay, wait," I said, through my laughter, "you grab one arm, I'll grab the other, and we'll get this done."

"Deal."

I put all of my weight into pushing the one metal arm in, as Zach did the same on the opposite side.

"Now pull!" Zach called out.

We completed four rounds before the game timed out.

"I call that a success," I said, reaching over to high-five Zach.

"We've got to go," Zach's bodyguard said. "Sound check."

Zach reached up and wiped the glisten of sweat off his forehead. "Oh yeah, that whole tour thing I'm supposed to be doing."

"I guess we should head back for that," I said.

We left the arcade, Zach setting his remaining coins on top of the machine for the next guest. I quickly swiped one as a memento from San Francisco. Not that I'll ever forget this day.

"Before I forget," I said, holding out my hand, "marker?"

He pulled the permanent marker from his pocket, handing it over. "What's the plan this time?"

I traced over the fading rest sign on his hand. "When you look at the rest sign, remember that I have one too. And that I'm always here for moral support, whether it be on or off the stage."

A honk interrupted the conversation, the taxi waiting.

"Thank you for coming on this adventure with me," I said.

"Thanks for the invite."

I wanted to remember this forever. The moment that Zach gave me a soft, genuine smile, his eyes focused on me and his serious features fallen away. He looked happy. And I felt like I was floating.

"Even if I did have to wake up at eight," Zach added. "I'd say it was worth it."

CHAPTER 9

I hadn't spoken to Connor since yelling at him in the Portland hotel kitchen. This wasn't uncommon for us, as we had very different schedules and lives—that's probably where our dissonance started in the first place. But unlike before, instead of roaming around the same house and avoiding each other, we were now trapped on the same bus. And you can't avoid someone in a space the size of a mall restroom.

I'd been lying in my bunk, staring at the ceiling for what felt like ever. We were back on the road, making the drive from San Francisco to Las Vegas. It'd been only a couple of hours, the drive scheduled to take over eight, and I was already going stir crazy. I went out into the kitchen area to get some water, where Connor was seated on the couch with a book in his lap.

"Hey," Connor said.

I grabbed my bottle of water, hoping that I could get back to my bunk before having to initiate a conversation. But luck wasn't on my side.

"Can we talk?" Connor asked.

Part of me really wanted to say no. But I was too tired to keep fighting, so I turned around and stared at him, waiting for him to speak.

"You seem like you're up a lot at night too," Connor said.

"I tend to have trouble sleeping in a narrow bunk bed. But I guess that's what we do for Connor Jackson."

He grimaced, and I knew my comment hit home.

"I was an ass. I *am* an ass. Sometimes I get wrapped up in my own head and don't take the time to think about how this affects everyone else, especially you. I guess these past few months . . . I guess I lost sight of everything non-tour-related. Including you. Us. Our family. And I'm really sorry."

This was the Connor that I missed. And it took everything I had not to run over and hug him, to let everything go. "You really hurt me." I gestured around the tour bus. "We're doing this all for you, Connor. *I'm* doing this all for you. But I have dreams and aspirations too."

"And I'm sorry. But I promise to do better."

I'd always been known for having a stubborn personality. And today was no different. "Then prove it."

And with that I went back to my bunk.

Skyline was talking amongst themselves as I approached the stage. I'd taken to the higher seats, wanting to sit in on some rehearsals today, and Skyline didn't see me. I couldn't help but eavesdrop. The seat folded out as I eased down onto it, trying to keep quiet.

"Let's take five," Jesse said. "Then we'll have to run the opening number again." He turned to face Aaron. "What's the deal with tomorrow morning?"

As Jesse was talking, Zach lay on the ground, closing his eyes.

"They canceled," Aaron said, with a shrug.

"What? Why?"

"Because they want Skyline, not the Aaron and Ross Show."

Ross laughed. It felt like I was intruding on a personal moment, hearing something that wasn't meant for me. I slowly stood up to leave.

"Did you offer me?" Jesse asked.

"Yeah, but they want Zach."

"Offer Zach," Zach said, cracking an eye open.

"That's not happening," Jesse snapped.

My head snapped back to the stage, curiosity getting the best of me. Against my better judgment, I sat back down to listen to the rest of their conversation.

"Why not?" Zach demanded.

"You know why, don't start this now."

Zach pushed himself up off the floor. "This is the third show that's canceled because I won't come to the interview."

"He's got a point," Ross said.

"Do we have a system?" Jesse asked.

Zach groaned. "Well yeah but—"

"And is the system working?" Jesse asked, interrupting Zach.

"Yeah, but—"

"There are no buts. Mom put me in charge on tour. Zach gets a *minimum* of eight hours of sleep per night. No external stressors, including interviews. And limited intake of the caffeine and sugar. We have a system, it's working, end of story."

"It's one interview," Zach argued.

"We have to be at the television studio at five a.m.," Aaron said. "I'm with Jesse here. That's not happening."

Zach shook his head, obviously pissed. "I'm not letting another station cancel on us."

"Let's talk about this later," Ross suggested. "We only have the stage for ten more minutes."

"I don't need you to watch my every step," Zach snapped at Jesse, ignoring Ross.

"I'm going to pretend like you didn't say that," Jesse answered, his jaw clenched.

"Take the tension down a notch." Aaron stepped between the two boys.

Jesse turned and walked off the stage.

"Fuck this," Zach said, and went off in the opposite direction.

"Is the Aaron and Ross Show really that bad?" Ross asked Aaron. "I mean, I thought we did pretty well during interviews."

"Go find Zach," Aaron said, shaking his head. "I'll go calm Jesse down."

The two boys disappeared and I tried to make sense of what I'd just seen. As I was comprehending the situation, Mackenzie came out onto the stage for her sound check. Alicia was laughing at whatever Mackenzie was saying. They adjusted Mackenzie's microphone, and I was able to pick up parts of her conversation.

The stagehand said something to Mackenzie, and she nodded. "'Finally Mine' is in the lineup tonight, we're axing 'Let's Get Crazy.'"

Mackenzie turned to someone offstage. "Are you coming to the studio with me today? I'm putting the final touches on this song to send to the label."

I thoroughly enjoyed watching Mackenzie's sound check. Her backup dancers were always energetic, and the three of them had good chemistry together.

As Mackenzie's sound check ended, I heard Aaron's voice. "Want me to make a Beans run? I'll grab you a green tea."

"That would be awesome," Jesse agreed. "My throat's killing me."

And then their voices disappeared. Thank God my hiding spot hadn't been exposed.

"Good afternoon."

A startled yelp escaped my lips as I turned to see Ross standing next to me. Ross busted out in laughter. "Did I actually scare you?"

"Where did you come from?"

He pointed to the righthand staircase. "I wasn't quiet about it."

And then Aaron was coming up the stairs. "Hey, Ross, I'm headed to Beans, do—" He paused when he saw me. "You found our hiding spot."

"I was definitely here first," I said, gesturing toward the empty balcony.

"We always take over the balconies at the shows," Ross said. "You may have gotten here first, but you stole our territory."

"Ross, Katelyn, want anything?"

I felt my heart do a flutter, and I silently cursed myself. *When would I stop fangirling over Skyline?* I went on an entire adventure yesterday with Zach. That should be enough for my Skyline-obsessed mind.

"No thanks," I said.

"I'll come with you," Ross said. "If we can go to CVS to get supplies for tonight."

Aaron cocked his head to the side, and the two had a silent conversation. I glanced away, feeling as though I was intruding.

Ross then appeared in my line of vision. "Hello?"

I looked at Ross, who said, "We're going swimming at the hotel tonight. It's a Skyline tradition. We'll come and get you."

"What?"

"If you're going to be hanging out with our brother, you should really know what you're getting yourself into with the Matthews family."

"Shut up, Ross. Are you coming or what?" Aaron said.

"See you at midnight, Katelyn. I'd suggest a swimsuit," Ross laughed on his way out.

There was a knock on my hotel room door. I checked my reflection in the mirror one last time. It'd taken me three tries to get my messy bun perfect, even though the rational part of me knew that it would be ruined as soon as I jumped into the pool. I was wearing a T-shirt and shorts over my bathing suit, but since the only thing I owned was a bikini, I wasn't sure if the T-shirt was ever going to come off. While waiting on the boys, I'd slipped on my comfy socks, and now as I went to put on my slides, I didn't bother taking them off. Answering my hotel room door to reveal Ross and Zach.

"Ready?" Ross asked, excitedly.

"Sure," I agreed, stepping outside my hotel room. The door shut behind me, my hotel room key safely tucked in my shorts pocket.

"Nice socks," Zach said, with a smile.

They both had polka dots on them, but one was neon pink and the other was bright blue.

"I gave up trying to match my socks," I said, as we reached the elevator. "I'm convinced that my dryer eats them."

"Sounds like Zach," Ross said, as we stepped into the elevator. "He says that about his underwear."

"Jesus Christ," Zach said. "Do you *have* a filter?"

"But you *do*."

Zach's cheeks turned pink.

"Jesse and Aaron are already done there," Ross said. "Scoping out the place."

"It's a pool," Zach said. "There isn't much to scope out."

"Grumpy," Ross muttered with a smirk.

We reached the ground level and headed outside. Paul was already standing next to the door, and he held it open as we walked out.

Immediately Ross dipped off to the side, and I quickly saw why when both Aaron and Jesse had water guns pointed at Zach.

"Oh no," Zach said. "Unfair ambush, I call reset."

Jesse and Aaron exchanged glances, and I ducked behind a chair as they soaked Zach.

"She's smart," Aaron said.

"We're not used to that," Jesse said.

Ross let out a loud whine. "Hurtful!"

"Where did you guys get water guns?" Zach asked.

"CVS," Aaron answered, as though it was the most obvious answer there was.

"We'll put down our guns if you come out!" Jesse called.

"She's not that stupid," Zach said.

"We really will," Aaron added. "Watch." He slid his water gun across the pool patio.

Jesse did the same.

Seems legit to me. I slowly stood up.

"Backup water guns!" Jesse called out.

Both he and Aaron soaked me with water guns they'd been storing behind potted plants.

"I'm not even surprised," Zach said, ditching his shirt before jumping into the pool.

I quickly grabbed the water gun that Aaron had discarded and used it to soak Aaron.

"Dammit!" Aaron called.

Jesse dove behind a chair before I could try to get him too. I took off my shorts and hopped into the pool, keeping my water gun with me.

"Swimming with a white shirt on is counterproductive," Ross said to me, as he jumped into the pool.

Not my smartest move. There was arguing behind me, and then a loud splash by Ross.

"You're going to die!" Aaron called out.

"Did you expect chaos?" Zach asked. "Because you definitely should've."

There was a loud yell behind me. Jesse sprinted across the patio and then cannonballed into the pool. With a swift motion, I pulled off my white shirt, placing it on the chair next to the water gun. I hadn't told the boys yet, but I planned on stealing the water gun to keep as a memento from our Las Vegas stop.

Aaron jumped into the pool last, jumping right on top of Ross. The two of them wrestled, while Jesse chanted, switching back and forth between Ross and Aaron. I went over and joined Zach on the edge of the pool, away from the action.

"I honestly think I was adopted," Zach said, as we watched them. "Or they were secretly raised by wolves."

"They're entertaining."

"That's a good word to describe them."

The water rippled as I splashed my feet in it.

"You seem really serious," Zach said.

"What do you mean?"

"Like, whenever we're joking around, you lighten up. But when we're sitting here, you get really intense."

"It's hard for me to open up to people sometimes."

"Because of your brother?"

"It's hard to adjust to new people, to tell whether they want to sincerely get to know me or want to get close to Connor." *But it's easy with you*, I wanted to add. The words felt stuck in my throat, and I quickly glanced away toward the chaos back in the pool, where Jesse was jumping on top of Ross to help Aaron take him down.

"I can see where that would get hard," Zach said. "People suck."

My eyes flickered over toward him. He looked as serious as I felt, like he was actually listening to what I had to say and internalizing it.

"Why do people suck?"

"They prejudge you," he said, a smile spreading across his face as Jesse and Aaron successfully managed to push Ross under. "They think they know you before they know you."

"Thanks for the help!" Ross called over to us, as he came to the surface gasping and sputtering for air. "You guys are the worst!"

We looked at each other and laughed.

"What are you guys doing?" Jesse asked. "This isn't sit-on-the-edge-of-the-pool time. This is night swimming."

"I think we should take him out," Zach said to me.

"I'm down with that."

We stood up and jumped into the pool, screeching at the top of our lungs.

PHOENIX, AZ
CHAPTER 10

I pressed my face against the tour bus window, watching as the storm raged around us. We'd been informed on our five-hour drive here that Phoenix was in the midst of their storm season. And I don't think I'd fully grasped what that meant until the thunderstorm had started. To make matters worse, I'd been scheduled to play a game tonight with the Phoenix Flyers. But by the looks of this storm, the fields were going to be flooded.

"Katelyn?" My mom was standing behind me, a sympathetic look on her face. "I just received news from the Phoenix Flyers' coach. The game's been canceled."

Disappointment seeped through me as I sat down on the tour bus couch with a groan. "Is it too much to ask for one game?"

Mom bent down, kissing the top of my head. "You're flying out for the Limitless Showcase while we're in Dallas, that's not too far off."

Nearly a week away.

"I guess."

"Can I do anything to cheer you up?" she asked. "We can do something else that's fun today."

I looked back over at the window, at the downpour of rain. "Not really."

"I'm sorry," she said.

"Unless you've suddenly become Zeus, the god of the sky and weather, I forgive you."

Connor came out from the bathroom. He had dark bags under his eyes, his face a shade paler than usual.

"Vegas get you last night?" I teased.

He sank down onto the couch next to me. "You could say that."

"Put some pep in your step, we're headed to stage for sound check in thirty minutes," Mom instructed. "Wash up, drink some caffeine—you made the decision to party all night and we're already rocking and rolling today."

And then I noticed the hickey. "You *really* had some fun last night."

Connor reached up, brushing his fingers across his neck. His eyes glanced toward Mom, who was absorbed in her phone. "*Shut. Up.*"

"Fine. But you owe me."

The tour bus door opened, my dad stepping inside. And he was drenched.

"Katelyn, I'm assuming your game is canceled today," Dad said.

I looked past him at the raging storm, a tightness in my chest as I realized it wasn't going to let up anytime soon. "Field's flooded."

"Everything is flooded," Dad said. "Be careful out there." He headed toward the back, grabbing a change of clothes on his way.

"If we're all up and going, let's head to the stage early," Mom said. "That way we can dry off before sound check."

With nothing better to do, I tagged along with them. Not that I necessarily wanted to sit through another sound check, but I didn't want to stay in the tour bus alone either. Connor and his band got onto the stage and I wandered away. I'd already seen enough sound checks for a lifetime.

I'd skipped the show last night to FaceTime Jenica about my pool adventure the night before. As I rounded the corner backstage, I was nearly plowed over by Zach.

"Hello there," I said.

He took a couple of steps back, clearly caught by surprise. "Shit, Katelyn, I'm sorry. I didn't see you there."

I glanced at the time on my phone. "This is an early call for you, barely one p.m."

"Okay, I'll accept the roast for almost running you over." He glanced down the hallway before looking back at me. "Where are you headed?"

"No clue. Anywhere."

"If you want you can come back to our dressing room."

The Skyline dressing room. Damn my fangirl heart.

"Sounds good."

Jesse was stretched out across the couch. He had a pillow across his eyes while he drank green tea. I looked to Zach for an explanation.

"His throat's killing him," Zach explained. "I think he should go to a doctor."

"No one asked you," Jesse called, before dissolving into coughs.

"As I said, he should go to a doctor." He plopped down in a chair. "You're welcome to sit anywhere."

Aaron and Ross were playing a videogame in the corner, the latter creating sound effects for the game.

"The game has sound effects built in!" Zach called. "You don't have to recreate them for us."

"*Bam!*" Ross called, as Aaron's car exploded. "It makes it that much better when I win."

Zach didn't comment any further, instead just shaking his head.

"What do you guys do before a show?" I asked, propping my feet up on a table.

"This," Aaron said, as they restarted their game.

"For like an hour," Zach said. "Then we have meet and greets and promotionals."

"Do we have any more tea?" Jesse called.

"We have this amazing guy called a *doctor*," Zach answered.

As the two of them continued to bicker, I took a moment to glance around the room. In the corner where Aaron and Ross were sitting on the floor, there was a TV plugged into the wall, with a gaming console hooked up. Next to them was a table of snacks, with a microwave on the end. And then the long couch that Jesse was stretched out on, along with the chair that I was seated on and another chair next to it. There was a smaller table between the couch and the two chairs, the one that my feet were currently propped up on. Over by the snack table, Zach produced a tea bag.

"Heat that up for me," Jesse said.

"Yes, your majesty."

Jesse threw a pillow at Zach, which Zach caught with ease and tossed back at Jesse.

Zach heated up a cup of tea and then dissolved a cough drop in it. Once the cough drop was completely gone, he handed the mug to Jesse.

"I want you to take care of me when I'm sick," I joked.

"He's only nice when you're sick," Ross called.

"I'll remember that next time you come to my room in the middle of the night," Zach snapped.

"I take it back!"

I raised an eyebrow toward Zach in question.

"He told you enough about me in the elevator," Zach mused. "Ross has nightmares. And then he thinks it's okay to climb into my bed in the middle of the night."

"I told you he's not nice," Ross huffed. "That's personal, you know."

"My underwear is too."

"Okay, we're even!"

It was easy to toss around jokes and bounce off the boys, easy to *exist*. Even when they were insulting each other, it was all light-hearted. Their ease and camaraderie made me feel wanted and included, things I'd been lacking within my own family lately.

"Yo, Zach," Ross said, standing up. "Come play in my place for a sec."

"No thanks," Zach said.

Ross let out a groan, but he paused the game before leaving the dressing room. Aaron dropped his controller, coming over to join Zach and me. "What kind of parties happen in your tour bus?" he asked me.

"What?"

"I'm curious how other people run their buses," Aaron plopped down on the couch.

Jesse let out a surprised shout. "You're sitting on my feet!" He dissolved into coughs, hiding his face away.

"Shut up, sickie," Aaron said.

"Our tour bus is boring," I clarified. "It has my parents on it."

"I'd prefer boring over a tour bus with *them*," said Zach.

"*Them* can hear you," Aaron said. "And nobody likes a party pooper."

"What do you guys do on your bus?" I asked.

"Play videogames and card games," Aaron said. "Dare each other to do stupid stuff. Write songs—"

"*You* do not write songs," Zach scoffed.

"Let Zach write songs while we screw off," Aaron corrected. "And mostly piss Zach off. That's the end game."

"A week into the tour and you're already winning," Zach muttered.

"Are you coming to the show tonight?" Aaron asked.

"Yeah, I am now. I was supposed to have a game tonight, but it got canceled because of all the rain."

"A game?"

"She plays soccer," Zach interjected. "And I bet she's really good at it."

The heat built in my cheeks. "Thanks."

"Of all people, I didn't expect Katelyn to suddenly get shy," Jesse teased.

The heat spread from my cheeks down the back of my neck. "I'm not."

"I think that's awesome," Aaron said. "How do you play on the road?"

"I guest-play with other teams," I said. "My team coach and my mom set it up."

"Okay," Ross called, coming back into the room. "I'm ready to finish kicking your ass."

Aaron clicked his tongue in disapproval. "Language in the presence of a lady."

Ross looked over at me. "I'm sure she says some words on the soccer field."

"How'd you know she played soccer?" Aaron asked.

Ross twitched a bit, and Zach immediately lowered his eyes.

"I know, no secrets," Ross said. "Suddenly I need to leave again."

I looked to Zach for an explanation, but Zach was glaring at Ross.

"Now," Ross added, before dashing out of the room.

"Weirdo," Aaron muttered. "Hope he remembers we have that live Q&A in fifteen."

Jesse pushed himself upright. "Go find him. I'll get everything set up."

I followed Jesse's lead, standing up as well. "Thanks for letting me hang out, guys."

"Anytime," Aaron said, with a wave.

Zach was avoiding my gaze, his eyes shifting over toward Jesse. *Guess that's my cue to leave.*

"See you guys around."

Connor was doing his sound check back at the stage, an energy drink in hand. My mom was in the audience, her iPad in her lap as she worked on what looked like a press release. I took a seat next to her.

"I'm sorry you're bored," Mom said. "If it wasn't pouring outside, I'd go with you on one of your tourist adventures."

"I might have given up on those."

She shook her head. "You need to find the right places and the right company."

I leaned back in my seat, a buzzing of energy pouring through my system. My body was going to explode if I didn't get on a soccer field soon.

PHOENIX, AZ
CHAPTER 11

Solo Katelyn was back on the town.

After two shows in Phoenix, we had two days off in a row. But we also had a sixteen-hour drive ahead of us. We were set to leave for Houston early this afternoon, but I couldn't stand another moment cooped up somewhere.

Of course today was clear skies, not a hint of rain. But there were no games scheduled today, with the fields still soaked from the storms over the past two days. So I found a cycling class to burn off the energy that I'd expected to burn off on the soccer field the other day.

Never having attended a cycling class before, I didn't have any expectations going in. But what I didn't expect was to get my ass kicked in the first fifteen minutes. My body was dripping with sweat at the end, my legs practically giving out as I dismounted the bike. It was one of the best workouts I'd had in a while. I purchased a sweat towel from the front desk, using it to clean myself off before changing out of my sweaty clothes. The towel would make a good memento from Arizona—after a good wash, of course.

I felt more refreshed than I had in days as I headed back to the tour bus. My body felt relaxed yet exhausted at the same time, and I felt like I could handle the long car ride ahead of us.

That is, until I walked into the chaos of the tour bus. Dad had his planner spilled out across the countertops, his Bluetooth in. Connor motioned for silence, beckoning for me to follow him back to the lounge area in the back of the bus. He slid the door shut.

"What's going on?" I asked.

"Lana's manager called," Connor said. "She wants a reconsideration of the contract."

I'd practically forgotten about the drama that was Lana Regas. "You broke up with her. What does she want?"

Connor grimaced. "She's threatening to leak everything."

Shit.

Connor's shoulders sagged. "This isn't how I would've wanted things to go, but I guess I'm not really being given much of a choice here."

With a tight chest, I reached over and placed my hand on his upper back as I tried to come up with any way to make this situation better. But I knew the video that Lana had, what she was threatening Connor with. One night, back when Lana and Connor's relationship was still very real, they'd gotten insanely drunk. They recorded a series of silly videos together, all on Lana's phone. And amongst those series of videos, they spilled secrets I'm not sure they'd ever admitted to themselves, let alone out loud.

After they both sobered up, the videos became a tactic. They agreed to an NDA, but after a rough year, I wasn't surprised that the contract was starting to break down.

"It's not that bad," I said. "Honestly, Connor. Maybe things are better this way."

I could tell he didn't agree, not that I blamed him. This wasn't the time for everything to come to light, not in the middle of his tour.

"Can you sue?" I offered.

He laughed at that. "If she's willing to pay to break the NDA, I don't think she cares about a lawsuit."

The lounge door opened, Dad standing outside. "We have a conference call with Lana's management at two."

Connor nodded.

"We're playing nice on this," Dad said. "She has the upper hand and she knows it. We'll let her blow her smoke and then see what she really wants."

"Okay."

"Katelyn, you might want to ride on Mackenzie's bus. This isn't going to be an easy conversation."

Sixteen hours on Mackenzie's tour bus? "This is one of the longest drives of the tour. Mackenzie's fine but I don't know her."

"What about Skyline?" Connor asked. "You've been hanging out with them."

"You really want me gone that badly?"

"I know Lana. This won't be a thirty-minute conversation." His voice had a heaviness to it, his shoulders visibly sagging.

"I'll call Jesse to make sure it's okay," Dad said. "If you're all right with that, Katelyn."

Connor actually laughed at that. "Are you kidding? Confined to a tour bus with Skyline all day long? That's her dream come true."

Dad didn't seem amused as he walked away.

"As if I haven't noticed you and the Zach-kid hanging out," Connor said, his smile growing. "Does he know about the poster you—"

"That wasn't me!" I shouted, as I dove on top of Connor. "That was Jenica and you know it."

"But you didn't take it down!"

We wrestled on the couch, Connor giggling the entire time as I tried to shove him onto the floor.

"Truce!" Connor called out. "You're stronger than me."

"Damn right."

Dad cleared his throat behind us. "Jesse said that would be fine. If you two are done?"

"This isn't over," I said to Connor. I grabbed my backpack, shoving a few essentials inside before following my dad out of the bus.

"I'm not trying to kick you out," Dad said. "I've just dealt with Lana's team before. And it's never a pleasant conversation."

Sometimes I think he forgets just how much I know, just how much I've heard. What Connor has told me. I know what Connor has gone through, what effect Lana's deal has had on him. But this wasn't a battle I was willing to fight.

Skyline's tour bus looked like ours on the outside. But from the pictures they'd posted online, I knew it was slightly different on the inside. They had only four bunks inside, whereas we had six. They still had a lounge in the back, containing an array of instruments while ours had been converted into a master bedroom for Connor. Dad knocked twice before taking a step back.

"Going to talk to my babysitters before you go?" I questioned. "Warn them about me?"

He was clearly unamused. "It's polite, Katelyn. They're allowing you to stay on their tour bus."

"How generous of them. Seeing as my dad kicked me out of mine."

Before our argument could continue, Jesse opened the door.

"Sorry," he said. "We were in the back."

"Bye, Dad."

He waved. "I'll call you later."

And with that my dad was dropping me off with four guys

without a second thought. I wasn't sure whether that said more about him or Skyline, for agreeing.

"Everything okay?" Jesse asked, as he closed the door behind me. "Your dad called and I figured you guys got into some sort of fight or something."

Ross was standing in the main area. "We figured we couldn't leave you on a tour bus with him if that's what went down."

"No fight, but thanks for thinking about me. He's talking business with Connor, and I guess it's for Connor Jackson's ears only."

"Not cool." Ross frowned.

Jesse gave Ross a pointed look. "Let's not comment on someone else's family?"

Ross held his hands up in mock surrender. "Just saying."

"We're playing *Call of Duty* in the back," Jesse said, nodding toward the back lounge. "By we, I mean Aaron and Ross."

"Jesse is doing business stuff," Ross said. "Very boring."

"So you're feeling better then?" I asked. "You sound a lot better too."

Jesse scoffed in response. "Of course I am. An overreaction by these idiots."

A very Jesse answer. I glanced around the small area, noticing that it was only the three boys.

Where is Zach?

"Zach's sleeping," Ross said, as though he'd read my mind. "He had a headache earlier."

Ross and I went back to the lounge room, Aaron still playing.

"Hey there," Aaron said, with a smile. He offered me the controller. "You play?"

"Never really been into videogames," I said.

Ross paused the game. "I'm sorry, what?"

Both Aaron and I laughed, and I felt some of the nerves start to dissipate as they continued their game.

"It's really simple," Ross said, as he handed me his controller. "Trust me."

"I don't," I said, as Aaron started the game. "But I guess I can give it a try."

My character was dead within the first two minutes.

"Solid effort," Aaron said, through his laughter.

"Absolutely not," Ross said, shaking his head. "You disgraced the game of *COD*."

The door opened, Jesse coming inside. "Are the Cheez-Its back here?"

Aaron tossed him the box. "Zach still asleep?"

Jesse nodded. "Sorry, Katelyn. You might be stuck with us for the evening."

"That gives her plenty of time to learn *COD*," Ross said. "Because so far it's pretty rough."

"I played for the first time," I teased. "That would be like me handing you a soccer ball and letting you loose."

"We played baseball," Ross said, pointing to him, Jesse, and Aaron. "The athleticism ended with me."

"Baseball and soccer aren't comparable," Aaron said. "But way to brag."

Jesse sat the Cheez-Its box on the ground, next to the door. "I'm going to watch a movie."

"Don't start the new Marvel movie yet," Ross called after him.

"Bet you he's watching Harry Potter," Aaron said to Ross.

Ross scoffed in response. "I'm not taking the bet because it's obviously true."

Through the many magazines I'd devoured about Skyline, I'd learned that Jesse was a Harry Potter nerd. "He's a Slytherin, right?"

"Yep," Ross said. "Says a lot about him right there."

"I'm a Ravenclaw," Aaron said, before pointing to Ross. "And he's a mix between a Hufflepuff and a Ravenclaw. A Ravenpuff. Or a Huffleclaw."

"And Zach is a Gryffindor," Ross said. "Basic."

Of course he is. "Guess that makes me basic too."

"Gryffindor?" Aaron asked. He tilted his head to the side, studying me. "Yeah, I can see it."

"I hear Harry Potter talk!" Jesse called out.

We went out to the main area, where Zach was sitting on one of the couches.

My heart did a flip in my chest as I witnessed Zach in pure form, a white T-shirt and black sweatpants with his hair sticking up in all the wrong places. It was clear he'd tried to smooth his hair down with his hands, but it was a perfect bedhead look. And I was swooning for it. As predicted, Harry Potter was playing on the screen. It looked like *The Chamber of Secrets*, but I wasn't sure.

"Feeling better?" Ross asked Zach.

Zach nodded, standing up as the two boys sat down. "I'm going to the back for a bit." He glanced over toward me. "Want to come?"

More than anything. "Sure."

I took a seat on the couch as Zach grabbed his guitar stashed in the corner.

"You going to write me a song?" I teased.

"I actually am in the middle of writing a song." His smile faded a little. "But I've got a killer headache, so no new melodies are coming from me today."

I tried not to think about the fact that Zach Matthews was sitting in front of me, a guitar in his hand. It was every dream I'd ever had coming true all at once.

"Sing an old melody then," I said.

He raised an eyebrow. "Like what?"

"I want to hear 'Honorable Mention.'"

A full-blown smile spread across his face. "You're kidding."

"Do you remember it?"

He strummed the guitar a few times, quietly humming. "I think so." He looked back up at me. "How did you remember 'Honorable Mention'?"

Because I'm obsessed with your work. "Just popped in my head."

"Shit, what key was that in?" he asked, as he continued to strum. "I think that was a C major?"

"C major, with a C, G, A minor, and F progression."

This time he fully paused, his eyes studying mine. "You play?"

My body felt numb as I gazed into his caramel brown eyes. "Sometimes. Not seriously."

He held out the guitar toward me. "Let's hear it then."

"You're not getting out of serenading me with 'Honorable Mention' that easily."

We paused as I took a moment to process what I'd said. I knew the blush was coming before I felt the heat rising.

Zach recovered first. "Of all songs to choose to be serenaded with, 'Honorable Mention' is a pretty shitty choice." I managed a small laugh, the embarrassment seeping through me. "But if you insist."

And he did just that. His voice was deep and gravelly, a contrast to the prepubescent Zach who had sung this song three years prior. It was an entirely different experience with only an acoustic guitar, and Zach's voice, and I never wanted it to end.

"That live up to your expectations?" Zach asked.

My racing heart answered for me. "Beyond exceeded."

He strummed his guitar, humming once again. "Give me something that won't make me cringe."

"Say what you want, 'Honorable Mention' is still one of my favorites."

He gave me a disapproving look. "We need to work on your taste in music."

That I had to laugh at.

"Give me something from the new EP," I said. "As a music fan, I feel as though it's my duty to give you my honest review."

A smile played on Zach's lips. "A music fan? Or a Skyline fan?"

"Music," I said.

"Right. Because all music fans know the chord progression for a deep cut off our first EP."

"This music fan does."

He let out a soft laugh, but began to strum again. "Okay. This one's called 'Henrietta.'"

"'Henrietta?'" I questioned.

"You'll see."

And with that, I was lost in the world of Zach Matthews's voice once again.

HOUSTON, TX
CHAPTER 12

Another sound check. Another meet and greet. Another show.

I couldn't even remember what city we were supposed to be in, what the schedule breakdown was. All I knew is that I couldn't sit through another repetitive routine.

Connor was off on a radio interview. Mackenzie had rented rehearsal space to practice the choreography for her new dance number. And I hadn't seen Skyline since I'd left their tour bus last night to sleep in ours.

Another me day.

I checked my Maps location. We were in the heart of Houston, Texas. There had to be some good food around here somewhere.

My phone buzzed as I started my walk, an Instagram Live notification from Skyline. I brought up the notification as I walked. It was almost like having company on my adventure. Almost.

"Hey, I'm Jesse."

"I'm Aaron."

"Ross."

"And I'm Zach. And we're Skyline."

It was a Q&A, the boys taking some time to announce some upcoming interviews they'd be doing and doing some promotional work for ticket sales for the tour.

"All right, I'm going to start scrolling for questions," Jesse said. "You have the next sixty seconds to spam us in the chat. To fill in those next sixty seconds, Aaron and Ross are going to arm wrestle."

A barbecue restaurant. It was only appropriate that I try something that Houston was famous for. I grabbed a menu, half listening to the Skyline live chat as I scanned the food choices.

"And we're done!" Jesse announced. "Ross the clear champion."

"That's only because he's a drummer," Aaron argued.

"That doesn't make any sense," Ross said.

I placed an order at the cashier's recommendation before taking a seat to wait for my food. The boys were scrolling through the chat, reading out some of the questions.

"Our next single is dropping mid-July," Ross said, with a smile. "We haven't released the name yet, but stick close because it'll be any day now."

"Yes, the rumors are true," Aaron said. "We are looking into headlining our own tour after we finish with Connor Jackson Live. More information to come on that when we get it."

"No, I don't spend fifteen minutes on my hair," Jesse said, looking into the camera. "What kind of question is that?"

"Yes he does!" Ross said. "If not more."

It felt like I was spending my lunch with the boys, my solo Katelyn adventure turning into a lunch date. As I finished up, I took one of the napkins with the restaurant's name printed on it. Memento for Houston? Check. As I tucked the napkin into my pocket, I couldn't help but realize how ridiculous the items were that

I'd picked up from each location so far. But that's what made them special, because they were *my* memories.

I walked back to the tour bus, dropping my napkin into my memento box before changing into Limitless Apparel shorts and a tournament T-shirt. I pulled on my sneakers, grabbing my soccer ball before heading back outside.

All I needed was a large, empty wall.

And the exact one was back where the crew buses were parked. It was a decent size, and nobody seemed to be around this area.

The repetitive sound of the soccer ball hitting my foot and then the wall brought on a calmness that had been lacking over the past few tour stops.

"Whoa, there."

I let out a surprised yelp, turning to see Zach coming up behind me.

And then the soccer ball hit me in the calf. Hard. "Ow, dammit."

He had a black journal in hand, a pen sticking out of his sweatpants' pocket. "Are you trying to dent the arena?"

As a force of habit, I picked up the tail of my shirt to wipe the sweat off my face. Only to then quickly realize I was flashing Zach my sports bra.

I quickly let my shirt fall back down, "Sorry, I was in my element."

"I could tell," he said. "I'd been standing there for like, three minutes, waiting for a chance to run past you without getting hit."

Oops. "Sorry about that."

"Nothing to be sorry about. Passion is something you should never apologize for."

"Thank you."

"Next time I cross your path, I'll bring you a towel," he said, with a teasing smile. "Though I think you look cute either way."

Before I had the chance to process, to respond, he was leaving. He continued into the arena, pulling his pen out and writing as he walked. I took a few moments to play with the soccer ball, doing some more intricate footwork before I slammed it against the arena wall again.

Wall, foot, repeat. This was my favorite way to spend a hot, summer afternoon.

And it did a really good job of keeping me from overthinking the fact that Zach Matthews had just called me cute.

"Can I get one of the Skyline shirts?" I asked my mom.

"What do you need a merch shirt for?"

"Because it's important to me."

She shook her head, but I could see her smile. "Yes, Katelyn. Go ahead and grab one."

I picked a simple white T-shirt with *Skyline* written across the front in block letters. On the back it had a professionally drawn portrait of the four boys. I also grabbed a *Connor Jackson Live* T-shirt, with the list of the tour dates on the back.

"Is that all you wanted?" Mom asked.

"For now."

"I'm guessing you're sitting in on the show tonight?"

I nodded, holding up my Skyline shirt. "Time to be the fangirl I truly am."

"You should get the boys to sign your shirt."

"Are you offering me a meet-and-greet pass?"

She shook her head. "You're too much."

"Is that a yes?"

"I don't have a meet-and-greet pass to see Skyline," she said. "Just go and see them yourself before the show."

Instead of crashing their meet and greet, I went back to the tour bus. Up until this point, I'd always found a way to entertain myself, to keep from getting bored. And it looks like that streak was coming to an end. After reorganizing my suitcase, catching up on my social media, and playing a round of solitaire, there wasn't much else I could force myself to do.

And then there was a knock on the door. Unsure who exactly would be taking the time to knock before entering, I slowly crept toward the door, peering out of the peephole.

Zach?

I quickly yanked open the door. "Hi!"

He offered up a smile. "I was trying to take a nap but have had a little too much caffeine to lie down. And your mom said you were looking for a friend."

Of course she did.

"Come in," I said, pulling him inside before closing the door behind him. "I was . . . cleaning."

He slipped his Vans off by the door before turning to face me with a quizzical expression. "Cleaning the tour bus?"

It sounded a lot better than playing cards alone. "A little."

We crossed over to the couch, and I realized this was his first time in our bus. "Want a tour?"

"Sure."

I spread my arms out wide. "This is the couch area."

"Living room?"

"I'm not sure it's big enough to be called its own room." I led him past the couch, placing my hands on the table where my cards were. "This is where we eat breakfast."

"That's usually what tables are for."

We then walked down the hallway. "These are the six bunk beds. My mom and dad sleep on the top two bunks. I have the middle left. And then the other three bunks store clothes." I pulled back the curtains of my suitcase bunk. "Here are where my clothes live."

Zach peered over my shoulder. "You sure do have a lot of soccer shirts."

"Are you calling me out?"

"Only slightly." And then he saw my memento box. "What is that?"

Pulling the box out, I handed it to him to sift through. "I like to collect an item from each city that means something to me."

He held up the napkin from today. "This means something to you?"

"That's where I had amazing barbecue for lunch," I said. "Each item is something that I'll remember."

He slowly nodded as his eyes swept over the contents. "Some people make scrapbooks. Some people journal. You collect *things*. I like it."

"I have one from everywhere we've been except Portland."

He raised an eyebrow in question. "Why Portland?"

"Because while on my run, I got so caught up in the city itself that I forgot to take a piece home."

"Understandable."

Zach's hand brushed against mine as he passed the box back to me, sending tingles down my spine. I turned away from him to put the box back, taking a deep breath to calm my nerves.

Pulling the curtain shut, I turned back toward Connor's room. "And this is where His Majesty sleeps."

"You mean he doesn't have a bunk?"

"Of course not." I pushed open the door to the back room. Inside was Connor's full-size bed, as well as his overspilling suitcase and acoustic guitar.

"I'd have to fight Jesse, Aaron, *and* Ross for this," Zach said. "No way I'd win that battle."

We made our way back to the couches, Zach pausing at the table covered in playing cards.

"What were you playing?" he asked. "You know, while you were cleaning."

Caught red-handed. "I might have played some solitaire."

He headed toward the door, slipping on his shoes. A sense of disappointment washed over me as I realized he was going to leave.

"I have something for you," he said, before opening the door.

I followed him outside. He stepped off to the side of the tour buses, picking up a rock. Reaching into his pocket, he pulled out his marker.

"What're you doing?" I asked.

He scribbled something on the rock, before turning around to face me. "For you."

I took the rock from him, flipping it over to see *Portland* written across it in bold letters.

"I definitely remember picking that up in Portland, don't you?" Zach asked, with a playful grin.

It was *perfect*.

DALLAS, TX
CHAPTER 13

I was set to fly out for the Limitless Apparel Showcase this afternoon. But trying to kill my nerves after our overnight travel was proving to be rather difficult. I took to pacing the "rooms" of the tour bus, much to my mom's dismay.

"Why don't you pop out for a bit?" she suggested. "Burn some of that excess energy."

"I can't. I have to pace. I have to think."

"It's eight in the morning; what do you have to think about?"

A knock came on our tour bus door, and my mom glanced toward me before answering it, as I was already heading toward the back of the bus on my pacing circle.

"Hi, Mrs. Jackson."

Ross.

My mom let him inside the bus. And of course I was still dressed in my pajamas: a pair of shorts with cats playing soccer and an over-sized Connor Jackson shirt. I looked absolutely ridiculous.

"Morning, Katelyn. I was checking to see what you're up to."

"Yes, Katelyn. What *are* you up to?" my mom teased.

I didn't have a good answer. "Thinking."

Mom let out a small laugh before retaking her seat on the couch.

"I was coming to see if you wanted to come to the studio with us this morning," he said. "We're recording a new song, and I thought it'd be fun with an audience."

"Such a difficult choice," Mom said. "Stay here and continue to *think*, or go with Skyline to the recording studio to hear their brand-new song."

My face flushed with embarrassment, my mom smirking behind Ross. She was exposing me in a way she knew I couldn't refuse.

"I'll come," I said. "Give me a minute to get dressed."

Ross's eyes flickered down to my cat shorts. "I mean, I don't know how you beat those shorts, but you can certainly try."

Mom ushered Ross off the bus, and I waited for the door to close before exploding.

"*Mom!* Could you *be* any more obvious?"

She shrugged. "I'm doing what is best for my daughter."

"You're embarrassing me."

"That's what moms are for."

As much as I wanted to continue the argument, I didn't have time to. I was nowhere near ready to go out into society. "This conversation isn't over."

She waved me along. "Want me to braid your hair? You know how adorable I think you look with those Dutch braids."

"Yes. But that doesn't make us good."

She just laughed.

I'd tried to organize my suitcase when the trip started by cloth-ing articles, but this far into the tour, it was hopeless. And of course today was the day I needed something other than Limitless Apparel running shorts and a tournament T-shirt, which seemed to be my entire wardrobe.

I managed to find a pair of high-waisted black shorts and a cropped, gray tank top. I locked myself in the bathroom as I got ready. There was knocking on the bathroom door as soon as I stripped off my pajamas.

"What are you doing?" Connor yelled.

"Go away!"

He let out a loud groan. "I need to use the restroom!"

"It's a girl emergency."

There was a moment of silence outside the door. "Oh. Okay."

I did my usual makeup routine, adding a pop of color with my chapstick.

"That's your definition of an emergency?" Connor demanded, as I came out of the bathroom. "Actually getting dressed?"

I knew that if I tried to explain, it would lead to more questions. Questions that I didn't want to answer, that I didn't know *how* to answer. "Shut up, Connor."

He surveyed me for a moment. "What's the special occasion?"

"What are you talking about?"

He gestured toward my outfit. "You're not wearing running shorts, for one. And your shirt is cropped."

Connor never notices what I'm wearing or what I'm doing. Why today, of all days? "I'm just getting dressed."

"Where are you going?" he asked, as I pulled on my black Vans.

"Out."

"With Zach?"

"No, with Skyline."

"Which includes Zach."

I looked up to see a teasing smile stretching across Connor's face. "You like him!"

"I thought you needed to use the bathroom," I said, as I pushed past him toward my mom.

"Katelyn likes Zach!" Connor sang, dancing around the narrow hallway.

"Katelyn likes who?" Dad asked, coming out of the back room and heading toward the bathroom.

"Nobody," I snapped, giving Connor a warning look.

Connor burst into laughter, collapsing on the floor.

"I want to file a petition for a new family," I muttered, as my mom stood up from the couch.

"Sit," Mom said, gesturing toward the couch. "They'll be here any minute."

I did as I was told, my mom twisting my hair into braids.

"I swear, if your hair isn't in a ponytail, it's in braids," she said. "You're going to break your hair."

"Alex Morgan still seems to have hair, so I think I'll be fine," I said, referring to my favorite soccer player.

A knock came on the tour bus door as my mom wrapped the last hair tie around the second braid.

"Perfect timing," she said, taking a step back from me. "Now go. Have fun. Stop thinking so much."

"What great mom advice."

She kissed my forehead before opening the tour bus door for me. And Ross then held open the taxi door for me.

"Welcome!" Jesse called from the front seat.

"Thanks." I climbed in.

Both Ross and Aaron were on their phones. Zach was asleep. He'd balled up his hoodie and was using it as a pillow against the window. I leaned back in my seat as the taxi started off onto the main road.

"What have you been up to this fine morning?" Ross asked, looking up from his phone.

"Nothing much," I said, answering Jenica's text about my flight.

We were originally supposed to get to Los Angeles around the same time, but Jenica's flight had been delayed. Which meant that we wouldn't be able to share a taxi along with our nerves and excitement.

"Your morning run then?" Aaron asked.

"What?" I asked, turning to face him. I know for a fact that I've never mentioned my morning to run to the boys. "How do you know that?"

"This is our sixth tour stop with you," Ross said, laughing. "We know a lot more than you give us credit for."

"Like what?" I challenged.

"Like how you only eat the yellow Sour Patch Kids," Aaron said, eyes glued to his phone.

"Or how you order a side salad practically every night from the place that delivers our pizza," Ross said. "But you still eat the pizza too."

"Or how your entire wardrobe consists of soccer T-shirts and running shorts," Jesse said.

"That's really freaky," I said. "And that last one was a little hurtful."

"Today it's different," Jesse pointed out.

I looked around at the guys. They were all wearing jeans and graphic shirts, except Zach. Zach was wearing a pair of black sweatpants and the familiar thin, white T-shirt. The taxi pulled up to the destination, and Jesse reached back to shake Zach a bit.

"I'd get out of the explosion zone," Ross warned, before ducking out of the car.

Zach rubbed his eyes for a few moments before looking between the two of us and then at the recording studio, putting the pieces together.

"Let's hop to it!" Jesse announced. "We have the space for only two hours." He turned to me. "We already laid down all the instrumental tracks, and today we're just completing the vocals so we don't need long."

Zach grunted before climbing out of the car, letting out a yawn.

"Good morning," I said to Zach.

"Morning," he answered, his voice hoarse from sleep.

We went back to the space that the boys had rented.

"Hey, guys," the guy at the console said, nodding at Jesse and Zach. He tilted his head at me, confusion written across his face.

He was a bit on the heavier side and had obvious laugh lines etched on his face. He had a little stubble on his face, as though he'd neglected to shave for a couple of days.

"And who's this?" he asked.

"Katelyn, this is our sound engineer Terrence," Ross said. "Terrence, this is our friend Katelyn."

"Nice to meet you, Katelyn," Terrence said, waving at me. He turned to face the guys. "Zach, my man, you look like you could use some caffeine."

"That's the understatement of the century," Zach grumbled.

"Oh great," Ross muttered. "We got Mr. Grumps-a-lot."

Zach glared at his brother.

"Good thing I have a green tea for you," Terrence handed Zach a hot mug. "I've got you, my man."

"All right, let's set up," Aaron said to Jesse and Ross. "Join us in a few, Zach."

Zach sat down on a couch and sipped the tea. "Thanks, Terrence, it's good."

"Katelyn, right?" Terrence asked once the guys were inside the recording room. I nodded, taking a seat in one of the empty chairs.

"How do you know these boys?"

"I'm Connor Jackson's younger sister."

"Ah, you're one lucky girl. These are four of the best guys I could ever want to work with."

Zach interrupted the conversation by laughing. "You're so full of it."

"Shut up and drink your tea," Terrence called over his shoulder.

"I finished it," he said, standing up. "Thanks again."

"No problem, kid."

"What's the name of the song?" I asked Zach.

"It's called 'L.A. Sunshine,'" Zach said. "I think you'll like it." He headed into the recording room. Terrence clicked his tongue as he leaned over the engineering equipment, having a quick conversation with the guys adjusting the machines.

The microphones came to life as the boys pulled on headphones. The sound was open, so we could hear what the guys were saying in the recording booth.

"I can hear you, Ross," Jesse said.

"We heard your fart," Aaron added.

"Disgusting," Zach said. "We're locked in a room together. Go fart outside."

"Are you boys ready?" Terrence asked.

"If I can sing through this stench," Zach muttered, shaking his head.

"Suck it up and get started," Terrence ordered. "We don't have too much time."

The next couple of hours flew by. It was a very surreal moment to be sitting in a studio with my favorite band, watching them record a brand-new song. And it was hard to process that this was actually happening.

Throughout the recording process, it was seemingly obvious that Zach was having a hard time. He continuously missed his count ins, was off the beat, and fumbled over the lyrics. And by the look on Jesse's face, this wasn't an everyday occurrence.

"That was a piece of work," Terrence said, once they finally finished recording.

"I get it," Zach muttered, ripping off his headphones.

"Don't egg him on," Jesse said, grabbing a Coke out of the refrigerator. "It's been a long session and he didn't come in with a great mood."

Zach came out of the recording room, stress lines creased along his face.

"Take a load off," I said, patting the seat next to me.

He sat down next to me, letting out a long sigh.

"Give me a few minutes here," Terrence said. "And then you guys can hear a rough cut of the final product."

"That's so cool," I said.

"Do you ever go to the studio with Connor?" Ross asked.

"No," I said. "He's in his tense mode when he's at the recording studio, and I don't want to be around that."

"His tense mode?"

"Like stressed-out and hyperfocused."

Ross thumbed in the direction of Zach. "Sounds like somebody we know."

"I can see you," Zach said pointedly.

"All right," Terrence announced, turning to face us. "For your listening pleasure, here's a rough cut of 'L.A. Sunshine.'"

After witnessing the hard work that went behind the recording of the song, it was satisfying to hear the end product. The song depicted a girl who was a little quirky, a little stubborn, but had a heart of gold. And who resembled the L.A. sunshine.

"You're the man, Terrence!" Ross said, reaching over to high-five him. "That sounds so good."

"It really does," Zach grinned.

"Now that Zach confirmed my opinion," Ross muttered.

"I sent you guys the file," Terrence said. "I'll keep working on it over the next couple of days and send you the finished product."

Jesse and Terrence started going over timelines as Aaron called for the taxi.

"We have to be back for sound check," Aaron said. "And Katelyn has a flight to catch."

"What did you think?" Ross asked me, as we walked out.

The fangirl poured out of me before I could stop it. "The overall beat is *sick*. And the line about two passions aligning into one? Absolutely brilliant."

"Glad you liked it," Ross said. "As our biggest fan and all, your opinion is valuable."

I resisted the urge to facepalm as I let out a groan, Ross clearly pleased with himself at my discomfort.

"Taxi's here, pick up the pace!" Aaron called out. "We'll get killed if we're late to sound check again."

My mom sifted through my duffel bag, double-checking that I'd packed everything I needed before heading to the airport. Once a momager, always a momager.

"Did I pack up to your standards?" I asked, as she zipped my duffel bag closed. "Is it Candace Jackson approved?"

She gave me a pointed look over her shoulder. "I'm your mom. I need to make sure you have everything you need before you fly to another state and realize you forgot to pack underwear."

"Thanks, Mom."

"Taxi's here!" Dad called from the front of the tour bus.

With my duffel bag over my shoulder, I headed outside with my mom following close behind.

"Be careful, honey," mom said, giving me a light hug and a kiss on the top of the head. "Call me when you land in L.A."

"I will."

"I hope you have lots and lots of fun."

It wasn't the ideal preshowcase speech, but I could tell she really was trying. "Thanks, Mom."

"Wait!"

Zach and Ross were sprinting toward our tour bus.

"We wanted to make sure we wished you good luck," Ross said, a bit breathlessly. "Unless that's bad luck. Then break a leg."

"I think you're thinking of theater," I said, with a laugh. "But thank you, Ross."

Ross saluted me. "By the time you get back, 'L.A. Sunshine' will be released as a single for the whole world to hear. Your seal of approval better be sincere."

"That's not what she needs to hear before she leaves," Zach said. "She's busy. Get out of here."

"Okay," Ross said, holding his hands up in mock surrender. "I can take the hint."

Zach turned to face me. "Good luck. I know you're going to do great." He held out a small box toward me. "For good luck?"

I took the box and opened it. Inside was a crystalized soccer necklace with my number engraved in the center, number two.

"It's beautiful," I breathed, looking up at Zach.

His usual, confident smile had been replaced by a nervous half smile. "I'm glad you like it."

I carefully put it back inside the box and gave him a tight hug, which he quickly returned.

"I'll see you when you get back," Zach said, tenderly.

"Would you two kiss already?" a voice called.

Zach's eyes widened, and his face turned bright red.

"Bye, Zach," I said, laughing. I slipped into the back of the car, still clasping the box in my hands.

LOS ANGELES, CA
CHAPTER 14

I shifted from foot to foot as I stood in line for check-in. We had to wait patiently in the queue to get our informational packets, which told us what room we'd be staying in and had our schedule breakdown. I stepped up to the table, my ID in hand.

"Welcome to the Limitless Apparel Showcase!" The redhead behind the table flashed me a bright, perky smile. "Name please?"

"Katelyn Jackson."

She leafed through her papers, finding my name and dorm room number. "Right this way!"

The nerves were starting to set in as I followed her down the hallway, realizing everything I'd worked for up until this point was resting on my performance over the next couple of days. The Limitless Apparel Showcase had the power to propel me to the next level in soccer, with scouts galore pouring in and out of the facilities.

I had to be on top of my game at all times, and that alone was enough to make me feel nauseated.

"Your room number is 319," she said and handed me a room key. "Have fun!"

"Thanks," I said, opening the door and heading inside.

She waited for me to get inside before leaving to greet the next set of girls, showing them to their dorm rooms.

I was the first one here, but I knew my bunkmate would be Jenica. Coach Jefferson had put a bug in the coordinator's ear to stick the two of us together for maximum performance. Jenica would want the bottom bunk, so I threw my stuff on top before walking over to the window. We didn't have a great view, staring off at some trees and a parking lot. Part of me wished we could see the fields from our window, but I knew that would only hike up my nerves even more.

The door opened, and I turned, expecting to see Jenica. But in walked Marci Adams. She paused when she saw me, the perky red-head oblivious to the obvious tension that instantly filled the room.

"Have fun!" she chirped, and walked away.

The door closed behind her, and we stood there in an awkward silence.

Marci crossed the room, throwing her stuff on the opposite set of bunks. "What a surprise. The universe must really like to screw with us."

"Of all people, I end up roomies with you."

"Feeling's mutual."

I took a seat on Jenica's bunk, leafing through my welcome packet as Marci unpacked. It wasn't a bad idea, to put some stuff away in the drawers. But I wasn't going to look like I was taking a hint from Marci. Instead, I pulled out today's schedule:

Dinner at six.

Conditioning from seven until nine.

Lights out at ten.

Getting started right away. I could feel the buzz in the pit of my stomach. I couldn't wait for Jenica to get here to share my excitement.

We were all seated on the turf soccer fields. As far as I could tell, everyone who'd been invited to the Showcase was here for the conditioning. The fake grass was sharp against my thighs, and although the sun had already set, the heat still hung in the air. There was a tall, well-built male standing next to the goal, an iPad in hand. He hadn't looked up yet, his eyes glued to the tablet.

"Sunscreen is a definite must for tomorrow," Jenica said. "Seriously, my skin might actually burn to a crisp."

As the time clicked to 7:01, the man cleared his throat, the chattering around the field immediately quieting down. "Welcome to your first conditioning session. I'm Coach Muldenhower, and I'll be your worst nightmare." His British accent came out strong as he stared us down, waiting for a response.

"Lord help me," Jenica whispered.

"You'll have two conditioning sessions per day. Each of them will be two hours, and each will be so brutal you'll crawl off the field at the end. Both are mandatory, meaning if you miss one, you have no chances of making the eighteen-girl team chosen on Friday."

The team of my dreams. "I'm going to die," I whispered to Jenica.

"I'll be right there with you," she whispered back.

"We always start with ten minutes of stretching," he called. "Followed by a ten-minute warm-up."

"There goes twenty minutes," I said.

"Then there's thirty minutes of plyometrics, thirty minutes of calisthenics, and thirty minutes of endurance testing. And then we'll finish with a ten-minute cooldown." He looked around us. "All of this will be done outside, which means we will take frequent water breaks to keep hydrated. However, keep in mind, this is conditioning, so you don't want to overdo the water." He looked at his watch. "We've wasted enough time with my intro, let's get started. Circle up, ladies."

The next two hours were *exceptionally* brutal. No amount of preparation could ready you for one of Coach Muldenhower's workouts.

"Good job, ladies," he called, as we sprawled out across the field. "Ice baths in the locker room."

"I'm good right here," I said to Jenica, my body aching.

"You're going to want it for later," Jenica said, as she pushed herself up off the ground.

"No," I groaned.

She nudged my side with her foot. "Get your ass up and let's get an ice bath before they're all taken."

I slowly pushed myself up off the floor and practically dragged myself to the locker room.

"It's time for *Drama Llama*," I reminded Jenica, as we headed into our dorm building.

"We have a communal dorm building TV," Jenica reminded. "That's a lot of people to convince to watch *Drama Llama*."

I headed into the main area where the TV was, and a few girls were sprawled across the couches. To my surprise, the intro to *Drama Llama* was playing on the TV. I hurried over to watch, Jenica right behind me.

The three girls introduced themselves as Amzley, Elizabeth, and Lauren.

"I'm Jenica."

"And I'm Katelyn."

The first girl's eyes widened. "I knew you looked familiar! Are you Katelyn Jackson? Connor Jackson's sister?"

There was always one. "Yeah."

"That's so cool!"

Amzley snorted. "She's obsessed."

"Am not."

"That's okay," I said, teasingly. "Jenica is too."

"A teeny bit," Jenica laughed. "He's even hotter in person." I closed my eyes and shook my head.

Drama Llama came back on, and I turned my attention to the gossip portion.

"Talk about juicy," the reporter said. "The hunky Connor Jackson was spotted walking the streets of Dallas, Texas, today with ex-girlfriend, supermodel Lana Regas." The picture flashed onto the screen, where Connor was walking down the sidewalk, a pair of sunglasses on and dressed in his usual designer clothing. He was looking off to the left. Lana was on his right, and she was dressed in a romper with a pair of sunglasses, and she was looking off to the right.

"The broken-up pair didn't seem too happy," the reporter continued. "And proceeded to have a minor dispute outside a coffee shop before going their separate ways."

I immediately pulled out my phone and sent a quick text to Connor. I knew that *Drama Llama* wasn't always accurate, but they did have a picture of the two of them together. And I wanted to know why.

Drama Llama went on to talk about the anticipated release of Mackenzie's new song.

My phone buzzed in my pocket, Connor's name popping up on the screen.

We had some loose ends to tie up. Fuck Drama
Llama for running a story. I've got enough to deal

with already, I don't need the paps blowing things
out of proportion.

Things definitely didn't end well between the two of them.

Be careful with what you say in public.
Someone could record you and it'd explode.

Connor was quick to answer back.

Good. I'm done talking about her and the video.

Ouch.

"Ignore him," Jenica whispered, as she'd been reading over my shoulder. "He's uptight about whatever went down with Lana; it'll blow over."

I put my phone facedown. "I need to know more juicy gossip. How long is this commercial break?"

"Hopefully we get to hear about the Nick and Lisa drama," Amzley said. "I've been following it for three days and I need new details."

LOS ANGELES, CA
CHAPTER 15

We were back to sitting on the turf. Unlike the night before, the sun was bright overhead, beaming directly down on the fields. I reached up and wiped a small bit of sweat that had already accumulated on the back of my neck.

"Welcome to your first full day of the Limitless Apparel Showcase!" a woman called.

A loud cheer came out from all of us. I let my head tip back, the sun grazing my face as I took in the moment. Took in the opportunity.

"Each of you has been assigned a locker," the lady announced. "Inside that locker is the latest Limitless footwear and clothing. You're expected to wear Limitless at all times."

Another loud cheer went up.

"Am I not allowed to wear my cleats?" I asked Jenica.

"But if you have your own Limitless cleats and gear, feel free to wear that too."

Relief coursed through my system. As silly as it seemed, my cleats meant everything to me. I could swap my shin guards, my prewrap, even my sliders, but I couldn't play without my cleats.

"We're going to go ahead and split you up," she called. "These groups will correspond with the schedule, so Group A, you'll follow schedule A, Group B schedule B and so on."

I exchanged nervous glances with Jenica. I knew I wasn't grouped with her. I was in Group C with girls I didn't know. We were released to our lockers, our first event in thirty minutes.

"It's time," Jenica said, catching up with me.

"What?" I asked.

"This is what we've been waiting for," she said, excitement written across her face. "A chance to show these people why we're the best girls in this sport."

"Blue pinny," Coach Fredrickson said, handing it to me.

I slipped on the Limitless pinny over my head, wincing at the stench of sweat. He handed out the rest of them in three other colors.

"These are small-sided groups," Coach Fredrickson reminded us. "Four people on a team, two teams on the field at a time. We'll go for five-minute intervals. Blue and yellow, you're up first."

I took the field, taking my position as sweeper. We had two midfielders and a striker.

The five-minute game was grueling. You were constantly moving, never able to stand still. I'm proud to say that they didn't score on us the entire time, while we managed three goals. Our team left the field at the end, and the red team took our place.

I drank a little water while I watched them play. The red team was dynamite, their footwork and passing much better than the yellow team. They ran circles around them and ended up with nine goals.

We took the yellow team's spot, having to face the red team.

Going up against the red team's striker was a challenge. She had good footwork, but so did I. She was fast, but not nearly as fast as Marci. I could easily match the striker's pace, preventing her from scoring. But they prevented us from scoring, too, ending with a nil–nil tie.

A few of the Limitless Showcase officials stood off to the side, taking notes on our performance. We did these drills for an hour, and I felt the weight of exhaustion at the end. But both my team and the red team ended the day undefeated.

I headed up to the locker rooms, having some time before my next session, and I was in need of an ice bath after my grueling morning.

"Hey!" Jenica called from an ice bath.

I quickly stripped down and joined her, letting out a groan as my body hit the cold water.

"That conditioning session this morning was death," Jenica said, with a wince.

"Tell me about it. I didn't know my body could hurt so much."

Coach Muldenhower had really put us through the wringer. After only two sessions with him, I felt more in shape than I'd ever been in.

"Hey, Jenica, are you coming?" a girl called, drying herself off from her ice bath.

"Is it time already?"

"Yup, we'll be late if we don't head out now."

"Bye, Katelyn," Jenica said, stepping out of the bath.

"Where are you headed?" I asked.

"Technical footwork," Jenica said, throwing her sweaty clothes back on. "An hour of juggling, step overs, and pullbacks."

I smiled at her. "Have fun."

"Sure will." She blew a kiss at me before heading out to her class.

Leaning back in the tub, I let the cold water numb my sore

muscles. I'd done ice baths before, but never two days in a row. I soaked in the ice bath for a few more minutes before climbing out and changing into new Limitless clothing. I headed down to the fields to observe what was happening.

"Katelyn Jackson?" a girl asked, jogging up to meet me.

"Yeah?"

"Nancy Torino, huge fan of your brother."

I didn't know how to answer, so I nodded in response.

"It must be weird for you to hear people say that," she said, running her fingers through her hair. "I wasn't trying to be weird. It seems so surreal that I would actually be standing here talking to you, because you're practically famous."

Me? Famous? "I'm most definitely not famous."

"Are you kidding me? You're so awesome. The Instagram stories Connor posts with you in them are hilarious." She shook her head. "Now you probably think I'm some sort of weirdo fan."

It was like talking to Jenica about anything Connor-related. "Not really."

"You're so lucky that you get to tour with Skyline too," she said. "What are they like?"

"They're all really sweet," I said as we reached the fields.

"What happened today was crazy though, right?"

I stopped short, raising my eyebrows at her. "What happened today?"

"You haven't seen the news?"

"No, I haven't had time."

"They did a live chat to promote their new song, 'L.A. Sunshine,' and Ross revealed that Zach wrote it with a specific girl in mind. Zach was pissed."

My heart began beating faster. "Oh."

"Yeah, I wonder who it's about."

"Me too," I muttered.

It couldn't be about me...right? He had *just given me that necklace, and I* was *from L.A.* No, I realized. I barely knew him, and he knew way more girls from L.A. than me.

Now was not the time for a distraction anyway.

"We're going to do the Beep Test to end the day," Coach Muldenhower announced.

My arms rested on the top of my head as I panted. This afternoon had been an incredibly hard conditioning session.

"How many of you have never taken the Beep Test?" Coach Muldenhower asked.

Three girls raised their hands.

"It's pretty simple," he explained. "The cones are set twenty meters apart. When the first beep goes off, you have until the next beep to reach the second cone. As the test continues, the beeps get quicker. There will come a point when you don't reach the cone before the beep. When that point comes you step out and that'll be your final score. There will be a winner."

I looked around, knowing that I had to come out on top. This was my chance. We started off on Level One, which was easy. It was just jogging between the cones. Nobody fell off. As the levels increased, the speed increased. People began to fall out around Level Five, which was understandable after the tough conditioning session we'd endured. My legs were on fire.

By the time we reached Level Nine, there were only two of us left. And of course my opponent *had* to be Marci.

The Limitless Showcase officials were standing off to the side, watching us. I was mentally and physically exhausted, as I knew she had to be, but I continued to push forward, unwilling to lose. As I went to turn on the cone, my foot slipped, and I went sliding out. I quickly jumped to my feet and went sprinting for the opposite cone, but I didn't make it in time. I lost to Marci.

"Good run, ladies," Coach Muldenhower called. "Let's do a cool-down."

I did the cooldown as instructed before trudging up toward the locker rooms for an ice bath, not wanting to talk to anyone.

"You did great, Katelyn," Jenica said, catching up with me.

"I lost."

"You were still in the top two! And you lost only because you slipped."

"I still lost. And to Marci of all people."

She squeezed my shoulder. "Don't be so hard on yourself, Kate. You did awesome out there."

Today was not going as planned.

Right now is usually when I'd vent to Jenica's mom about my soccer struggles. She'd probably tell me I was overreacting. And then I'd tell her the story again to try to persuade her to see why I was most definitely not being dramatic. And then she'd tell me again that I was overreacting, and she'd tell me that it was going to work itself out.

But Jenica's mom wasn't at this tournament. And Jenica was as dramatic as I was, so going to her would exacerbate the problem. And my own mother would nod along to my story and try to offer advice without really understanding the situation, which would frustrate me even more. I flopped back on my dorm room bed with a groan, willing myself to gain the motivation I'd lost after this morning. As I was contemplating my next steps, my phone buzzed next to my head.

hi it's zach. connor gave me your number.

A smile spread across my face as I read Zach's text.

"That's a much different Katelyn than I left," Jenica said, as she came out of the shower. "Smiling Katelyn is my favorite Katelyn."

"Why would you take a shower before full-field scrimmages?" I asked, with a slight laugh.

"Because I felt gross. Two showers a day never hurt anyone." She peered over my shoulder, glancing at the text from Zach. "Oooh! I understand the smile now. What are you going to say back?" she asked, as her towel dropped to the floor.

"Whoa, give me a warning!" I called out, before glancing back down at my phone.

"Play it cool!" Jenica said. "Like him texting you is no big deal."

"It isn't."

She laughed at that, peering over my shoulder again as she pulled on a T-shirt. "Right."

"What do you think I should say back?"

She pursed her lips together. "Something like, *oh hey there* with a winky face."

Point proven. "Shut up."

"We need to go anyway. Mull over it during scrimmages."

As we went down to the field, I began readying myself for the full-field scrimmages. It was time to prove that earlier was a fluke, and that I truly deserved a spot on this team.

I got a blue pinny and was placed as starting sweeper. Jenica was also handed a blue pinny, and she was starting striker.

"Looks like we've proven something," I said to her, as we waited for the rest of the assignments.

"I told you it was our time."

We took our positions on the field, and I watched as Marci was handed a red pinny. Starting striker on the opposing team.

Playing with these girls was like playing a whole new level of soccer. My club team was good, but these girls were dynamite. My outside wings didn't stab; they actually contained players. And when the offenders got around the wings, my goalie actually communicated with me, and together we made an unstoppable team.

"I'm Rhonda," my left wing said, as we pushed forward while our team had the ball.

"Katelyn," I said, a bit breathlessly since I'd just chased down the opposing team's midfielder.

"Hey, Katelyn," Nancy said. She was playing right defender.

I answered with a wave.

The opposing team regained control of the ball, and our defense kicked into action.

I ended up clearing the ball, something I almost never do. But their offense was swarming us, and I didn't have much of a choice. As the game progressed, substitutions began to happen. During the second quarter Jenica was pulled, and at halftime they replaced the entire team, including me. I sat the bench for the first part of the third quarter, watching as the new team took on the new red team.

We'd been winning 1–0 when we were pulled, but the red team ended up scoring within the first seven minutes of the third quarter, tying up the game. Jenica was the first one subbed back in with strict instructions to score another goal. At the end of the third quarter, Rhonda, Nancy, and I were subbed back in with strict instructions not to let another goal through.

"I hate sitting on the bench," Rhonda said as we took our positions.

"I'm not used to it," I admitted, focusing in on the game.

"Yeah, me neither."

"It's weird when they put the best all together in one camp," Nancy said. "I'm not used to having this much of a challenge."

Rhonda and I nodded in agreement.

We weren't trying to be cocky, which is how it might've sounded to people listening in on our conversation. This camp was for the best of the best in our sport, bringing in players from all around the United States. There were fifty-two of us. And I personally loved the challenge. There weren't many times I got to test out my footwork and endurance—usually the only challenge was Marci. And that was rare, although I had played her quite a few times these past few months.

And then Marci was subbed back in.

"I thought they only let talent in," Marci muttered, as we stood next to one another at the halfway line.

"I guess you must've slipped through. It happens."

The opposing team began their passing game, something that Marci wasn't used to. On her team they'd usually chip it, knowing she could outrun almost anybody. But here they played the game like it was meant to be played, with footwork and trickery.

The right midfielder got the cross off just in the right spot.

Marci and I both jumped for it, but my head connected with it before hers, sending the ball back in our direction.

"You may have the speed," I said, once we were both back on the ground, "but I have everything else."

"You wish," Marci spat. "Don't think this is over, Jackson."

The ball was crossed, and Jenica jumped up and headed it into the goal. I let out a screech, jumping up and down with excitement.

"Nice goal," I said, jogging up to meet her. "I think we're looking at the next Abby Wambach."

"I don't want to brag," Jenica said, "but I do believe my head is blessed."

We returned to our positions, ready to finish out the game. The blues ended up winning 2–1, and the losing team had to run sprints.

"You girls have two hours before lights out!" one of the coaches called.

We trooped back to our dorm building, eager to catch what was left of *Drama Llama*.

"I love it here," Jenica confessed. "I love the level of competition."

"Me too," I agreed. "It's definitely a challenge, and sometimes I really hate Coach Muldenhower, but I don't think I ever want to leave."

Another Beep Test. A chance at redemption.

"This is your final chance to prove to me why you deserve a spot on this team!" Coach Muldenhower called, as the next beep went off.

I sprinted to the other cone, determined to win this time.

There were only four of us left: me, Marci, Jenica, and another girl. Then there were three, and then . . . it was between Marci and me again.

"And we're down to our last two!" Coach Muldenhower called, as the beep went off.

Marci and I sprinted to the cone, and I was determined not to slip this time. This went on for several agonizing minutes, neither one of us caving. And then, miraculously, Marci slipped as we were taking off toward the opposite cone. I pulled in a deep breath, feeling my lungs expand to their capacity as I realized that I was the overall winner.

"Congratulations!" Coach Muldenhower boomed at me. "Cool down and then hit the locker rooms for some ice baths."

I did a quick cooldown before heading to catch up with Marci. As someone who had lost by a slip before, I knew how shitty it felt to be bested by someone due to a mistake versus a competition.

"What do you want?" she spat.

"To say I know how you feel," I said, with a shrug. "That was me last time. I'm sorry."

She quickened her pace. "No, you're not."

"I really am." I caught up with her again, my legs on fire. "I'm not some soccer robot. I do have feelings for other people."

"Is that supposed to be some sort of dig?" she snapped.

"Maybe," I shot back. I immediately regretted it. "No, it's not supposed to be a dig. I was trying to be nice."

"I don't need your pity," Marci said, ripping the locker room door open. "So go away."

My body was too physically tired to continue arguing. "Okay." I fell back, letting her race ahead.

Why did she have to be so infuriating?

Jenica held up a black dress. "I think this would look good on you?"

"Me? In a dress?"

She folded her arms across her chest, her eyes narrowing. "It's a banquet, Katelyn. It never hurt anyone to wear a dress."

"You can't show up in jeans," Nancy added. "This is a big deal. And we all know you made the final team."

"Thanks, but I'm not so confident."

Nancy and Jenica shared an exasperated look.

"Put on the dress," Jenica said. "You're impossible, I swear."

The dress was tight through the waist, and then flared out at the bottom, ending midthigh. It had two thick tank-top straps at the top, and the back was open.

"That looks so much better on you than it ever did on me," Jenica said. "Sandals? Flats? What are we feeling? I know you won't do heels."

There was no way I could balance in heels.

"Why did you pack so many options?" I asked, as she removed some shoes from her suitcase.

"There's no such thing as overpacking, Kate. You always have to be prepared."

My duffel bag contained a variety of sports bras, T-shirts, and running shorts. As well as one pair of jeans. Clearly I didn't get the overpacking gene.

"I feel like you're one of those people who can rock a sneaker-and-dress look," Jenica said. She handed me a pair of black-and-white Converse. "Try these."

Our dorm room door opened as I was slipping on the shoes, and Jenica's mom came in. "You can't answer a phone call?"

Jenica let out a squeal, running into her mother's arms. "I'm sorry! I was helping Kate with a fashion crisis."

"I'm so proud of you," Jenica's mom said, kissing the top of her head. She flashed me a smile. "Of both my girls."

I stood in front of the full-length mirror as Jenica and her mom caught up, taking in my reflection. My hair fell straight around my shoulders, the dress accentuating a figure I didn't know I had. And Jenica was right, the sneakers were more my style. I was used to being sporty and athletic. But today, I felt pretty. Feminine. A little outside of my comfort zone, but I liked it.

"What kind of food is down there?" Jenica asked her mom.

"Your heaven," she said. "A barbecue buffet."

My mouth watered as my stomach growled.

"So much for all that conditioning," Jenica said, patting her stomach. "My toned abs were nice for three days."

Over the next hour, parents showed up for Marci and our fourth roommate. I put on my fake smile for them, trying to cover up the hurt that my parents didn't show up. Because it really stung.

"Ready to go?" Jenica asked me.

I clasped the soccer necklace Zach had given me around my neck and then smiled. "Yeah."

"That's so pretty," Jenica breathed, running her fingers over my necklace. "Where'd you get it?"

"Zach gave it to me."

Jenica gasped. "Oh my God, of course he did."

We went downstairs, meeting up with the rest of the girls. My ribs felt as though they were caving in as I looked at all of the girls and their supportive parents.

An elbow nudged into my side, and I looked over at Jenica, who was staring at me with a curious expression.

"What?" I asked.

I followed her gaze toward the dorm room building door. My mom was standing there, her eyes flickering around the room.

"Mom?" I asked.

"Katelyn!" She looked just as excited to see me as her voice grew louder. I ran over to meet her, throwing my arms around her.

"Who is this woman?" she asked, holding me at arm's length. "You look beautiful, dear."

"You came," I said, tears building in my eyes.

My mom had *actually come* to support me.

"Of course I came," she said. "It's your banquet night. I couldn't miss that."

"What about the tour?"

"Your father's a capable man, I'm sure he can handle it." She took my hand in hers. "Now let's go find some food."

We walked to the banquet hall with Momma Terry and Jenica.

"How has the Showcase been?" Mom asked, as we found our seats in the banquet hall.

"Tough," I admitted, sitting between her and Jenica. "But hopefully it's all worth it."

My mom clasped her hands on the table, leaning toward me. "So if you make the final team, your first game is in three days, correct?"

"Three days," I said, wiggling my fingers. "Here in L.A."

"Of course I'm packed to stay," she said. "As I already know you've made the team. And I'm so, so excited for your tour with the team!"

I had the entire schedule memorized. "We get to play one game in L.A., and then one in London and one in Paris," I explained, "and our coach will be the coach from the U.S. Women's National Team!"

"How exciting," Mom squealed.

After we grabbed our delicious barbecue feast from the buffet, the lights in the room dimmed, and I turned to face the podium with a makeshift stage. A woman stood up there and welcomed us to the Limitless Apparel Showcase and then thanked us for suffering through the camp.

"We're going to call the names of the eighteen girls who have made our Elite Team," the lady announced. "When your name is called, we need you to come to the stage, shake all the hands on your way, and then stay on stage until all the names have been called."

Mom reached over to me, squeezing my shoulder in support as my stomach churned in anticipation.

"We're going to start with offense and work our way back to goalie," the lady announced.

Jenica was anxiously holding her mom's hand next to me, her eyes filled with tears.

"The first thing we noticed about this girl was her technique," the lady started. "She has great footwork and amazing stamina. Everyone give a round of applause for Kimberly Grant."

We clapped as the girl stood up. She was the striker who'd given me the hardest time with her footwork.

"This next girl has fire," the lady said. "She's a goal-scoring machine, and some of the coaches believe she could be the next Abby Wambach with her header goals. Please welcome Jenica Terry."

I jumped up out of my seat, screaming as she made her way to the stage, tears in her eyes. The lady continued to announce players through the strikers and midfielders before reaching the defense.

"This next girl has containment skills like you wouldn't believe," the lady announced. "It's almost impossible to get around her. Please welcome Nancy Torino."

I flashed her a thumbs-up as she took the stage.

"Our final defender," the lady said, "is truly something special. She's one of the fastest girls on the field, and one of the most aggressive. There isn't a ball that's getting past her. She's willing to lay her life down for the game. Please give a round of applause to Katelyn Jackson."

I could faintly hear the cheers around me, but my heart was soaring as I ascended the stairs to the stage. I numbly shook the hands of the people along the way and accepted the medal put around my neck and the plaque put into my hands.

"I told you it was our time!" Jenica squealed, giving me a tight hug as I took my spot alongside the others.

The lady called out two goalies, and as I mentally counted the girls, I realized it was only seventeen.

"There's one spot left," the lady said. "This spot was tough to fill. This girl brought a certain fire to the field, something that couldn't be ignored. A level of competitiveness that brings out the best of those around her. Our final spot goes to Marci Adams."

Of course.

That night, my mom insisted that she pack up my stuff to make sure she got everything. As I scrolled through my phone, I realized I never responded to Zach. *I'd left Zach Matthews on Read.*

"Jenica!" I screeched.

She dropped her cleats in surprise.

"Katelyn!" my mom called out, in a scolding tone. "Relax."

"Jenica, the text."

Confusion crossed her face, quickly replaced by a panicked expression. "Oh no."

"What do I say *now?*"

How do I explain to Zach Matthews that I'd accidentally never responded to his text? She came over and reread the text with me.

hi it's zach. connor gave me your number.

"All you can do is change your number and pretend you never got it," Jenica said.

Of course that would be her response. "You're no help."

"Or you could respond and apologize profusely. And you should send him that picture of you earlier tonight with the necklace. That'll distract him."

Jenica had forced me to take a photo in the outfit from the banquet, and you could see the necklace he gave me shining around my neck.

"Let me draft it," Jenica said. "I promise I won't send it."

"I don't trust you."

She opened her mouth, and then quickly snapped it shut. "Fair enough."

I'm so sorry! I read your text before a game and was going to respond afterward. I'm the worst kind of friend.

"Don't call yourself a friend," Jenica said. "He's clearly into you."

"He's clearly into someone else."

She let out a frustrated groan. "You're so dense, Katelyn. Delete the friend part."

> *I'm so sorry! I read your text before a game and was going to respond afterward. I'm the worst kind of person.*

"Better," she said. "Now you're going to double text him to show how sorry you are. So send that one, and then send the picture next."

My finger hovered over the send button, my heart flipping in my chest. I couldn't explain why I was so nervous, but the thought of sending a text to Zach Matthews sent me into a panic.

And then Jenica pressed it for me before I had time to think about it.

"Jenica!" I screeched.

"Katelyn!" my mom scolded, once again.

"Sorry, sorry."

Jenica took my phone from me, pulling up the photo from earlier. "And now we thank him."

"Don't you dare send it without letting me—"

She handed my phone back to me. "Too late. Sent."

"And this is why I don't trust you."

She'd sent the picture of me from earlier tonight. And then a follow-up text. *Like it? ;)*

"Jenica!"

This time my mom stopped what she was doing to turn and face me. "There are other people in this building, Katelyn. What in the world is going on?"

"Jenica is ruining my life."

"I'm fixing it," Jenica corrected. "I took the step she wouldn't take."

My mom shook her head in disapproval. "You two girls fight like sisters, I swear."

"I can't believe you sent that," I said, staring at the winky face. "I'm going to die of embarrassment."

"You're welcome."

"Are you ready to go?" Jenica's mom asked, coming into the room. "The taxi's here."

"I'll see you tomorrow morning," Jenica said, with a wave. "There'd better be news."

"I'm not talking to you."

She wrapped her arms around me. "I love you!"

"I'm so mad at you."

She called over her shoulder as she left. "I want all the juicy details!"

I looked back down at my phone, staring at the Sent receipt underneath the text. No text bubbles. No response. This was going to be the longest wait of my life. My mom called for a taxi to take us home. I wouldn't even have the chance to see Zach after that text message.

He was never going to talk to me again.

LOS ANGELES, CA
CHAPTER 17

Nothing felt better than a full night of sleep back home in my own bed. My mom was making breakfast when I came downstairs, the smell of pancakes wafting through the air.

"I love you," I said, as I sat down on a bar stool at the kitchen island. "This smells so good."

She blew me a kiss, and then pointed to her Bluetooth. I grabbed myself a glass of milk as she talked on the phone.

"Okay, I'll see you then," she said. "Love you. Bye now."

"Was that Connor?" I asked.

She shook her head. "Your dad." She came around and kissed my forehead. "Good morning."

"I'm so excited for pancakes."

"Some things never change." She flipped the pancake in the pan. "I used to make you and Connor Saturday morning breakfast every weekend. And the two of you would fight over what you wanted every single time."

I'd forgotten about Saturday morning breakfast fights. "Connor for French toast, me for pancakes."

"You almost always won," she said. "You sure do know how to get your way. You must get that from your momma."

"What did Dad want?" I asked.

"Your soccer game is between the New Orleans and Orlando shows, so he and Connor are going to fly in for the game."

That couldn't be right. "Dad and Connor are going to fly here from Louisiana to see my game?"

"Connor's idea."

Wow. I didn't know how to quite react to the fact that Connor was going to hop on a five-hour flight to come and watch me play. Connor never came to see me play. Neither did my dad for that matter.

"And this wasn't under your influence?" I asked.

She shook her head. "I was always going to come to your game, of course. But Connor said he wanted to come, and of course your father is excited to see you play too."

I highly doubt that. But I appreciated the lie nonetheless. "Wow."

She handed me a plate, two pancakes stacked on top. "Next batch is cooking." My mom knew me too well.

As I dug into my pancakes, my phone buzzed on the counter next to me. I glanced down to see Zach's name on my home screen. My fork dropped out of my hand in surprise. Zach had not only read the winky face text, but had actually responded. My hands shook in anticipation as I opened up my text messages. Hopefully he didn't think I was being too forward.

beautiful, as always.

I let out a loud gasp, causing my mom to look over at me in alarm. "Are you choking?"

Zach Matthews called me beautiful. I didn't know how to react, let alone how to respond.

"I need to call Jenica."

The entire team was staying at a hotel that had been booked by the Elite team, which meant I had to pack another duffel bag to drive fifteen minutes down the street.

So much for sleeping in my own bed anymore.

We were assigned roommates, but immediately everyone began switching room keys. Jenica and I quickly ended up in the same room.

"What are we thinking?" Jenica asked, as she claimed the bed closest to the air conditioner. "Sushi for dinner?"

"It's barely lunchtime!" I said, with a slight laugh.

There was a knock on our door. "Team bus leaves in fifteen minutes!"

"I cannot wait to take a nap after practice."

We headed downstairs to the lobby, waiting with the other girls.

"It's our first Elite team practice together," Jenica whispered. "How exciting!"

"You're way too peppy, I'm going to need you to tone it down at least seven notches," Nancy said.

"Exactly," I teased.

A van pulled up in front of the hotel, and we piled inside. I greeted people as I passed them to find a seat.

"Are you ready for this?" Jenica asked, as we found seats.

"Nervous," I admitted.

"Don't be," she chastised. "Remember, we were born for this."

The bus ride was short, but long enough for my mind to race with the overwhelming possibilities and scenarios of what was about to happen. The eighteen of us filed out onto the field, nervously chatting amongst one another.

Coach Tom Wright was setting up cones on the field, chatting with two girls whose backs were turned to us. I immediately recognized them, even with their backs turned. They were Morgan Lopez and Charity Williams, two U.S. Women's National Team players. Charity was a striker and Morgan was a defender.

"You have five minutes to get your gear on," Coach said, turning to face us.

We dug through our bags, pulling on our stuff. Lucky for me, I already had my shin guards and socks on. I switched out my slides for my cleats and then grabbed a soccer ball, juggling while I waited. A couple of other girls copied me, working on their juggling while we waited, including Jenica once she was ready. Others sat around and waited, talking and giggling.

"What's your name?" Coach asked, coming over to me.

My mouth went dry as I stared up at him. "Katelyn Jackson," I managed to choke out.

"Everyone take note," Coach announced. "What Katelyn's doing is what you should be doing when you have spare time."

My legs felt like Jell-O. Coach Tom *had noticed me.*

"You can't fangirl every time he speaks," Jenica said to me. "He's our coach now."

"All right, ladies, gather around," Coach called, waving us over.

Nervous energy coursed through my veins as we sat in a semicircle.

"Welcome to the Elite Limitless Showcase World Tour," Coach announced. "Wow, that is a mouthful. I'm Coach Tom, and I have two of my players with me. Charity is a striker on the U.S. Women's National Team, and Morgan is a defender. They're going to help me with today's practice."

We clapped in excitement as Charity and Morgan waved at us.

"We have three days to practice together before our first game," Coach Tom continued. "Today I will be watching you to get an idea of my starters. Starters will be announced during game warm-ups, so nobody needs to ask me before then. Give me your best. Is that a deal?"

I was unsure of what his schedule was exactly, but I knew that I'd constantly give 100 percent to be on that starter list.

"Then let's get started," he said, clapping his hands together. "Morgan, why don't you demonstrate the first drill here?"

I lay down on the floor of our hotel room floor with a groan. "My hamstrings are so tight."

"Let's stretch them out," Jenica said. "Leg up."

I obediently put my left leg straight up in the air, Jenica applying light pressure to stretch out the back of my leg.

"My body doesn't hurt as badly as I thought it was going to," Jenica said. "Probably because of the hell we went through at the Showcase."

"I'd say we're pretty well conditioned at the moment," I agreed.

"How do you think you did at practice?" Jenica asked. "Other leg."

I did as she asked. "I gave it my best."

"Same here," Jenica said. "Though I did make a couple of rookie mistakes."

"You can't dwell on the little things," I chastised. "Your overall performance is what's most important."

A knock came on our door as Jenica finished stretching me out. She went and answered it as I pushed myself up.

"Just seeing if you guys wanted to grab dinner and watch Netflix or something?" Nancy's voice said.

"Yeah!" I called out. "Come in, I'll turn it on."

"Take a seat anywhere," Jenica said. "I'm ordering sushi. Want some?"

"She's been talking about sushi since lunch," I said to Nancy. "As soon as we got here, she was asking me about dinner."

"I'm too wired to sleep," Jenica whined. "And what's the next best thing to sleeping? Eating."

We found an old sitcom to binge, and the food showed up halfway through the second episode.

"Who's your roommate?" I asked Nancy.

"Marci."

The face I made must've conveyed my opinion, as Nancy was quick to defend.

"I like her," Nancy said. "We bonded over our love of romance books."

Marci didn't strike me as a romance book reader. "Interesting."

Nancy leaned in toward me. "And she'd kill me if I told you, but she's a total Mack fan."

"Mackenzie? Really?"

"I can see it," Jenica said. "She's a bad bitch. Mack sings about being a boss bitch. Makes sense."

"I'm going to call it a night," Nancy said, standing up. "Same thing tomorrow?"

Jenica and I both nodded.

"See you."

Jenica flopped down on her bed. "I'm still too wired to sleep."

"How are you wired? I'm exhausted."

"Are you going to bed now?"

"I'm going to scroll through my social media until I fall asleep."

She let out a loud yawn. "Sounds like a good idea to me."

LOS ANGELES, CA
CHAPTER 18

My eyes scanned the airport as I waited for Connor and my dad. I rose to my tiptoes, standing up to see over the crowd. My entire family coming to my game. I never thought I'd see the day. And I couldn't be more nervous.

I saw my dad first. He was walking in front of Connor, who had his head ducked and sunglasses on. It didn't stop him from being recognized by at least ten different people as they tried to come down the escalator.

I hugged my dad first, much to his surprise. "Thank you for coming to my game, Dad."

"I couldn't be prouder of you, Katelyn. I'm very excited to see you play."

It didn't sound scripted. "Really?"

"Very much so."

And then Connor pulled me in for a hug. "Congrats, baby sis."

"Thanks, Connor," I said, holding him tightly. "And thanks for flying home for me."

"I promised," he reminded me. "I want to support you like you've always supported me."

And then I saw Zach.

"Oh, and I brought some friends," Connor said. "You might've met them before, they're on the same tour as me? The young one has a massive—"

"Hi, Katelyn," Jesse said, quick to interrupt Connor. "Hope you don't mind that we crashed your party. Connor wouldn't stop jabbering on about how talented you are, so we wanted to come and see you play."

Connor? Talking to his tour mates? About me?

"Who is this social butterfly?" I asked Connor. "Do I know you?"

I gave Jesse a quick hug, as well as Ross and Aaron.

"Come and drop your stuff in the car," my mom said. "You all must be exhausted. Let's get you home."

And then it was only Zach and me.

"How's the tour without me?" I asked.

"Not the same."

I didn't want to overthink it, but it was hard not to when he'd flown to another state to watch me play. "Thanks for coming."

"I don't know much about soccer," Zach admitted. "But I know you play it well, so I'll just cheer for you."

"You don't know that, seeing as you've never seen me."

"I also know you're way too humble."

Ross's voice called out over the airport noise. "Would you two stop flirting and come on?"

I nearly choked.

"I'm going to kill him," Zach muttered. The tips of his ears were red, along with his cheeks. "Sorry."

We went out to the car Skyline had ordered. I could hear my mom arguing with Jesse as we approached.

"Don't be silly," she said. "Here's our address. You're coming to dinner at our house tonight."

"Say 'Yes, Ma'am,'" Aaron said to Jesse, as he took the note from my mom. "You're fighting a losing battle."

"Thank you," Jesse said.

I slid into the car next to Connor, my mom driving and my dad in the passenger seat.

"The game's tomorrow, right?" Connor asked.

"Yup, we've been training all day. I have to go back to the hotel tonight, but my coach said that I can spend the evening with you guys."

We pulled up to the house, and both Connor and I leapt out and took off for the closest bathroom. One thing I had on Connor was speed, and I locked myself in the bathroom before he was able to.

"You're so annoying!" Connor shouted.

"Just for that, I'm going to take my sweet time. Use the one upstairs!"

I spent the next fifteen minutes in the bathroom to piss Connor off. As I opened the door, he was standing right there and gave me an all-knowing grin. "Skyline started the tour while you were busy."

"Good?"

"If I recall, don't you have some posters on your walls?"

A brick settled in my stomach as I realized.

"If only you'd been quicker," Connor said.

"No!"

I quickly ran upstairs, but was too late into the self-guided house tour. The boys were all in my room, laughter loud and clear.

"You're a Skyline fan, huh?" Aaron asked, as I came running in.

Crap.

"More importantly," Ross said, gesturing toward my Zach poster. "She's a Zach fan."

Now would be a great time to get struck by lightning. Or for an infamous California earthquake. Anything to get me out of this embarrassing situation.

"Leave her alone," Zach said. But even he was holding back laughter.

"I've been signing your posters," Ross said. "I can't reach the one on the top of that wall. But I got the rest."

There was nothing I could say to defend myself. "Thanks."

"We're going to go unpack," Jesse said, ushering Aaron and Ross out of the room.

"Unpack?" Ross questioned. "We're not at our hotel. And we're only here for two—"

"Walk," Aaron ordered.

He closed the door behind him, leaving Zach and me, alone, again. This seemed to be a recurring theme.

Zach shoved his hands in his pockets. "You didn't say anything about the song."

Between the Limitless Showcase and the flirty texts, I'd almost forgotten that he'd written a love song.

My heart felt as though it plummeted in my chest. "It was really good. I hope whoever you wrote it about loved it."

I tried to keep the bitterness out, tried to remain positive. *I mean . . . it couldn't—*

"I don't know if she did," Zach said. "I hope she heard it. Listened to it."

I bit my lip, trying to hold back the ugly jealousy threatening to bubble up and drown the hope I still had. "Have you talked to her about it?"

He shook his head. "I dropped a few hints. A lot of obvious ones. But she's not seeming to get them."

As desperately as I wanted to be selfish, to ask him if it was me, I was scared I'd embarrass myself.

"You honestly don't have a clue, do you?" Zach asked.

I stared at him, my heart beating so hard I thought it would leap out of my chest.

"The song was about you, Katelyn. I wrote the song *for you*."

I stepped back, my mind racing. *Did Zach just . . . The song is . . . Who?* All I could do was stare at him with wide eyes. And he stared back at me, waiting for me to say something. Zach Matthews had written a song about me, Katelyn Jackson. *Me.* For a second, I could only gape at him. What alternate reality had I been thrust into? Was I dreaming?

I needed to say something.

"Me?" I managed to choke out.

"Yeah, you."

"That . . . must have been very frustrating," I said, my words coming very slowly. "To write a song about someone so oblivious."

And he'd been waiting for me to realize. Giving me gifts, sending me texts, waiting for me to say something.

"I thought it was about some other girl," I said, my voice coming out as a whisper. "I didn't want to hope . . ."

Before I could finish my thought, Zach's hand reached out and cupped my cheek. His gaze burned into mine as he spoke his words slowly and deliberately. "And how'd that make you feel?"

My mind went blank as I reached up to touch his hand. I tried to come up with a response that would explain how jealous I'd been of a nonexistent girl. "Bad," I whispered.

He reached out, pulling me forward to close the space I'd opened between us. I let out a short gasp in surprise, and then he was kissing me.

At first I didn't kiss him back, my mind unable to comprehend what exactly was happening. But then my shoulders relaxed and I kissed him, warmth spreading through me as our lips molded together.

Zach Matthews liked me. And I hadn't realized it.

As we pulled away, I couldn't help but stare into Zach's eyes, my heart soaring in my chest. "I really like the song."

"Good. Because it's about you, in case you hadn't noticed."

"There better be talking happening in there!" Connor called out from down the hall. "I speak for all of us when I say we're tired of trying to find ways to get the two of you alone."

"Don't mind us," Aaron added.

"Your next song should be about annoying brothers," I giggled.

"I could write an entire album about that," he replied, and kissed me again.

Jenica and I stood side by side, staring in the full-length mirror in the hotel room. We'd received our uniforms this morning. And we hadn't taken them off since.

"Another selfie?" Jenica asked.

"I want at least a thousand."

A knock came on the door as Jenica took a few more pictures of us.

"Bus in ten!"

I grabbed my soccer bag, making sure it was packed before hauling it over my shoulder. My slides were waiting by the door, and I shoved my feet in them as we walked out. "Are we ready?"

"No," Jenica answered. "But let's do this."

The bus ride to the field was intense, everyone trying to get themselves into game mode. We were instructed to be completely in uniform before we got off the bus, so as we pulled up, I switched my slides out for my cleats.

We filed off the bus one by one. The captains of the team would be announced to us before the start of the game, along with starters. We took a seat in a circle before our warm-ups, sipping on water as Coach Tom pulled out his starter list.

"Strikers, Jenica and Marci."

I reached behind my back, high-fiving Jenica behind hers.

"Midfielders, Sky and Wilma. Stopper, Ashley. Defensive wings, Nancy and Gabriella. Sweeper, Katelyn. Goalie, Cassandra. Any questions?"

Jenica reached around her back, the two of us high-fiving once again.

Starting team. We'd worked our asses off for this.

Our pregame warm-up was crucial—the other team would be studying and criticizing us. This was our first game as a team.

"Marci Adams and Katelyn Jackson," Coach Tom called, waving us over.

I exchanged confused glances with Jenica before jogging over to him, my stomach flip-flopping.

"Congratulations," he said, handing the two of us captain bands.

"Thank you," we said in unison.

"Make us proud," Coach said as the refs called for captains.

I slipped my captain band around my shin guard before heading to the center of the field. All of the handwork and dedication had led up to this moment . . . and I had to share it with Marci. As excited as I was supposed to be, I still felt a bit disappointed that I didn't get to share centerfield with my best friend. And worst off, I was being forced to share it with *her*.

My eyes traveled over to the stands while waiting for the other team's captains. The stands weren't packed, so it was easy to spot my family and the Matthews brothers. They were sitting together toward the top of the stands on the U.S. side. I gave them a thumbs-up, receiving a series of waves in return.

"All right, introduce yourselves," the ref ordered.

I exchanged names with both the girls from the other team, who were from China.

"All right, since you are the visiting team, you'll call it in the air," the refs said to our opponents.

They called it correctly and asked for kickoff. Marci chose our side of the field and then we parted ways, heading back to our own teams.

I'd never played in front of my entire family, let alone Skyline. Or Zach. And as shallow as it sounded, I really wanted to make a good impression.

"Goalie, you ready?" the ref called to our goalie, Cassandra.

Cassandra flashed him a thumbs-up, as did the other team's goalie.

They started off like dynamite, tearing down the field.

By the end of the first half, I'd been taken out four times, and I'd slide-tackled three. The entire right side of my body was caked with dirt.

"They're running circles around you," Coach announced, as we grabbed some water. "It's the kick-and-run game, which is what you do before you learn ball control, ladies."

He made a couple of substitutions, one of them to my defense, taking out Gabriella and putting in another right-wing defender by the name of Bianca.

"All right, ladies, bring this home," Coach Tom ordered.

We retook the field, but this time I wasn't as nervous, knowing what to expect. We had kickoff this time, and we drove the ball right down the field, but as our midfielder went to cross it in, the goalie caught it right out of the air. I could hear Cassandra cussing from half field.

The ball bounced around midfield, nobody taking clear possession. But I watched as our team finally started finding rhythm. Our midfielder crossed it in and Jenica's head connected with the ball, sending it flying into the top left corner of the goal. I stood there for a moment, stunned at what happened. Our team met up in the center of the field, celebrating, as Jenica jumped into my arms.

We retook our positions, some of the pressure taken off with a lead, but not much because it was only one goal.

Pretty soon their team had the ball again and one of their midfielders was streaking down the left side. She tripped up Nancy, giving her the full line.

"Cover me!" I called to Nancy, switching positions with her.

I reached the midfielder as she was going to cross the ball, resulting in the ball slamming into my face with full force. I stumbled backward in surprise, my butt hitting the grass. But I didn't stay down for long, standing back up before I could be pulled out.

"Are you all right?" Nancy asked me worriedly.

My face was burning, and I had tears in my eyes, but I wasn't in pain necessarily. Just more in shock.

"Yeah, I'm okay," I said, wiping my hand under my nose. I was happy to see that there wasn't any blood.

"What's your name?" the ref asked me.

"Katelyn," I said, looking over at him. "Katelyn Jackson."

The ref looked to Nancy for confirmation, who nodded.

"Do you need to go off?"

"No, I'm fine," I promised, my vision finally completely clearing. I blinked a few more times and then smiled at the ref. "Honestly."

"All right, we'll drop-kick it here then," the ref decided.

Nancy took the dropkick, and I took my position as sweeper back.

"You sure you're with it?" Cassandra asked me.

"For the most part," I said, watching as Nancy took control of the ball and booted it out.

Our offense had two separate rushes, both ending in a scoop by the opposing team's goalie. But as it turns out, third time's the charm. Marci had control of the ball and had a breakaway toward the goal. The goalie came out and Marci slid the ball into the bottom right corner of the goal, giving us a 2–0 lead. The team celebrated in the center of the field again. I didn't pick Marci up in my arms like I had Jenica, but I did give her a smile and a nod.

"Watch out for their kickoff," I called out, knowing the chip-and-run game all too well.

Bianca cut off the midfielder, controlling the ball to send it up to our midfield as the ref called time.

End of the game.

"You had one hell of a second half, Katelyn," Coach Tom said.

"Thank you," I said.

"If you keep up performances like that, we might have something to talk about at the end of this tour."

I looked up at him in surprise, unsure of what he was implying.

He didn't say anything else before addressing the team as a whole, giving us a postgame speech and then reminding us of team curfew at ten p.m. He promised to see us for a light practice tomorrow morning at ten. I packed up my stuff and joined Jenica on our walk across the field.

"You kicked ass," Jenica said.

"Same to you, Ms. Wambach," I said.

"You're caked in dirt," she said, checking out my right side. My uniform and leg were all covered.

"Battle scars," I said, with a laugh.

"And your nose is kind of looking a little swollen."

"Really?" I felt around it, the pain hardly noticeable over the coursing of my adrenaline.

"Maybe Zach finds clown noses attractive."

"Screw off."

At the mention of Zach, I immediately started looking around for them. My family and the Skyline boys had watched me play. And I'd done a pretty damn good job today, if I do say so myself.

My mom was the first one waiting for me. "Are you okay, sweetie?" She took my face in her hands.

"I'm fine, Mom."

"That was a hard hit to the face you took," she said.

"It wasn't a *nice* hit to the face," I joked.

Connor's hoodie was tied tight around his face, as usual. He loosened the hoodie a bit, letting it fall. "It looks like I have a lot to apologize for. I didn't realize how damn good you are. Which makes me a really bad brother."

I was shaking my head before he finished. "We've both been a little caught up lately. But thank you for coming today. Seriously."

"I'd suggest dinner to celebrate, but I have an idea that someone else may want to have dinner with you," Mom said with a wink.

I gave them all hugs, promising my parents to text them later tonight, before heading off to find Skyline. As it turned out, they were in the parking lot, signing autographs.

Jenica tagged along with me as I insisted that she had to meet Zach. It was time to acquaint him with my best friend.

Zach excused himself from the group once he saw me, and jogged over. He took my bag, slinging it over his shoulder. "Wow, Katelyn."

"What?" I asked, reaching up to feel my nose. "Is it swollen?"

"No, I'm talking about your soccer skills. I mean, I've never seen anything like it."

Before I could respond, his fingers entwined with mine. I didn't know how to react to the fact that I was casually holding hands with Zach Matthews. His hand was rough and callused from playing guitar, but my fingers held tight and somehow it felt perfect.

"So I'm Jenica." She thrust her hand out toward him.

Right. Jenica.

"This is my best friend," I said. "The one who scored the goal today."

"Zach," he said, reaching out his hand to shake hers. "Pleasure to meet you."

She flashed him a smile. "Oh, cutie, the pleasure is all mine."

And I shouldn't be surprised. "Now Jenica is leaving. Bye."

"See you tonight, curfew at ten." She waved at Zach one last time before skipping away.

I held up my hand before Zach could speak. "Don't ask."

Jesse waved us over. "The taxi is almost here. We can talk about the plan in the car."

I narrowed my eyes at Zach, trying to read his mind as to what he was thinking for tonight. But his expression remained neutral. The boys said good-bye to their fan group before we climbed into the car, Zach and I taking the third-row seat.

Exhaustion seeped through me as I leaned back in my seat. My limbs felt heavy, my body aching as I dropped my head onto Zach's shoulder.

"Tired?" he murmured.

"Mm-hm."

He reached up, smoothing my hair back. "You're sweaty."

"Wow, thanks."

"Do you care to tell us why you've been holding out?" Ross asked me.

"What?" I asked, raising my eyebrows at him.

"What was that?"

"That was soccer."

"No, what those other people were playing was soccer," Ross corrected. "What *you* were playing was Death Soccer."

I couldn't help but laugh, curling up in Zach's arms as he put them around me. "Death Soccer?"

"Yeah, sacrificing yourself for the game."

"You do what you've got to do."

"I'm glad we took the time to do this," Jesse said. "You kicked ass."

My eyes slipped shut, Zach's hand running up and down my arm as I drifted in and out of consciousness.

"Is she asleep?" I heard Jesse ask, after a few minutes.

"I think so," Ross answered.

"Zach, are you feeling any better?" Jesse asked. "Because we're not going to go out for dinner if you're feeling ill."

"Drop me off at the hotel," Zach said, dismissively. "I don't think Katelyn's really in a dinner mood either."

"All right," Jesse agreed, after a few seconds.

The car was silent for a few moments, before Jesse spoke up again. "What kind of sick is it, Zach?"

"What?" Zach asked.

"I don't want to leave you at the hotel if you think you're going to have a seizure," Jesse stated, bluntly.

"Jesus Christ, Jesse," Zach said, his voice taking a hard edge, "I think I know when I'm feeling ill and when I'm feeling like I'm going to have a seizure."

"Chill out," I heard Aaron say, a little softer than they had been speaking.

"Hey!" Ross shouted.

I quickly jerked out of my half-conscious state, my body pulling out of Zach's arms.

"What the hell?" Zach demanded.

"Turn up the radio," Ross ordered.

" . . . opinion on Zach from Skyline?" the radio announcer finished asking.

"Zach's a great kid," I heard my brother's voice saying.

It was strange hearing Connor's voice on the radio so soon after seeing him, but I also knew that he'd been doing press in L.A., so he must've prerecorded this earlier today.

"Are you confirming that he and your sister, Katelyn Jackson, are a couple?" the radio guy asked.

"I didn't say that," Connor said. "I said that Zach's a great kid."

"You're not going to give us any kind of hint?"

"They're both great people," Connor said.

"Okay, okay," the radio announcer conceded. "Let's talk about the Connor Jackson Live Tour."

They started talking about the tour, and Jesse reached over and turned it back down.

"Oh boy," Aaron said, with a bit of a forced laugh. "We've got drama on our hands."

I went from being Connor Jackson's sister to Zach Matthews's new rumored girlfriend. How did I get myself into this mess?

"I'm not much for the rumor mill," Zach said. "Let it be."

"They'll be onto a new topic in a few days," I added. "If I've learned anything by watching *Drama Llama*, nothing sticks for long."

"Hey, Katelyn," Jesse said, "now that you're awake, what were you wanting to do for dinner?"

They didn't know that I'd heard their earlier conversation.

"Whatever you guys are doing," I said, placing my head back on Zach's chest.

"What if we stayed at the hotel and called in for room service?" Zach asked.

"Sounds like heaven," I mumbled, closing my eyes.

We pulled up to the boys' hotel, and Ross had to get out so that Zach and I could climb out of the third-row seat.

"Thanks, guys," I said.

The boys waved before pulling away. I followed Zach inside and up to his suite, which he shared with Jesse.

"If you want to take a shower, I'm sure I can find something for you to change into," Zach said, as we stepped inside.

A hot shower sounded heavenly. "Thank you."

He handed me a room service menu. "Pick out what you want and I'll order it while you're showering."

"Hamburger," I said, my mouth watering at the thought. "And fries."

"But there's chicken parmesan on the menu."

"But there's a hamburger on the menu."

I stepped into the shower, as suggested, my body grimy and sweaty. The jets hit my sore, aching muscles, and I let out a sigh of relief. I'd usually be collapsing into bed right about now, but I couldn't ignore the buzz of excitement at the thought of having an entire evening alone with Zach now that we were . . . whatever we were. More than friends, at least.

Once I was finished, I wrapped a fluffy towel around myself and forced my wet hair into a braid.

"Can you pass me my soccer bag?" I asked through the door. "I have clean clothes in there."

He opened the door, handing me my soccer bag with his arm over his eyes. A giggle escaped my lips as I accepted the bag from him before closing the door.

After I changed and came out, Zach was lying across a bed in the main area of the suite, watching Netflix.

"Our food should be here any minute," he said. "You smell a lot better."

I threw a pillow at him in response.

There was a knock on the hotel room door, and Zach went and accepted our food.

"Fries," I breathed, immediately stuffing them into my mouth.

Zach sat with his back resting against the backboard of the bed. He placed his chicken parmesan in his lap. I stayed lying across the bed, reaching up onto the cart to eat fries every once in a while as we watched TV. This, to me, was the perfect evening in. No pressure, no expectations. Just some French fries and a night in with Zach.

Zach was picking at the chicken parmesan he'd been so excited for. I couldn't help but think back to the conversation I'd been half-awake for in the car. "Are you feeling okay?"

His eyes flickered away from the TV, and he raised an eyebrow at me in question. "Me?"

"Obviously. It's just, you seemed so hungry a minute ago and now you're not touching your food."

"Sometimes my seizure meds take it out of me. But I'm fine."

Zach and I had never openly talked about his epilepsy. I sat up. I'd always been a Skyline fan, but this was something more. I wanted Zach to know that his story mattered to me, that it was more than the flashing lights and the fame. I cared about *him*.

I was hesitant to ask, but the words slipped out before I could filter them. "Is it because of the dosage?"

"That's probably part of it." He yawned, putting his half-finished plate of chicken off to the side.

I couldn't tell if Zach's yawn was showing disinterest, so I risked another question. "What would happen if you lowered the dosage?"

"That's always an option, if I wanted more seizures."

"Oh."

"It's not so bad, honestly. Some days are harder than others, but I've got a pretty good system down. It's been two years since my grand mal seizure."

"That sounds terrifying."

He reached over, taking a discarded tomato off my plate.

"You're chastising me about not eating my food, yet you pulled the best part off your burger."

"Tomatoes are gross."

His head tilted to the side as he studied me. "You're exhausted."

I nodded. "It's been a long day."

He pulled me close to him, and I folded myself into his arms, resting my cheek on his chest. He bent down, his lips pressing against mine.

There was nothing that compared to kissing Zach Matthews.

"You know what I want to do?" I asked.

"No telling."

"I want to watch some TV and cuddle with you."

My head fell to his chest, and he ran his fingers down my back as Netflix autoplay put on a new movie.

"Is this how two lazy people spend a date night?" Zach asked, his voice soft and welcoming.

His chest rose and fell beneath me, and I flashed a smile at him. He bent over and gave me a quick kiss.

"I kind of like it," he confessed.

"Don't let me fall asleep," I said, as I let out a long yawn. "My parents would kill me if they found out I slept here instead of back at the hotel with the team."

"I'll get you back home after this movie."

I tried to fight the exhaustion, but gave in as I let my eyes slide shut. I couldn't imagine a more perfect place to be.

I was startled awake by the sound of a slamming door. Sleep clouded my eyes as Zach's voice began speaking.

"Seriously, *nothing* happened," Zach said. "We fell asleep."

"So did I . . . in Ross and Aaron's room, I can't believe I did that," Jesse said, sounding both confused and apologetic. He'd clearly just rushed into the room; the door was still open and the bodyguard was standing behind him—he sussed out the situation pretty quickly and ducked back out into the hall.

I reached over and grabbed my phone.

7:30? *A.M.*?

"Shit!" I was going to throw up. I did not sleep in Zach's hotel room. "I'm so dead."

"We'll figure it out," Zach said.

If my parents catch wind of this . . . "I'll be grounded until college. Probably worse."

"Nobody's getting grounded, okay? Relax," Jesse said

There were multiple missed calls and panicked texts from Jenica. "I'm going to get kicked off the team." I pushed myself up out of Zach's bed, grabbing my bag. "I didn't make curfew last night. I'm so screwed."

My hands were shaking as I tried to collect my thoughts, my mind whirling.

My phone buzzed, a new text from Jenica.

You better be here in the next thirty minutes.

"I can get you there," Jesse said. "And I won't mention anything to your parents."

"Thank you, Jesse."

He looked at Zach. "But . . . we're going to have to talk about this."

"Chill," Zach muttered, opening the door for me. "Save the lecture for a more appropriate time."

The three of us headed downstairs, Jesse calling for a car as we went down the elevator.

I called Jenica as we reached the lobby.

"Girl, you owe me big time," Jenica said. "I'll tell you the excruciating tale of how I kept Coach believing you were here last night later. Right now, you need to get your ass here before the team bus arrives."

"I'm leaving right now, I should be there any minute."

"I'm going to meet you in the lobby with your duffel bag. You're going to take a phone call outside and then come back in like you've been here the whole time. Don't question me, just do it."

I was never going to live this down with her. "Understood." I hung up with her, bouncing on my heels as I tried to keep calm.

"Sorry about last night," Zach said quietly. "I must've fallen asleep too."

"It's not your fault."

The taxi pulled up.

"I'll text you later?" I said to Zach.

He gave me a quick kiss. "I'm sorry, again."

"Not your fault."

The hotel that my team was at was only a couple of miles away, and I had the driver stop around the block so I could step out without being seen. As Jenica instructed, I pressed my phone to my ear as I walked into the lobby. Coach was standing there, along with a few team members.

"Okay, thanks, got it," I said, faking a conversation. "I've got to go now though, okay? Bye."

"Our infamous sleeper," Coach said, with a laugh. "How long did you sleep yesterday, Katelyn? Like fifteen hours?"

Jenica raised an eyebrow at me.

I played along. "I was exhausted after the game."

"We missed you at team dinner," Marci said, with an all-knowing smile.

The team bus pulled up, and I hung back with Jenica as Coach loaded up.

"Do you know what I went through last night?" Jenica whispered. "I left the shower running. I stuffed pillows under the comforter and took a picture for Coach. I brought back leftovers for your pillow stand-in. It was a very stressful evening and morning for me, Katelyn Jackson."

"I'm sorry!" I whispered back. "I fell asleep in Zach's hotel room."

"Yeah, I figured that out after the eighth unanswered phone call."

I held out my arms toward her. "Best friend hug?"

"Absolutely not. You owe me . . . I don't even know how much you owe me yet. But it's a lot."

We loaded on the team bus, and Jenica gave me the silent treatment the entire drive to the fields. We had a team practice before dispersing for the next ten days—then we were heading to London and Paris.

The timeline had to work around the U.S. Women's National Team schedule, which meant my sleeping schedule for the next month was completely screwed. Being in a different time zone every week wasn't easy on the body.

"So?" Jenica asked me, as we finished warm-ups. "Were all my efforts in vain?" she demanded. "Are you and the Matthews brother an item?"

"We lay around, kissed a lot, and cuddled."

"Damn, that's cute."

"Am I forgiven?"

She groaned, letting her head fall back. "Forgiven. Just promise me you won't ever put me through that again."

I held out my pinky. "Promise."

She locked pinkies with me. "And you still owe me."

"Deal."

I'd only been home for four days, and it was like a hurricane had come through my room. Clothes were strewn everywhere, laundry baskets piled on top of one another, and shoes were piled in the corner.

My bag was repacked for the next two weeks, ready to fly out to rejoin the Connor Jackson Live Tour. The boys had flown out this morning after our timing mix-up to play a show tonight in Orlando, and my mom and I were flying out tomorrow to meet them in Jacksonville.

It was total and complete chaos, but I found myself excited to get back to the tour. Excited to get back to Zach.

"It feels like you're leaving all over again," Jenica said. She'd made herself comfortable on my bed. We were both exhausted and sore after a full day of training.

"I know, but I'm coming right back. And then we'll be doing some traveling, playing some soccer, and living our best life together."

My phone buzzed, and Jenica got to it before me.

"It's the boyfriend," Jenica teased. "Wants to know if you'll be there before the show tomorrow."

I held out my hand. "Give me my phone."

"Don't worry, I'll answer him for you."

"I'd rather you didn't."

She handed me my phone back. "Too bad, I already did."

> most definitely. can't wait to
> see you snookums.

It didn't even surprise me anymore. "I hate you so much."

"That's a fraction of my payback for what the two of you put me through with Coach. This, my friend, is only the beginning."

My mom knocked on the door, peeking inside. "I'm ordering dinner, do you girls have a preference?"

"Pizza!" Jenica called out, before I had the chance to answer.

"Pizza is good by me. Thanks, Mom."

She closed the door, and I sat down next to Jenica.

"One last round of *Drama Llama* before you leave me again?" she asked, picking up my remote.

"*DL* and pizza, the perfect night."

JACKSONVILLE, FL
CHAPTER 20

My afternoon run quickly turned into a fight against the humidity. It felt like I was sucking water into my lungs, sweat pouring down every inch of my body. The sun was sucking the life out of me, my face burning with the intensity of the heat.

Florida in the summer is hell on Earth.

I dragged myself up to my hotel room, contemplating the true necessity of a shower versus collapsing in a sweaty pile on the bed.

The need for a shower won out.

As I finished my cold shower, my phone went off, a FaceTime request from Zach. The phone call rang through as I quickly threw on a pair of sweatpants and a T-shirt before immediately calling him back.

He answered backstage at the arena. "Are you in Jacksonville?"

"I took the worst run of my life, honestly almost died."

"Never go outside in the afternoon in Florida," Zach laughed. "It's a death wish."

"A little late with the reminder."

"Are you coming to the show?" Zach asked.

"My body has no idea what time zone we're in right now. I'm going to keep it low-key tonight and try to go to sleep at a decent time to get myself back on track."

As I was talking, I could see myself relaxing into the bed, my head resting on my pillow. I was much more tired than I'd originally thought.

"You're going to fall asleep before we hang up," Zach said, with a teasing smile.

"I've been traveling nonstop," I whined. "I'm not made for this tour life. I miss my bed."

"I'll text you after the show. If you're still awake you can come night swimming with us," Zach said.

As much as I wanted to, I knew as soon as my eyes closed I would be out for the night. "I'll try my best."

"Get some rest. If nothing else, I'll see you tomorrow."

"Have a good show. I'll be rooting for you in my sleep." I blew him a kiss as he ended the call.

I plugged in my phone before pulling the comforter over me, closing my eyes.

It was only seven, but I needed a good, twelve-hour nap.

I woke up to the sound of voices, ones that sounded awfully close.

"Shouldn't we make sure she's alive?"

That sounded like Connor.

"Is she breathing? Can you see her chest moving?"

Connor again.

"Did you ever stop to consider maybe she's tired?"

Definitely Zach.

I pried my eyes open to see Zach and Connor both leaning over me.

"She's awake!" Connor exclaimed. "She's alive!"

"Of course she's alive," Zach said. "Sorry, Kate."

I reached up to rub my eyes, taking a moment to take in my surroundings. "What the hell are you guys doing?"

"You've been asleep for, like, twelve hours," Connor said. "I was worried."

I flipped over my phone to see it was seven a.m. "Oh."

"I figured you were probably exhausted," Zach said. "And I'm guessing you don't want to go to breakfast, since we woke you up."

"But we have to get moving," Connor added. "Tour buses are scheduled to leave in half an hour. We've got to drive to Atlanta for the show tonight."

"How did you guys get in here?" I asked.

Connor flashed me a room key. "The rooms are under my name."

I pulled the covers back up to my neck. "I absolutely do not want to get out of bed and go anywhere. But if you want to bring me breakfast, I won't complain."

Connor threw his hands up, looking at Zach. "That's all you, bro."

"Wow, thank you, oh-so-kind-and-considerate brother," I said.

"You've got a boyfriend now, that's what they're good for." Connor walked out of the room, chuckling to himself.

We had never approached the boyfriend-girlfriend topic. And this wasn't when I wanted to have the conversation, half-awake in my pajamas.

Zach was also clearly thrown off guard, silent as he stood next to my bed.

"We need to head to the buses," Zach said. "I'll grab breakfast and meet you there?"

"Sounds like a plan."

I forced myself to get out of the comfort and warmth of my bed, my feet stepping onto the cold tile of the bathroom floor as I closed the door behind me. Brush my teeth. Run a hairbrush through my hair. Wash my face. How do people wake up next to their boyfriends in the morning? I'd always be so self-conscious about my morning breath and rat's nest hair.

Leaving the hotel room, I made my way down to where the buses were parked. Zach was standing outside of my bus, his gaze on his phone. Hopefully the weird tension had passed. I took a sidled up next to him, glancing over at the text he was sending to Jesse.

"Where's the food?"

"Jesse is grabbing fast food, he should be here any minute."

"How is it that most of the time we've spent together so far involves food?"

"Because we're two lazy people."

"Very true."

Zach answered a text before tucking his phone away in his pocket. Silence hung between us, and I realized that the awkward tension hadn't passed. This was something we were going to have to address.

Luckily, Zach also came to that same conclusion. "I guess we should probably talk about the whole boyfriend-girlfriend thing and what that means?"

"Yeah, maybe."

He ran his fingers through his hair, and I could feel the anxiety radiating from him. I'd thought that we were on the same page, both happy at the pace at which we were moving and open to whatever came next. But maybe that had been something I'd been inferring; maybe Zach was on a different wavelength.

"How public do you want to go with this?" Zach asked. "Being someone in the public eye, if I mention I have a girlfriend, it'll blow up."

Was I ready for all of that? I'd watched the fame consume Connor, watched it change him, whether he realized it or not. Everybody changes with fame.

"I'm not going to lie, I'm nervous," I said. "I don't really know how to be in the spotlight. That's more Connor's thing than mine."

"Then we keep doing what we're doing," Zach said.

I felt torn. While I liked having Zach all to myself, I wanted to be able to scream from the rooftops that I, Katelyn Jackson, was falling head over heels for Zachary Matthews. I wanted to be able to tell people that he wrote a song for me, that he anxiously waited for me to realize for over a week before finally telling me himself. I wanted to be able to share our story.

"You're being awfully quiet," Zach said. "Let me in."

"I like you, Zach."

"That's good, because I like you too."

"And I want to be able to tell people that."

"Like, publicly?"

"I don't want to have to keep this a secret. I want everyone to know how taken you are."

"How taken I am?" he said.

"That you and I are together and that you're off the market and that I like you."

"I'll only do whatever you're comfortable with."

I leaned in, and he immediately did so, too, giving me a slow kiss. There was a sense of passion behind it, urgency almost. I tugged Zach's shirt closer to me. He reached around my neck, and I rose up on my tiptoes, pressing myself into him.

This is the part of Zach I wanted all to myself. I didn't want to have to keep our relationship secret, but I wanted to be able to keep a part of him for me. And it was going to be hard to find that line.

"Can you do me one favor?" I whispered.

Zach nodded, his forehead pressed against mine. "Of course."

"Please break the news on *Drama Llama*."

He threw his head back in laughter, his shoulders shaking.

"I'm not kidding!"

He looked back at me. "I know you're not. And that's what makes it so funny."

"Can you?"

He reached up to wipe the tears of laughter from the corners of his eyes. "Of course *we* can."

ATLANTA, GA
CHAPTER 21

My mom was waiting for me in the hotel room once I got out of the shower. She was sitting on my bed, her iPad in hand as she flipped through her emails.

"Good morning," I said.

She glanced up, flashing me a smile. "Good morning, hon. I wanted to catch you before you left."

"I didn't really plan on going anywhere," I said, as I sat down next to her. "What's up?"

She set down her iPad, angling herself to face me. "I noticed that you've been spending a lot of time with the young Zach boy."

I already felt uncomfortable. "Yeah."

"I need to remind you that you have to be safe," she said.

Oh no. "We are not having *the* talk."

"Don't make any decisions that you'll regret later," Mom said, "He's a nice kid, but you've got soccer, and big dreams too."

I quickly shook my head, my face immediately flushing red. "Nope. Nothing like that. We're not ... nope."

My mom reached out and placed her hand on my knee. "You know you can always come and talk to me, right? About anything?'

"Sure do, Mom. Absolutely." I desperately tried to shut this down.

"Your father and I were discussing some boundaries," she said. "Some rules to make sure that you're being safe and that we're monitoring you as parents."

It was bound to come sooner or later. My mom had been more than lenient in letting me spend all of my free time with Zach. "Like what?"

"A curfew of midnight, unless we discuss something else ahead of time. Absolutely no sleepovers, and if he's over in a hotel room with you, then the door cannot be fully closed. Whenever you're on his bus or in a hotel room, you need to text us and let us know where you are."

Basically every rule I've broken up until now. "Understood."

"We trust you, Katelyn. Don't let us regret that."

And a little dose of guilt to wrap up the conversation. "I won't, Mom."

She leaned in and kissed my forehead before standing up. "Are you coming down to the arena?"

I'd already gone on my morning run and done some ball skill work this morning. And it was only nine a.m.

"I might take a nap," I said. "Maybe later?"

I pulled out my phone as she left, pulling up my social media.

SKYLINE'S NEW SONG? ZACH MATTHEWS REVEALS THAT
HE WROTE IT FOR CONNOR JACKSON'S SISTER

As I kept scrolling, the headlines kept pouring in.

I searched for the *Drama Llama* story, and wasn't disappointed by the headline.

When Zach said he was going to break the news, he meant immediately.

My phone buzzed with a text from Zach, and I quickly opened it in surprise. It was way too early for Zach to be awake.

Drama Llama wants a live interview tonight with us during their show. You in?

My jaw dropped as I read the text. My favorite gossip show wanted to do an interview with me?

Of course I'm in!!!

Zach sent back a laughing emoji before FaceTiming me.

"You're up early," I answered.

"Very. I wanted to take advantage of the day with you."

I raised an eyebrow in question.

"Atlanta is one of my favorite cities," he said. "So I want to spend the day with you."

My heart did a flip as I shared a smile with him. "You woke up early to spend the day with me?"

"I figured we could meet downstairs in thirty?" he suggested. "I'll definitely need some coffee as our first stop."

"Deal."

||||||||||

Zach was already in the downstairs lobby. Contrary to his usual white T-shirt and sweatpants, he was wearing a short-sleeve, light blue button-up shirt and a pair of khaki shorts.

"You clean up well," I said.

"We stepped out of our comfort zones today, I see."

I stood up on my toes, giving him a good morning kiss. "What's the plan for today?"

"The plan is to make you the ultimate Atlanta tourist."

"First stop, Beans?"

"Absolutely. Caffeine is a must."

Zach's hand made his way into mine as we walked a few blocks to the nearest coffee shop.

"I like swinging hands with you," I said, as I swung his arm all the way up into the air.

"And I like coffee," he answered.

After we had our coffees we came back outside and waited for the car to pick us up.

"Where to now?" I asked.

He pulled up his phone, opening up the Notes app. "I have it all planned out. And our first stop is the Coke factory."

"The Coke factory? Like Coca-Cola?"

"I told you, I'm going to make you a professional Atlanta tourist."

The drive was relatively short but it gave me enough time to try to pry more information from Zach about our schedule for the day.

"My lips are sealed," Zach said.

"Okay, okay," I surrendered. "But what do you do at the Coke factory?"

"You can try Coke from around the world."

"What's so special about drinking Coke?"

"Many countries have their own version," Zach said. "I prefer the option from Brazil."

As it turned out, the Coke factory was an entire experience. We took a picture with the Coca-Cola polar bear, walked through the history of Coke, and then did a taste test of beverages around the world.

"I definitely prefer the Italian Coke flavor."

"That's a good one too," Zach agreed. "Doesn't compare to Brazil though."

We didn't even do a quarter of the activities offered before Zach was pulling me away. But not before I snagged a copy of our picture with the mascot as my Atlanta keepsake.

"Where are we headed to?" I asked, as we left the factory.

"Lunch reservations at White Oak Kitchen & Cocktails."

"When you said you had the whole day planned out?"

"I meant the *whole day*."

I leaned into Zach as we stood in line for the Skyview. It was Zach's last item on the itinerary for today, and he was insistent that we had to be here in time to watch the sunset.

"It's basically like the London Eye," I said.

"Except in Georgia."

"Thanks for the observation."

We stood up the front, Zach handing over our tickets.

"We're going to watch the sunset in this tube?" I asked, as we stepped inside the Skyview.

"You've asked too many questions today," Zach said. "You've reached your question limit."

"I'm a curious person! Especially when my boyfriend is being cryptic."

He leaned in to kiss me, cutting me off before I could continue with my questions. I rose up on my toes, dropping the subject for the sake of the kiss.

"I wanted to make today special for you," Zach said, quietly. "I know we've only just started this whole relationship thing, but you're going to be leaving soon for your Showcase and we're going to be playing some back-to-back shows coming up. I wanted us to be able to get away for a day before the chaos sets in."

How did I get so lucky?

CHARLESTON AND BEAUFORT, SOUTH CAROLINA
CHAPTER 22

Last night was the first night in a long while I hadn't tuned into *Drama Llama*. Mostly because I'd been *on* the show. Also I was so tired after a day out with Zach, the interview, and then having to be up at an ungodly hour this morning for the five-hour bus ride to Charleston. So now I was having a FaceTime watch session with Jenica from the tour bus.

"The show was epic," Jenica gushed, as I pulled up the stream on my laptop. "You looked like a poised professional."

"I highly doubt that."

I'd been so nervous that I held Zach's hand under the table the entire time. And I knew my hand was sweaty, but Zach never complained. Our interview was at the start of the show, apparently the highlight of yesterday's gossip news. Must've been a slow news day.

"Ready?" Jenica asked.

I shared my screen with her, the two of us watching together. "Okay, let's watch this train wreck."

Zach and I came up on the corner of the screen. We'd done the livestream from the hotel's meeting room, with Jesse micromanaging in the background.

"Today we have Zach Matthews and Katelyn Jackson live-streaming in with us," the host introduced. *"As you all know, Zach Matthews is the lead singer of Skyline. But what you may not know is that he recently announced his relationship with Katelyn Jackson, the younger sister to pop star Connor Jackson."*

And there I was, with my wet hair braid and faded concealer. A day out in the Atlanta heat hadn't done me any good.

"And here they are now," Jake said. *"Welcome to the show, guys!"*

Zach waved, and I glanced toward him and then back at the camera before doing an awkward late wave.

"Oh no," I groaned.

"Stop," Jenica scolded. "You're cute."

"Walk us through how this happened," Jake said. *"One minute you're singing the opening number for Connor Jackson, and the next minute you're getting together with his sister?"*

Thankfully, most of the questions had been directed at Zach. But there was one question that had been directed toward me, and I was anxious to see what I looked like answering it. Because I was a mess on the inside.

"So, Katelyn," Jake said.

"He said your name!" Jenica squealed. "My best friend is famous."

On the livestream, my cheeks flushed red. *"Yes?"*

"We know all about Zach Matthews here," Jake said. *"But we don't really know much about you. An inside source tells us that you're into soccer. Tell us a bit about that."*

"And this is where I totally freeze," I said to Jenica.

"It's not that bad," Jenica argued.

On the livestream, I was staring at the camera. In total silence.

"My brothers and I got the chance to see her play last week," Zach said, *jumping in to save the moment. "She's a natural out on the field."*

I reached up and tugged on the bottom of my braid. *"Much like music is Zach's passion, soccer is mine. And since I'm touring with the band, I get to see Zach live and in action practically every night. It was really special to be able to share something I'm passionate about with him too."*

I let out a groan. "That didn't answer his question at all."

"It was still good!" Jenica said.

"It was a politician answer and it's embarrassing."

The interview wrapped up from there, and then the livestream shut off.

"Do I get the Llama approval?" I asked Jenica.

Jake answered for me. "So what do you think, DL?"

The Drama Llama mascot is the one who gives the approval ratings after each segment. It's a six-foot-tall llama statue that stands in the corner of the room. Enough green votes from the Drama Llama team and it'll give off a loud, gurgling noise. If there are more red votes than green, the llama gives off a spitting noise.

I anxiously awaited the response, my eyes wide in anticipation.

The Drama Llama let off a gurgling noise.

"I got the DL approval!" I shouted. "I'm Drama Llama–approved!"

"Of course you are," Jenica said. "You were adorable. And you and Zach are the cutest couple on the market right now."

"Shut up."

A text came in, a loud *ding* going off.

"I bet that's lover boy," Jenica crooned.

"Shut up again."

We ended the call before I checked my text.

come to our tour bus?

Of course Jenica would be right.

My mom doesn't want us alone together . . .

I hated that I even had to say that. But my mom was trusting me, and the last thing I wanted was to get grounded on a tour bus.

my brothers are here. unfortunately.

I let him know I was coming before heading over to his bus. I waved at Paul standing outside the door before knocking.

"Hey!" Zach said, answering with a full-blown smile.

"Wow, you seem chipper for noon!"

"I had a doctor's appointment this morning."

"Where?"

"It was virtual, with my neurologist," he said. "A medication check. Everything's all good."

He leaned over into the crook of his elbow, a deep cough escaping. He ushered me inside, closing the door behind me. I was very used to seeing Aaron and Ross playing videogames in the corner, but this morning Aaron was noticeably missing, Ross playing by himself.

"Are you okay?" I asked.

"Just a scratchy throat."

"You should rest up tonight," I said. "Before your hometown show tomorrow night."

His eyes lit up. "Speaking of my hometown, my mom wants to cook dinner for everyone tonight. Including you."

"Your mom wants to meet me?"

"Jesse won't shut up about you."

I teased, "Jesse, huh?"

"Yeah, that guy's got a motormouth."

"I'm flattered."

He rubbed the back of his neck with a shy smirk.

This was a big step, one that I had to be ready to take. It was one thing for Zach to be around my parents—it was more business than anything. But meeting with and having dinner with Zach's mom was a commitment. She was inviting me into their home, setting a plate for me, cooking an extra meal for me. It was all very nerve-wracking.

"I'm nervous," I admitted. "Has *Jesse* said good things about me?"

"Nothing but the best."

"Okay," I found myself saying. "Of course, I'd *love* to have dinner with your mom."

"Good, because it was never really an option."

The bus door opened, and Jesse came in with Beans in hand.

"Drink," Jesse ordered, handing the Beans drink to Zach. "Green tea, honey, and a dissolved cough drop."

Zach did as he was told, wincing as he took a sip.

"Are you coming tonight?" Jesse asked me.

I nodded. "I've heard that I've been spoken about."

"Yeah?" Jesse asked, in a teasing tone. "I may have heard your name once or twice."

"Shut up, both of you," Zach ordered.

Jesse continued laughing to himself as he turned to leave. "I hope you like Southern food," he said to me. "I don't think my mom can cook anything but."

"We're headed over there about three," Zach said. "I'll come by your hotel room?"

"Sure, we're just going over there to check in now, so that should give me enough time to look presentable."

"You always look beautiful to me," he said.

I leaned in for a kiss, and was immediately met with gagging noises from Ross.

"Should I apologize for him?" Zach whispered.

"No, I'm used to it by now."

He gave me a quick kiss, met with a loud *boo*.

"After all the work your brothers did to get us together, you think he'd be a little more appreciative," I said.

"Ross is dumb."

I turned and waved at him. "You annoy me! See you at three!"

Ross waved back, laughing.

"Seriously, though," Zach said, as I opened their door. "Thank you for coming. My mom is really excited."

"Any woman who can raise the four of you and remain sane is my hero. And I can't wait to meet her."

I did a twirl in front of the hotel mirror, trying to decide if my ripped black shorts were the right choice for tonight. Maybe I should go with a more traditional blue jean, in case Ms. Matthews is one of those hate-against-ripped-jeans type of people. I changed into a pair of high-waisted blue jean shorts and a slouchy, gray V-neck, doing another twirl to determine if this outfit was better. I'd even straightened my hair and put on some mascara with a touch of concealer.

A knock came on my hotel room door as I was trying out a French tuck.

This outfit was going to have to be the one. I slipped on my shoes as I answered the door, Ross standing there.

"Ready?" he asked.

I nodded, a bit confused. *Where's Zach?*

"Jesse already called for the car," Ross said, as we headed toward the elevator. "And Zach was taking a nap, so I've saved you from his grumpiness."

"Thanks for looking out for me."

The rest of the boys were already downstairs, waiting on the car.

Zach had a to-go cup in his hand, drinking what I guessed to be tea for his throat.

"Give me a minute," Zach mumbled. "I'm not awake yet."

The elevator opened, and Connor and Mackenzie stepped out.

"We have two cars," Jesse said, checking his phone. "Since my mom is apparently throwing a dinner party."

"Ross has talked up your mom's cooking the entire tour," Mackenzie said. "I have to taste her mashed potatoes."

"Only the best this country has ever tasted," Ross said, proudly.

The first car pulled up, and Connor and Mackenzie climbed in with Aaron and Ross.

Leaving the second car for Jesse, Zach, and me.

"Did I tell you that you look cute yet?" Zach asked.

"No, but thank you, this was my fourth outfit. And the only reason it stuck was because Ross was knocking on the door."

"I didn't say it yet," Zach teased. "But you look cute."

"Less talking, more drinking," Jesse ordered. "We want a voice for the show tomorrow. Katelyn already knows you think she's cute. Everyone knows you think Katelyn's cute."

The second car pulled up, and Jesse took the front while Zach and I took the back.

"We're in for a long haul," Jesse said, glancing back at me. "So get comfy."

The drive from Charleston to Beaufort was just under two hours. As we got closer to their hometown, the brothers began to exchange stories.

"Has Zach ever told you about Francisco the Elephant?" Jesse asked me.

"No!" Zach groaned.

"When Zach was still seven, I convinced him that we had a pet elephant named Francisco," Jesse said. "And I got Aaron and Ross to go along with it."

"How?" I asked.

"The elephant could fly," Zach explained. "And whenever they said he was there, I'd look, and they'd say he flew away."

"You believed them?" I asked Zach, incredulously.

"I was seven," he defended.

Jesse barked out a laugh, clearly pleased with himself. "We kept that one going for months."

"When did you finally figure it out?" I asked Zach, unable to contain my own laughs.

"He didn't," Jesse said.

"My mom told me," Zach muttered.

This time I doubled over, my stomach cramping as we howled with laughter.

"I was seven," Zach repeated.

I managed to sit up, reaching over and resting my hand on his shoulder. "You're adorable."

"We played all kinds of tricks on Zach," Jesse said. "He was so gullible as a kid."

"You'd be gullible too if your three older brothers all insisted that something was true," Zach muttered, shaking his head.

Jesse began laughing all over again. "We once convinced him that there was no color red."

That couldn't be true. "What?"

"It screwed me up," Zach said, laughing as he shook his head.

"We convinced him that the color red was a figment of his imagination," Jesse explained.

"You guys were so mean!" I said, much to Jesse's delight.

Jesse nodded. "That one was bad," he admitted. "We made him cry."

"You cried?"

"Wouldn't you cry if you were six and you thought you were crazy?"

And then we were all laughing again.

The car came to a stop in front of a modest, one-story home. The paint was peeling off in certain places, and the porch was in need of a few new wooden planks. But it looked homey.

"I wish she'd let me fix up the outside," Jesse grumbled, as we stepped out.

"Don't start today," Zach said, with a shake of his head. "She's stubborn and she doesn't want us to pay to fix it up."

"I'd do it myself."

"And she wouldn't let you."

Clearly this was an ongoing battle between them.

Zach wrapped his hand around mine. "Are you ready?"

I followed them up to the front door, following Zach's instructions to avoid the second stair that led up to the porch. Jesse went right inside, and I went behind him, feeling the anxiety building inside.

"Are you okay?" Zach asked me.

"Fine," I breathed.

"You don't need to be nervous," he promised. "There isn't a person on this planet my mom doesn't like."

We reached the kitchen, and there was a woman in there cooking and ordering around Aaron and Ross. Her back was to us. She had long, blond hair, the same color as Aaron's. And she was short, barely over five feet.

"Hey, Mom!" Jesse called.

The kitchen looked like it was well loved, the wooden cabinets chipped in areas and the refrigerator decorated with Christmas cards and school photos. Ms. Matthews was wearing an apron tied around her waist, a spatula in hand as she turned to face us. She had caramel brown eyes that had a certain sparkle in them.

"Hey, baby," she said, taking Jesse in her arms. He was much taller than her, but he bent down to kiss her cheek.

Zach wrapped his arms around his mom next, and she showered him with kisses.

"All right, Mom," he said, in his raspy voice.

She held him at arm's length, raising her eyebrows at him. "You don't get to have an attitude with your mama."

"Yes, ma'am. Sorry."

And then she looked over at me, her hands still on Zach's arms. "And who's this pretty girl?"

"Katelyn Jackson," Jesse said, with a smirk.

"Come on over here, don't be shy," she said, waving me over.

I tentatively made my way over, and she crushed me in a hug. "Welcome home, sweetie!"

My arms wrapped around her. "Thank you."

"Now Aaron and Ross," she said, releasing me. "Have you finished setting the table?"

They nodded.

"Then the rest of you boys can start putting out the food. And Zachary Matthews, have you been drinking some tea for that throat of yours?"

"Zachary?" I teased.

He cast me a disapproving look before looking back at his mom. "Yes, ma'am."

"Not enough. Mama will warm you up something good."

"Thanks, Mom."

She handed him a bowl of mashed potatoes. "Off you go."

"What can I help with?" I asked.

"Nonsense," she said, shaking her head. "You're a guest here."

"No really," I protested. "I want to help."

"That goes against every Southern bone in my body," she said, swatting me.

I was already falling in love with her. "Please?"

"I think not." She untied the apron from around her waist. "Your brother and Mackenzie are out back. Connor said something about a bonfire tonight in the pit, although it's the middle of summer. They're out there scoping it out."

I peered out of the large, sliding glass doors next to the table to see Connor gathering firewood as he chatted with Mackenzie.

"Zachary Matthews!" Ms. Matthews called out.

Zach came back into the kitchen. "Yes, ma'am?"

"Show Katelyn around the house while I finish up supper."

"Yes, ma'am."

I followed him out of the kitchen and into what I guessed was the living room. It had an old, faded couch along with a small TV. The walls were plastered with family pictures, and in the middle hung their mom's VIP pass to tonight's show.

"This is the living room," Zach said.

"This is so cute," I said, studying the pictures, which showed the boys growing up, starting with only Jesse and progressing throughout the years.

"Mortifying."

I leaned over, knocking my shoulder against his. "This doesn't even compare to the highly embarrassing posters you saw in my room."

He led me down a hallway and opened the first door. "Jesse's room."

There was a bed in the center with a dark blue bedspread loosely thrown over it. His room was decorated with posters of different bands and race cars—Formula One, NASCAR, and Indy 500. There was a desk tucked away in the corner with papers strewn across it, and a TV mounted on the wall.

"It's cute," I said, as we headed to the next room.

"You think everything's cute," he said. He opened the next door. "This is Aaron's room."

The bed had a green comforter, haphazardly made. There was a desk shoved in the corner and a TV mounted up on the wall, with game controllers and games littered across the room.

We left his room and headed to the next room in the hallway. "This is mine and Ross's room."

The first thing I noticed was the black line of tape down the center of the room. It extended up the wall as well. There were two beds in this room, one with a blue comforter and the other plaid. It was set up much like the other two rooms, with two desks. The only noticeable difference was that there wasn't a TV.

"My bed's the one with the blue bedspread," Zach explained.

His side of the room was neat and tidy, not a thing out of place. The other side of the room was a complete mess. Papers and clothes were strewn everywhere, posters were hung loosely up on the wall.

"What's with the black divider?" I asked.

"Because Ross is horribly messy and one day I got so pissed off that I divided the room. My mom wasn't too thrilled."

I stepped farther into his room to take a closer look, as it was only fair since he did the same with mine. Zach's desk was organized chaos. Scratched-out lyrics and half-written songs were piled in the corner. There were textbooks stacked on the floor, next to the desk. And a couple of books rested in the middle.

Over on his nightstand, there was a coaster with a cup of stale water sitting on top, along with some various snacks and another book, this one with a bookmark inside.

Zach came over behind me, wrapping his arms around me.

"Did you bring me a memento?" I asked.

He leaned over me, reaching down onto his nightstand and wiggling his bookmark out of his book. "I'm very forgetful, so I'll never remember what page I was on. But you can have my most prized possession."

It was more than a bookmark. It was a postcard for an advertisement for Skyline's first show. The graphics were clearly made on Paint, Zach's signature scribbled across the bottom.

"I spent four days making that," he said. "Thought it was a work of art."

"Zach, this is something special. I can't take this."

He slid the postcard into my back pocket, sending a shiver down my spine as he did. "I insist. It's a part of my hometown, a part of my story. And I want to share it with you."

He wrapped his arms around me once again. "I can think of a better bookmark."

"And what's that?"

"A picture of my beautiful girlfriend."

I leaned my head back, and he bent down to give me a kiss.

"Let's make out a bit," Zach whispered.

"No! I'm here to meet your mom for the first time. I can't make out with you in your bedroom. That's like, the number one rule."

He threw his head back in laughter. "The number one rule? No making out with your boyfriend while his mom cooks dinner?"

"Yes, absolutely. That and I don't have time to be sick, so keep your germs to yourself."

Zach's door opened, Ross peeking his head inside.

"I was sent to make sure you guys weren't doing anything inappropriate," Ross said.

I pulled away from Zach's arms. "We're just looking around."

"Clearly," Ross said, with a smirk. "Mom said that there are condoms in—"

"Good-bye!" Zach called out.

"*In the basket underneath the bathroom sink!*" Ross shouted, before closing the door.

Zach let out a groan, reaching up and burying his face in his hands. "Dammit, Ross."

At the rate my cheeks were burning, I knew they had to be bright red.

"Maybe we should go back and see if they need any help?" I suggested.

Zach let his hands fall back down to his sides. "Yeah."

My mouth watered at the sight of all the food laid out on the table. There was fried chicken, mashed potatoes with gravy, cornbread, and green beans.

"Would you like some sweet tea?" Ms. Matthews asked me. "Or something else?"

"Sweet tea sounds great," I said. "But I can get—"

"Nonsense," she said, waving me away. "Take a seat."

I did as I was told, feeling guilty that she was waiting on me. Zach took a sip of the tea his mom had made him, remaining silent.

"Did you give her a nice tour?" Ms. Matthews asked, coming back and handing me a glass of sweet tea.

"I guess," Zach answered, with a shrug.

"Did you see the boys' rooms?" Ms. Matthews asked. "I should've made them pick up."

"Never," Ross grumbled, stuffing some mashed potatoes in his mouth.

I loaded up on food, much to Ms. Matthews's delight, and began to chow down on the mashed potatoes.

"Ross was absolutely right," Mackenzie said. "These are amazing."

"Oh, stop it," Ms. Matthews said, as Ross enthusiastically nodded.

"You're coming to the show tomorrow night, right?" Jesse asked.

"I wouldn't miss it for the world," she said, with a smile.

"Does work know?" Zach asked.

"I handled work," his mom said, waving Zach off. "I've had it on my calendar for months."

"Mom, can you make a whole bunch of mashed potatoes and let us take it with us?" Ross asked, his mouth full of potatoes.

"You boys, I swear." She turned to look at me. "So, Katelyn, have my boys been minding their manners around you?"

"Yes, ma'am," I answered, with a smile.

"Feel free to whip them into shape if they need it," she said, with a nod. "I have no doubt Mackenzie already does so."

Mackenzie nodded. "Just whenever they're late."

"We can hear you," Aaron pointed out.

"That was the point, dear," Ms. Matthews said.

As dinner progressed, the table broke off into different side conversations, and I found myself in a conversation with Ms. Matthews and Zach.

"What do you do during the day?" Ms. Matthews asked me.

"I usually hang out around the arena," I answered.

"She bums around in our dressing room," Zach teased.

"There isn't much for me to do. I'm not in rehearsals or meet and greets, so I kind of hang around."

"And she plays soccer," Zach said. "Really well too."

I reached up to tug on my shirt sleeves, feeling my muscles coil.

"She made a team that gets to travel the world and play for the U.S. Women's National Team's coach," Zach continued. "And when we went and watched her play, she was the best one out there."

"You're totally biased."

"Even so, it's true."

"That's amazing," Ms. Matthews interrupted. "You have quite some talent."

"Thank you."

She turned her attention over to Jesse. "Now about this manager business, what's the name of the lady you're going to hire?"

"Marlene Sanders," Jesse said, before stuffing green beans into his mouth.

"You guys decided on a new manager?" I asked.

"Jesse and I met with her yesterday when Zach was out. She's going to fly in for the Charleston show tomorrow night," Aaron answered.

"You boys better introduce her to me," Ms. Matthews said.

"Yes, ma'am," they all chimed in unison.

After dinner I helped clean up, despite Ms. Matthew's protests. I felt a tug on my arm, and I turned to see Zach. He nodded toward the sliding glass doors. "Your brother is all about this midsummer bonfire."

Of course he is. There was an assortment of chairs surrounding the bonfire pit, and I took a seat in the folding camping chair while Zach took a beach chair.

Connor finished stacking the wood, and then glanced over toward Jesse. "How are we starting this thing?"

Jesse produced a lighter from underneath his seat. "We use a lighter, unless you're a master of kindling firewood."

"Hell no."

I watched as Jesse lit different ends of the woodpile, until the fire engulfed the pit.

"Well?" Mackenzie asked, glancing toward Connor.

He took a seat on the bar stool next to me. "What?"

"You wanted this bonfire so bad. What's the plan?" She looked around at all of us. "Is there anything more cliché than a group of singers sitting around a bonfire?" Connor pulled out a guitar from behind his stool. Mackenzie laughed. "Of course. I can't deal with you guys."

"I'm not a singer," I pointed out. "But it *is* very cliché."

Connor strummed the guitar a few times. "Okay, give me something."

"What do you know?" Mackenzie questioned.

Connor spent endless hours watching YouTube tutorials and learning songs on his guitar. I doubt there's a song he doesn't know.

"I'll start with a classic," Connor said.

We started off with "Sweet Caroline," which quickly turned into Ross and I seeing who could sing louder than one another.

"That's not considered singing at this point," Jesse said, with a shake of his head.

I interlaced my fingers with Zach's, our hands swinging between the chairs as Connor started up on "Yellow Submarine."

"You better not be singing!" Jesse called over toward Zach. "Drink your green tea."

Zach flipped him off. But he reached down and grabbed his drink, taking a sip in silence.

"It's okay," I said, flashing him a smile. "I'll sing loud enough for the both of us."

Zach laughed. "Oh how lucky we are."

The next evening, I met Ms. Matthews by the VIP entrance. The boys had finished sound check, and they'd asked me to bring their mom back to them.

"Hi, Ms. Matthews."

She reached over, giving me a tight hug. "Hi, sugar."

Security checked her pass as she followed me inside.

"How are my boys today?" she asked.

"I saw them only briefly, but they seemed to be doing pretty well. Zach's on vocal rest."

Her lips pulled into a frown. "I knew he should've gone to the doctor. He's going to give himself a throat infection if he doesn't take care of himself."

That was the most mom thing I'd heard in a while. "He's very stubborn."

"That, darlin', I know."

"This is Connor's dressing room," I said, jabbing my thumb toward his door. "And this is Skyline's. And that down there is Mackenzie's."

I knocked twice and then opened the door to Skyline's dressing room. Ross and Jesse were watching Netflix, and Zach was asleep on the couch.

"Hey, Mom!" Jesse said, cheerfully. "And Katelyn."

"Hey, honeybee," Ms. Matthews said, with a smile.

I waved at them. "What did the doctor say about Zach?"

Jesse's eyes flickered over to Zach, who was still asleep.

"Vocal rest," Jesse said to his mom. "I gave him some cough medicine and he was knocked out in about twenty minutes."

"He shouldn't be singing," Ms. Matthews said.

"Don't start, Mom," Jesse warned.

"You know I won't ever interfere in your band business," she said, waving him off. "Just giving my nursing advice."

My eyes flickered around the room. "Where's Aaron?"

Ross shrugged. "Haven't seen him."

"Katelyn Jackson to stage!" Connor's voice called.

Ms. Matthews glanced around. "Now who was that?"

"My brother," I said, with a laugh. "I'll go find out what's going on."

"I'll walk you," Jesse said, following me out.

He ushered me out of the door, closing it behind us.

"What are you doing?" I asked.

"I need to talk to you, I don't want to upset my mom. So walk with me for a sec."

That didn't sound good. We walked a bit down the hallway before Jesse stopped me.

"You're spending a lot of time with Zach," Jesse said, his lips pulled into a slight frown.

"Don't tell me you're here to give me *the talk* too!"

He took a step back, his eyebrows furrowing together in confusion. "No."

"Oh."

"No, I'm more referring to Zach's health."

This time it was my turn to be confused. "His throat?"

"Kind of. When Zach's immune system is down, he's more prone to seizures. He's been seizure-free for over a month now, but I just want to make sure that you're prepared for the worst."

I felt a tight squeeze in my chest. "I . . . I don't think I am."

"No one ever is. I want to make sure you remember the training?"

"I took notes that day; I'm pretty sure they're still in my phone."

"Do you have my number?"

I pulled my phone out, checking my contacts. "Saved it during the epilepsy training."

"If you even *think* something's off, never hesitate to call me. Shoot me a text right now so I know I have your number."

I did as he asked, my name popping up on his screen.

"I figured I already had it, wanted to be sure."

Connor's voice came back over the PA system. "Katelyn Jackson! Meet me at the stage."

"You'd better get going," Jesse said.

My nerves felt frayed as I took a step back. "I've never really been in an emergency medical situation before."

"I understand," Jesse said. "Call me anytime you need to. Now go to the stage."

"Thanks, Jesse."

I made my way to the stage, surprised to see Connor sitting in the middle with food spread out around him.

"What's this?" I asked, as he handed me a prepackaged Olive Garden salad.

"A preshow dinner," he answered, with a smile. "Let's catch up."

I took a seat, grabbing a breadstick. "I'm more interested in hearing the latest with you. You and Mackenzie seemed awfully close at the campfire."

"You of all people know that's not a thing."

"Do I?"

He didn't answer, picking up a breadstick. "Lana and I are over. I don't know what comes next."

"Let's not focus on next. Let's focus on now."

He picked up his water, taking a sip. "Let's toast to that."

I picked up my water too. "To the now."

"To the now."

It was the first time I'd been to a show in over a week. I was sitting in the VIP section with Ms. Matthews, half watching Mackenzie's set in anticipation for Skyline.

"My boys are on next?" Ms. Matthews asked, once Mackenzie exited the stage.

I nodded.

The lights dimmed, and the arena went crazy. The spotlights came on, four lights for the four members of Skyline.

"I'm Jesse."

"I'm Ross."

"I'm Aaron."

"And I'm Zach," Zach finished, his voice hoarse. "And we're Skyline."

The crowd went crazy, stomping their feet.

"For those of you who don't know, this is our home state!" Aaron called out.

Screams came up around the arena.

"And tonight we'd like to welcome a very special guest," Ross said. "Our mom's out there in the audience tonight. Love ya!"

More screaming ensued, and Ms. Matthews waved.

To my surprise, Ms. Matthews sang along with all the songs, smiling and dancing the entire time. She was truly their biggest supporter.

After their set I offered to take her back to their dressing room, but she refused, saying that she wanted to stick around for Connor.

Connor's set went flawlessly, including "Illusion," when he successfully disappeared off the stage, and "Shades," which was perfect now that he didn't have a wobbly chair to contend with.

"Your brother is incredibly talented," Ms. Matthews said, once he left the stage. "That was amazing."

"That's not the end," I said, with a smile.

The crowd began to chant for an encore, the lights still off on the stage and in the arena. Then the spotlight came up on Mackenzie, and the crowd went crazy.

The song went beautifully. It was like everybody was on top of their game tonight, even Zach.

"That was spectacular!" Ms. Matthews exclaimed, once the song was finished.

"*Now* the show's over," I shouted to Ms. Matthews.

"That was delightful," she said, as I led her back to Skyline's dressing room.

"You liked it?" I asked, knocking twice on their door. I entered the room, where they were all talking and high-fiving each other, still high from the show.

"I'll see you guys later," I said, leaving them to spend their only night with their mom.

CHARLOTTE, NC
CHAPTER 23

For the first time in a while, I wasn't spending my day with Zach. My mom had insisted that we share a mother-daughter day, so we were headed out to get mani-pedis and possibly facials. I had to admit that my skin was in desperate need of a good exfoliation.

"Don't take the calluses off my feet," I said to the pedicurist. "I need those for soccer."

"Gross, Katelyn."

"You don't know how long it took me to build these. I rely on them for games."

I leaned back in my chair, letting the massage settings dig into my muscles. I let out a sigh of contentment, my eyes slipping shut.

"We should do this more often," Mom said.

"It's nice to be spoiled sometimes."

"Sometimes?"

"Very funny."

My toes were painted with a clear gloss, with my fingernails painted red, white, and blue to match the U.S. team colors.

"Are you sure you don't want color on your toes?" the pedicurist asked.

"They'll only get ruined during practice and games. Not worth it."

She was clearly confused but didn't ask any further questions.

"What's the latest?" Mom asked me. "I feel like I hardly see you these days; you're always off with Zach."

"Nothing to report," I said, with a shrug. "We like hanging out."

"You guys were gone for a full day in Atlanta. I kept checking your location, and you two were always somewhere different."

"First off, stop tracking me." She laughed in response. "And he had this whole tourist day planned, so we went to the Coke factory and then out to lunch, and then spent the afternoon in Centennial Park before doing the Skyview for sunset. And then we had to get back to the hotel for a livestream at eight."

"Busy girl these days. As long as you're happy."

"I'm very happy."

After the mani-pedi was complete, we were led to another room for a dual facial. I pocketed the receipt for the mani-pedi as we walked; it would be my memento for this tour stop. It wasn't often I got a spa day with my mom.

"I feel like after touring for so long, I could use a good exfoliation and deep hydration," Mom said.

"My oily skin disagrees with the deep hydration," I said. "But I could definitely use a good exfoliation too."

We laid faceup on the tables, a technician assigned to each table. Much like with the pedicure, my eyes slipped shut in contentment. I wasn't accustomed to getting facials, and was very surprised when the technician massaged my face. I quickly realized how much tension I was holding in my jaw and let out an audible groan once it was released.

"You okay over there?" Mom asked.

"This is perfect, Mom," I said. "Thank you."

She reached out, grabbing my hand between the facial beds. "I love you, daughter of mine."

"I love you too, Momma."

I slipped backstage at the arena, trying to be discreet as I kept an eye out for Zach. This was the first time since I'd returned from L.A. that I'd gone all day without even speaking to him.

He'd texted me earlier, but to honor our mother-daughter day, I hadn't responded. But after a late lunch and gossip session, we were back in time for meet and greets. And I was dying to see Zach. I peeked out into the arena, where Connor was holding his preshow meet and greet and sound check. I slipped backstage again to avoid the fans, taking the long way back outside.

I found Skyline's meet and greet off to the side of the arena. It was outside, in a shaded and cool area. They were in the midst of signing photos and merchandise, much too distracted to notice me slip into line.

The girl in front of me turned to see who'd gotten into line behind her, a look of confusion flickering across her face. "Excuse me? Aren't you Katelyn Jackson?"

Okay, maybe I didn't completely think my plan through.

"Yeah."

"Why are you waiting to meet Skyline?" she asked, staring at me like I was an idiot. "You're dating Zach."

"It's a surprise," I said. "Don't tell him."

She slowly turned back around in line, probably thinking that I was crazy. Which was fair.

The line slowly inched forward, and I ended up waiting an hour to meet Skyline. I played a game on my phone as I waited, helping to pass the time spent waiting to see my own boyfriend.

I positioned myself so that I was directly behind Paul, none of the boys taking notice of me as they greeted the girl in front of me.

"It's so cool to finally meet you," she said to Jesse, handing over a poster for him to sign.

"It's cool to meet *you*," Jesse said, with a smile. "What's your name?"

"Anne, spelled *A-N-N-E*."

I wasn't able to hear the rest of her conversation with the boys, my view blocked so that I could only see Aaron and Jesse. I tried to peek around Paul to get a good look at Zach, and in the process caught eyes with Jesse.

He was in the process of taking photos with Anne, but that didn't stop him from letting out a loud laugh, causing Aaron to glance at him in confusion.

"Just a funny thought," Jesse said, dismissively.

And then it was my turn.

"And what are you doing here?" Jesse asked me, as I stepped up to greet the boys.

"I'm here to meet you," I said. "Obviously."

"Got anything for me to sign?"

I glanced around, seeing if there was anything I could grab. And then I held out my arm. "I'd love for you to sign my forearm."

Jesse laughed, taking my arm in his hand and scribbling his name in permanent marker across it.

I held out my arm toward Aaron as well, who just signed it with a shake of his head. "You know, Katelyn, if you want our autographs all you have to do is ask."

"Not to mention that I already autographed all of the posters in your room," Ross added, as he signed my arm as well. "So I should really start charging you."

And then I was face-to-face with Zach.

He had a sign to the left of him, with the words *Vocal Rest* written on it in big, bold letters.

A smile played on his lips as he scribbled his signature across my arm, before leaning in to give me a kiss.

I heard a few gasps behind me.

Zach pointed to the *Vocal Rest* sign, and then pointed toward his phone.

I nodded. "I was having a day out with my mom. But after the show tonight, if it's not past curfew, maybe we can grab dinner? Watch a movie?"

Zach eagerly nodded. He pointed to his watch and then phone.

"You'll text me after?"

He nodded again.

"Are we going to take some pictures?" Jesse asked. "Or are you two going to flirt all day?"

"I would love some photos," I said, slinging my arms around Ross and Zach before smiling for the camera.

I was ninety-five percent sure that Ross held up bunny ears above me.

"Funny face!" Ross announced, and the boys all cracked up before doing as they were told. The next few minutes were spent with each of the boys, aside from Zach, shouting out different faces to make.

"Okay, time to move along," Ross said, shooing me away. "You two can text later. We've got a few more people who want to play charades with Zach."

I waved good-bye before heading back to Connor's dressing room, excited for another lazy date night.

This time Zach came over to my hotel room and my mom agreed to a curfew extension, with conditions. We had to leave the door cracked and use separate covers if we were going to lie in bed.

I'd ordered Zach chicken noodle soup from room service. He'd made it through most of his set at the show, but they'd had to cut it short due to Zach's voice being unable to hold out.

Jesse had let Zach come over with strict vocal rest instructions. I'd promised to take care of him, and although I could tell Jesse was skeptical, he didn't question any further. And now we were back to watching Netflix while eating room service food, half cuddling while also keeping an eye out for my ever-present mother.

The last thing I wanted was for my mom to catch us making out.

"It's so rude when Netflix asks me if I'm still watching," I said, as I confirmed that we were, indeed, still binge-watching while grubbing out.

I rested my head on Zach's shoulder as he lightly ran his fingers through my hair with one hand, using the other hand to sip his chamomile tea.

Conversation wasn't needed as the two of us sat in content silence, my arms half-wrapped around him as he massaged my scalp.

As the episode ended, I heard a *clunk* noise. I turned to see that the tea had fallen off the edge of the nightstand. There hadn't been anything left inside, the cup hitting the floor and rolling.

Zach's gaze was focused on the teacup.

"How did that happen?" I asked.

He didn't answer, not that I expected him to out loud. But he didn't acknowledge my question, either, continuing to stare at the dropped teacup.

"Did it slip off?" I asked.

No response.

"Zach?"

I cupped two fingers under his chin, turning his face toward mine. "Zach, are you okay?"

He blinked a few times, reaching up to run his fingers through his hair. Something didn't seem right. My heart raced as I sat up on my knees, snapping my fingers. "Zach? Can you nod? Show me that you're hearing me?"

His gaze rested on me, but it was as though he was seeing right through me, his eyes continuously blinking as it seemed he was trying to focus.

This definitely wasn't right.

I fumbled for my phone, my body feeling shaky as I tried to think through my next steps. I immediately called Jesse.

"Katelyn?" Jesse asked, as he answered the phone. "Everything okay?"

"I don't think so. Zach's not acting right."

"I'll be right there. Do you need me to stay on the phone? Is he saying anything?"

I held my hand over the speaker. "Zach?"

No response.

"No, he's not saying anything. He looks lost."

My hotel room door flew open, an out-of-breath Jesse coming inside.

"Did you sprint down the hall?" I ended our phone call.

Jesse nodded as he walked around Zach's side of the bed, kneeling down next to him. "Zach?"

Zach reached up and ran his hand down his face, his gaze resting on mine once again.

I wanted to reach out and hold him, to calm whatever was happening inside of him. But according to the training, I was supposed to stay hands off. So I sat back.

"Zach," I said, softly. "Can you hear me?"

"Bad news is that he's in your bed, so getting him back to our room will be a bit of a nightmare," Jesse said, quietly.

He pulled out his phone, sending a text. "Hopefully Aaron is still awake so he can help me out."

"What should I do?" I asked.

Jesse shook his head. "Nothing you can do. It should only be a couple of minutes tops."

Maybe I can't help what's going on inside of his brain, but I could at least try to keep him calm. I began speaking quietly to him, in soothing tones. Zach's hand reached up, and he rubbed it across his eyes.

"Hey, bud," Jesse said. "You coming around?"

Zach slowly nodded.

"Okay, good," Jesse said.

Aaron came to the door, a water bottle in hand. "Ross woke me up."

"I'll need your help getting him back to the room," Jesse said. "He's not come around quite yet, but you'll need to take one arm and I can take the other."

Aaron nodded, leaning against the doorway. "I've got the w-a-t-e-r when he's ready."

Why would Aaron spell it out?

"We want Zach to say it," Jesse said, answering my unasked question. "That's how we know he's coming to and not just repeating us."

Zach raised both arms above his head, before resting his forearms on top of it.

"You're okay," Jesse said. "I'm here. Katelyn's here. Aaron's here. You're okay."

"Okay," Zach said, his voice hoarse.

I'd never been so happy to hear someone speak.

Jesse reached up, gently lowering Zach's arms back to his sides. "Let's release some pressure from your head."

Zach nodded. "Water?"

Aaron tossed the bottle to Jesse.

"Here," Jesse said, cracking it open for him. "Drink slowly."

He took a few slow sips, lightly squeezing my hand.

"Ouch," Zach said, handing Jesse the water back. "Hurt my throat."

"Oh shit, I didn't think about that," Aaron said.

Jesse waved him off. "How's the head?"

"Hurts."

I ran my fingers through his hair, wishing that I could rub the pain away. "I'm sorry."

Jesse stood up. "Let's go get some rest, okay?"

Aaron came over by Jesse's side.

Jesse handed me the room key. "We'll need you to open the door. Hopefully I don't end up having to carry the kid."

I climbed out of the bed, shoving my feet into my slippers. "What's your room number?"

"It's 416," Jesse said, as he grabbed Zach's hand. "Ready, bud?"

Zach hoisted himself up, stumbling into Aaron. Jesse slung Zach's right arm around his shoulders, Aaron taking his left.

"Think you can walk?" Jesse asked. "Is this enough?"

"Yeah," Zach said.

The four of us made our way down the hallway, very slowly. I held the door open for the boys, and they got Zach into bed.

"That's your bed," Aaron said to Jesse.

"Doesn't really matter right now."

I pulled back the comforter, making sure Zach was comfortable.

"I'll see you tomorrow," I said, bending down to kiss his forehead. "Please get some sleep."

"I'll walk her back," Aaron said to Jesse. "You good here?"

Jesse nodded as he eased down onto the other bed. "I'll call you if I need anything."

"I'm coming back," Aaron said. "You need sleep."

Jesse didn't respond, but it was clear that he wasn't budging.

"Thank you, Katelyn," Jesse said, as I turned to leave.

"I don't really think I did anything," I said, with a bit of a forced smile.

"You kept him calm," Aaron said. "You haven't seen Zach when people get upset after his seizures. Remaining calm and speaking in a slow, soothing voice is the absolute best way to ensure that it's as smooth as it can be."

I felt like they were saying that to appease me, but I nodded anyway. "Thanks."

"See you tomorrow," Jesse said.

Aaron walked me back to my room, where my mom was waiting.

"Did Zach go back to his room?" Mom asked.

Aaron and I exchanged glances.

"Yeah," I answered. "He wasn't feeling well."

"I know he was on vocal rest today," she said, with a bit of a frown. "I hope he starts feeling better soon."

"Thanks again, Katelyn," Aaron said. "See you tomorrow."

I waved good-bye as he headed back down the hall.

"Such a nice group of boys," Mom said.

I leaned into her, my heart feeling heavy. "I know."

Mom bent down and kissed the top of my head. "Are you sure you're okay?"

"Just tired."

"Get some rest, then. It'll be an early morning to head out on the bus, but you can go right back to sleep once we're loaded up."

"I will. Love you, Mom."

"Love you too, Katie."

She closed the door as she left, and I flopped down in my bed.

My eyes were heavy, but my body was wired. I couldn't sleep without knowing that Zach was okay.

CHAPTER 24

In the city that never sleeps, I felt like a walking zombie. I hadn't been able to sleep at all, my mind replaying the events of the night.

When I'd sat back in that epilepsy training, I was concerned about whether or not I could help Zach on my own during a seizure. And now that I had seen what it looked like, my mind couldn't comprehend what had happened. One second we were watching TV, and the next it was like he had checked out. And if it was terrifying for me to witness, I couldn't imagine how it felt on Zach's end.

Once Jesse knew that I wasn't sleeping, he sent me text updates every hour. They were just letting me know that Zach was still asleep, but I still appreciated it nonetheless.

For the first time in a long while, I skipped my morning run. My body was too exhausted to fathom getting out of bed for exercise purposes, especially at four in the morning. We'd started the almost ten-hour drive at five—Jesse told me their bodyguard helped move Zach to the tour bus before everyone else had boarded so the rest of the crew wouldn't see his condition—and by three in the afternoon we were still in traffic.

I was sitting on the couch, constantly checking my phone to see if Zach had texted me yet. Jesse said he'd woken up a little after twelve; however Jesse also said Zach was usually a bit slower the day after a seizure.

"Want to play a card game?" Connor asked me.

Connor sat down at the table, a deck of cards in his hand.

"Sure," I agreed, making my way over to the booth seat.

"You look exhausted," Connor commented.

"I didn't sleep much last night," I said. "I have a lot on my mind."

"Amen to that, baby sis."

He dealt out the cards for a game of rummy. "Mind if I play some music?"

"Play away. I'm not really in the conversation mood."

"Same."

Connor scrolled through his phone and ended up playing through the top charts.

We didn't make it to the hotel until nearly five—twelve straight hours on the bus, due to traffic. We were all itching to get out and stretch our legs, to leave the confined space that the bus had to offer.

"That was a long drive," Mom said, as the bus parked in the designated garage for the hotel. "New York traffic is no joke."

There was no show tonight, thankfully; however I was scheduled to fly out to L.A. tomorrow to meet up with the team. Which meant that I had only this evening to be a tourist.

"What's your plan?" Connor asked me, once we were checked into the hotel.

"I need to find my commemorative item for NYC," I said. "I'm not sure where to look."

"Times Square," Connor said. "You can find all the cheap tourist stuff there, as well as experience the most tourist part of the city."

"I think the Statue of Liberty might be the top tourist attraction spot."

Connor raised an eyebrow in question. "You think the Statue of Liberty ranks above Times Square?"

"Absolutely."

"We'll have to agree that you're wrong."

"It's agree to disagree, dumbass."

Connor smirked. "Except when I'm always right. Can I go with you?"

"You want to go on an item hunt with me?"

He nodded. "And I'm going to convince you to get a bobblehead of some sort. Not sure what kind yet, but I feel like a bobblehead is a must in a collection of miscellaneous tacky items."

I let my mom know where we were headed before the two of us took off walking toward Times Square. I'd forgotten how exhausting it was to travel with Connor. He had his bodyguard, Eddie, and was stopped every block for a photo or an autograph.

What should've been a ten-minute walk ended up taking nearly forty-five.

"Sorry," Connor apologized, as he jogged to catch up to me once again.

I'd taken to standing off to the side as Connor signed something. His fans weren't interested in me; they wanted a one-on-one moment with Connor. And I didn't want to third wheel on that.

"For what?" I asked.

"For holding you up."

"You're not holding me up," I said, with a shake of my head. "I like the walk. It's much better than being cooped up in that bus."

Times Square was even worse—there were people that you could pay to take a picture with who got annoyed with the requests from fans to take pictures with Connor. This was definitely a lot harder than going out with Zach.

"I should've worn a hat," Connor said.

But I knew that he'd never purposely duck his fans. There were times when I'd watched him go out of his way to make sure he got to see them. And while it could be tedious to have to stand around and wait for him, it's also an awe-inspiring moment to see people clamoring after your brother.

This was the guy who I yelled at for leaving the toilet seat up in the middle of the night and who tried to sing opera in the shower. There were people who would die for a chance to meet him, to get to spend a couple of seconds with him. And as a fangirl myself, I more than understood it. Connor stopped at a corner store, buying a hoodie. He pulled it on, tying the strings tight around his face.

"You always look ridiculous when you do that," I said, with a laugh.

"I can meet everyone after we complete our mission," Connor said. "But right now I want to find you the perfect bobblehead."

"And who said I agreed to getting a bobblehead?"

"Me. And I'm always right, remember?"

"You're definitely a pain in my ass."

We made our way through the many shops along Times Square. Connor was insistent that we had to find the perfect item, and I found it amusing to watch as he tested out each and every bobble-head.

"What about a mini Statue of Liberty?" I asked.

"Nope," Connor declined. "Not cool enough."

In our seventh store, Connor held up a bobblehead for me to see—a rat with two buck teeth, dressed in an NYC hat.

"What is *that*?" I asked, as I took it from him. "It's hideously cute."

"It represents the Subway Rat," Connor said. "Something you'll probably experience before you leave tomorrow, so . . . a realistic object."

"It's a rat," I said, unable to contain my laughter.

"It's perfect."

And that's how I ended up adding an NYC bobblehead rat to my collection.

There was a knock on my hotel room door as I finished packing my suitcase the next morning. I'd already showered and dressed for my flight, so I'd had to stuff all of my belongings back into the suitcase in order to fly to L.A. My body was never going to understand time zones again. I opened the door to reveal Zach standing outside, with two coffees in hand.

"Hey," he said, his voice still hoarse.

I immediately wrapped my arms around him, pulling both him and the drinks in close. I hadn't seen him at all the day before, and I wanted to give him his space, but I missed him terribly.

"I know," Zach said, quietly. "I'm sorry."

Despite my mom's rule, I brought him inside and closed the door behind us.

Zach handed me a drink. "It's an Iced Caramel Macchiato."

I took a sip, savoring the sweet flavor. "Yum."

He took a seat on the edge of my bed, resting his drink on my bedside table. "We need to talk."

"Okay."

I rested my drink next to his before standing in front of him, a few feet back.

Zach's eyes flickered around the room, and I could feel the nervous energy radiating off him. And so I bent over, cupping his cheeks in my hands as I gave him a tender kiss.

He pulled away. "I understand if you can't do this anymore."

What? I took a step back once again.

"I know my seizures can be a lot to deal with," he continued. "Jesse said that was a pretty mild one, but that was a taste of the broken connections in my brain. Sometimes things just . . . stop working. And I don't want you to feel like you have to take care of me or watch me or—"

I cut him off with another kiss, before pressing my lips against his ear. "Listen to me very closely, Zachary Matthews. You having epilepsy doesn't change how I feel about you." I took a seat next to him, taking his hands in mine. "I won't lie, it was a little scary for me. But the only thing it changes is that I want to learn more about partial seizures, learn more about what I can do. This doesn't change anything between us."

He leaned in, resting his forehead on mine. "Are you sure?"

"More than sure. I like you. And I want to keep doing this with you."

He pulled away from me, his shoulders visibly relaxing. "I like you too. I wanted to make sure that you were okay after seeing that, seeing me like that."

"The only thing on my mind right now, and for the past day and a half, is you. I just wanted you to be okay."

His lips curved into a small smile. "I am. And I will be."

There was a knock on the door.

"That's probably Jesse," Zach said, with an eye roll. "He wants me to do an urgent care trip to make sure my voice is okay."

"Then you should."

He shrugged as he stood up, grabbing his drink. "And give into Jesse that easy? Where's the fun in that?"

As Zach predicted, it was Jesse on the other side of the door.

"We've got to go," Jesse said. "Sound check is coming up soon and we still have some stuff to do."

I stood up, giving Zach one last kiss before he left. Before I left. "Try not to miss me too much," I said.

"I'll do my best."

LONDON, ENGLAND
CHAPTER 25

The team was flying to London for our next game stop. Yesterday I had flown from New York to L.A., so my body clock already felt like it was three hours later than it was. But London was eight hours ahead of L.A. time, and by the time we arrived it would be eight p.m., but it would feel like three p.m. And to make matters worse, we'd have to be in bed early for practice the next day. I feared my body clock would never be the same again.

Coach handed us our boarding passes after we checked our bags, and we made our way over to the security line. I stood with Jenica, the two of us catching up on the latest gossip.

Marci and Nancy came up behind us.

"There's our little rebel," Marci said.

"Rebel?"

"Don't act like you forgot our last practice," Jenica said, with a huff. "You still owe me big time for pulling off the cover-up of the century."

Falling asleep in Zach's room, leaving my best friend scrambling with Coach Tom: not my proudest moment.

"And how does she know?" I asked.

"I brought Marci with me to come over and watch *Drama Llama*," Nancy explained. "And then . . . you weren't there."

"Was the Zach-boy worth nearly losing your spot on the team?" Marci asked with a smirk. "Because that doesn't sound very captain-like to me."

I was instantly annoyed . . . but Marci *had* kept my secret, so I held my tongue.

"For the record," Jenica said, "as her best friend, *I'm* the only one allowed to give her a hard time."

I glanced over my shoulder at Marci. "I'll call truce if she will."

Marci's lips pressed together in annoyance. "I'll call truce if she will."

"Deal," Jenica said. "Now both of you shut up and don't ruin this for me. I've never been out of the country."

"And we're going to both England *and* France," Nancy said. "I can't wait."

∿∿∿

The wake-up call came at nine a.m. I was pretty sure I hadn't fallen asleep until seven.

Coach knew our bodies would be trying to adjust to the time difference, so he proposed yoga at ten a.m. We had no idea what tortures he had planned for the rest of the day after that.

After tossing and turning all night due to jet lag, my aching body wasn't quite ready to let go of the hotel room bed.

"No!" I groaned, pulling my pillow over my face. "I can't do it."

We didn't have much time to lie around and protest, as Coach Tom had explicitly stated the night before that he wanted us downstairs by 9:30.

Jenica and I rode the elevator down in silence.

"Good morning, ladies," Coach Tom said, with a bright smile.

"Oh, it is way too early for this," Nancy muttered.

We piled onto the bus in silence. For most of us it was too early to try to start conversations.

"All right, ladies," Coach announced, once the bus was on its way to the stadium, "here's the plan for the day. After yoga, you're free to sightsee for the rest of the day."

A cheer came up from around the bus, the team excited.

"Curfew is at ten p.m. sharp," he ordered. "I will be doing room checks. If you're not in your room by ten, you will not play tomorrow. I am very serious about this rule, ladies."

"Hey, Nancy," I said, turning in my seat to face her. "How good are you at keeping time?"

"Oh, trust me," she said, raising her eyebrows at me. "We will all be in that hotel room before ten. Chances are we'll be half-asleep by dinnertime anyway."

"It's up to you," Jenica informed her, turning around to face Nancy. "Because Katelyn and I suck when it comes to curfews."

"Don't worry," Nancy promised. "I got you."

We pulled into the stadium and all filed off the bus and onto the fields, which were still wet with morning dew.

"Hey," Marci said, joining me in the front of the team.

"Hey."

"Do you mind if I, um, tag along with you guys while you sightsee today?" she muttered.

My knee-jerk reaction was to answer with a sarcastic *what happened to the rest of your friends?* remark. But I also knew what it was like to be on the outside of a team.

"Of course not," I said.

"Cool, thanks."

Coach was standing by the entrance of the stadium next to a woman with a British accent.

"Everyone take a mat," he ordered, as we approached them.

We each took a mat as we passed the British woman, who I assumed was our yoga instructor.

"Have you ever done yoga before?" Marci asked me, as we laid our mats out at the head of the team as instructed by Coach Tom.

"Nope," I said, shaking my head.

"Awesome," she muttered. "We're stuck at the front of the team and we're going to look like idiots."

"Well, at least it won't just be one of us."

"I guess that's true."

Coach silenced us with a whistle. "All right, ladies! Let's listen to what Ms. Jackie here has to say."

"Shoot me now," Marci muttered, as the yoga instructor started us in downward dog.

Our first stop on our sightseeing adventure was caffeine.

"I want to visit Buckingham Palace," Nancy said, as we left our hotel lobby.

"How do we get there?" Marci asked.

I glanced around the group. "I'm not sure anyone here has experience in London."

"Found a Beans!" Jenica announced, holding up her phone. "This way."

Nancy let out a long yawn, causing a chain reaction amongst the four of us. "There's no way I'd make it through the day without a coffee. A massage would be nice too."

"Cassie and her friends were booking massages at the hotel," I pointed out, as we hurried across the street.

"Jealous," she muttered. "But I'd rather sightsee."

"Have you guys seen the London team at all?" Jenica asked, switching the subject.

We all three shook our heads.

"I hear they're a powerhouse," Jenica said, showing us the news article on it. "And that they work on a dual striker system, like us, but a flat-back defense."

"You can crash a flat-back defense," I said, with a nod. "You two definitely have the speed."

"Marci has the speed," Jenica corrected. "I mean, once we slide that ball through, it's a simple footrace. And Marci, you can have them beat every time."

"What's so powerhouse about them?" I asked, as we reached Beans.

"Their defender Elizabeth," Jenica read off. "She has the fastest sprint times in her city."

"Katelyn and I have the fastest sprint times on the team," Marci said, as we entered the coffee shop. "I bet we can give them a run for their money."

I ordered a shot of espresso and a blueberry muffin before finding a seat in the small coffee shop. I pulled out my phone.

"I have the directions to get to Buckingham Palace," I said, studying the map. "We need to find the nearest subway station so I can figure it out."

Nancy cleared her throat. "It's called *the Tube* here," she said, in a terrible British accent.

"Never do that again," I said, as Jenica laughed.

Once Nancy's coffee was ready, we took our Beans to-go, heading to the nearest station as I followed my phone's directions to Buckingham Palace.

"Are we sure we want to trust Katelyn?" Jenica teased.

"Shut up and follow me."

I stood back as Jenica snapped picture after picture of Buckingham Palace.

"You're such a tourist," I teased.

"Be nice," she ordered, snapping a picture of my face.

I walked away from her, FaceTiming Zach. He was quick to answer.

"Welcome to London," I said, showing him my surroundings. "Here we have the Royal Family."

"Very nice."

I flipped the camera back around to face me. "Next sight I'll be calling you from is the London Eye."

"Looking forward to it."

We spent the day like true tourists, taking a ton of photos and having fish and chips for dinner.

"We should head back," Nancy said, as we came out of an ice cream shop.

Jenica pulled out her guide to London. "We can totally fit in one more thing."

"No," Marci said, firmly. "We're heading back."

"But there's so much more to see," Jenica argued. "We have time for one more thing, I'm sure of it."

I couldn't help but nod along. "Maybe we could fit—"

"We're heading back," Marci confirmed. "You two are the worst at this."

Jenica let out a frustrated groan but folded her map back up and trudged along behind.

I googled the address of our hotel and routed the way back, combining my map with the subway station.

"You're, like, a whiz at this," Nancy said, watching as I picked out our route.

"It's not hard once you get used to it," I said, pointing to the train we needed to get on. "We should be back with plenty of time to spare."

"Thirty minutes isn't plenty of time," Nancy said. "But we shouldn't have an issue."

Our subway came up, and we took the route back to our hotel.

"Are you sure this is right?" Nancy asked, as we came up out of the subway station.

"According to my phone our hotel should be less than a mile ahead," I said, showing it to her. But as I looked around, I didn't recognize any of it.

"Where's the Beans in the distance?" Jenica asked.

"I have a bad feeling about this," I muttered, as we rounded the corner to where my phone promised the hotel was.

We stopped outside a fast-food restaurant, and my stomach started twisting into knots.

We were lost.

"Oh shit," Jenica mumbled, looking around.

Nancy was hyperventilating while Marci pulled out her phone, cross-referencing her map with mine.

"It definitely says our hotel is right here," she confirmed. "What the hell?"

"Good ol' Apple Maps," Jenica muttered, shaking her head. "What are we going to do?"

"Oh my God," Nancy groaned. "We're not going to be able to play tomorrow! My entire life is ruined."

"Chill out," I ordered, flipping through my phone to find the number to the hotel.

My phone went off, Zach's picture popping up. I sent him to voicemail, instead calling the hotel.

"Yes," I said, as someone answered, "my name is Katelyn Jackson, a guest at your hotel. I'm currently lost, can you give me the street name your hotel is located on?"

She did, and I thanked her and hung up. I typed it into my phone, only to find out it was across the city.

"Come on," I said, running to flag down a cab.

"Do you know how expensive that cab will be?" Marci demanded.

"It's on me," I promised. "Well, it's on my emergency charge card. I'll explain it to my parents later."

A cab pulled over and we piled in, me in shotgun, giving the cab driver the name of the hotel and the street name it was on. He gave us a once-over before obliging our request, taking off in the direction of our hotel.

Feeling bad about sending Zach to voicemail, I sent him a quick text, promising to call him when I had a minute.

"We have less than twenty minutes," I heard Nancy say.

"Just breathe," I promised. "I'll handle it."

We pulled up to the hotel four minutes past curfew. My heart was pounding in my chest and my hands were clammy as we walked into the hotel lobby, and my heart stopped as I saw Coach Tom standing there, his arms folded across his chest. I heard Nancy gulp next to me.

"You ladies do realize it's 10:04," he said.

I stepped forward, my mouth dry. "It's my fault, sir. I got us lost on the way back."

"It's not only her fault," Jenica piped up, stepping forward.

"It's all of our faults," Marci confirmed, with Nancy's backup.

"But I'm the one that got us lost," I said, giving them a look. I was trying to let at least three of us play tomorrow. We needed that.

"Trust is something that's earned, ladies," Coach Tom said. "And since two of you are my captains, I trust that you are telling the truth, and that you were simply lost."

I felt nauseated enough to puke, my eyes widening as he spoke.

"You'll be eligible to play in the game tomorrow," Coach Tom confirmed, "and this right here? This is mentioned to no one."

"Yes, sir," we chimed in unison.

"And there will be consequences."

"Yes, sir."

"Good, now get upstairs."

We scurried into the elevator, waiting for the doors to close before we spoke again.

"I can't believe that just happened," Jenica squealed, her hand over her heart.

"I wouldn't be so happy if I were you," Marci mumbled.

"Why not?" I asked, a smile on my face.

"Because he mentioned there would be consequences," she explained. "And I have a feeling that won't be pleasant."

We piled out of the elevator and went into our hotel room. My adrenaline was still pumping, and I changed into my pajamas before calling Zach back.

"Is everything all right?" he asked, answering his phone.

"Everything's fine," I said, as I lay out across my bed. "Only a little drama. More importantly though, what time is it for you? Where are you?"

"It's five in Pittsburgh right now," he said. "And my brothers are arguing, which is *so rare* for them, as you know. Today it's about personal space on the tour bus, as we don't have much of a break for the next ten days. Being cooped up on this bus together is going to be literal hell."

"Go to bed!" Jenica called out from the bathroom. "We don't have time for your gushing."

I flipped her off as Zach laughed. "Was that Jenica?"

"Yes, and she can *shut up*."

She peeked out from the bathroom to glare at me. "You owe me. So *you* shut up."

"I think maybe you should go to bed," Zach said.

"I think you're right," I said. "Talk to you tomorrow?"

He hummed in agreement. "Good night."

"Good night."

I hung up and plugged in my phone before turning over and staring at the ceiling, willing sleep to come.

"And now comes the jet lag," Jenica said, as she climbed into her own bed.

The joys of traveling.

LONDON, ENGLAND
CHAPTER 26

During the bus ride on the way to the game, Coach Tom announced that it was going to be live-streamed, and then sent out a link for us to share. I forwarded the email to my mom and sent a quick text to Zach to let him know that my mom had the link, in case he wanted to watch too.

The pit of my stomach was bottoming out as we emptied out onto the fields, ready for our pregame warm-ups. The buzz continued throughout the pregame water break and then pregame chats.

"I'm making only one change to my starting lineup," Coach Tom announced.

I knew he was going to replace me after what happened yesterday.

"Bianca will be going in for Gabriella," he announced, and relief coursed through my system.

"Captains!" the ref called, and Marci and I took the field.

I called tails, and it landed on tails, giving us kickoff and them their choice of the field. They gave us the sun.

After one last pregame pep talk from Coach Tom, we took the field, Nancy on my left and Bianca on my right.

"They have a dual-striker system," I explained to Bianca, as we waited for London to take the field. "Number three is said to be one of the best players in London, and she has some of the fastest sprint times in this part of the city. So play to contain."

Bianca nodded, and we did a quick handshake before taking our positions. London took the field, number three on the left side of the field, Nancy's side. I nodded at Nancy, who flashed me a thumbs-up, letting me know she could handle it.

We started with the kickoff, and knowing that they had a flat-back system, sent it back to our midfield so they could launch it. We sorely underestimated London. They were on our midfield in seconds and had the ball faster than we anticipated.

"Contain!" I shouted to Nancy, as I covered their star forward. "Midfield, I need backup!"

The London offense was swarming us, fast. I'd never seen anything like it, yet it was beautiful. Their midfielder tripped Nancy up and crossed the ball in. I jumped up to get my head on it, but it went over me, and instead number three made contact with it, sending it into our goal. We stood there, stunned, as the ref blew the whistle, signaling that it was indeed a goal.

"The hell just happened?" Bianca asked, as Cassandra dug the ball out of the goal.

"They scored in less than ten seconds," I said. "That's what happened."

Coach Tom was yelling at us from the sideline, but I could tell he was as baffled as we were.

It was time to step up our game. We kicked off again, and instead of shooting it back to our midfield, Jenica launched it over their flat-back defense. I pushed the defense up as our offense moved the ball up the field, keeping their defense on their toes.

We lost the ball, giving them a goal kick.

I backpedaled as the ball was kicked, jumping up to head it back up to our offense.

Number three yelled at the other striker on London's team, telling her that it was her fault they'd lost the ball. The defense pushed back up, catching number three offside without her realizing, and as the ball was launched into our backfield, she took off and the ref blew the whistle.

"What?" she demanded, stomping her foot.

"You were offside," the other striker informed her. "Maybe you should watch where you stand."

"I want her off the field!" number three shouted at their coach, pointing at the striker.

If they kept this behavior up, they'd self-destruct before the half.

The rest of the first half was spent bouncing the ball back and forth, no clear control and no more goals. As the ref blew the whistle to signal halftime, I turned to glance toward the bench, where Coach Tom was waiting with his arms folded. This wasn't going to be a fun chat.

"You girls have had so many opportunities," Coach Tom informed us, as we gathered around. "You have to connect with those crosses, you have to find those breakaways, it's the little things that we aren't finishing on."

I nodded, taking a sip of water as I watched the London team out of the corner of my eye. Number three was having a heated conversation with the other starting striker.

"As for our defense," Coach Tom said, snapping me back to our team, "would anyone like to tell me what happened? How they scored?"

I exchanged glances with Nancy and Bianca, unsure of what to say.

"Anyone?" Coach Tom prompted.

"We still don't know," I admitted. "It was like a swarm of London, and I saw the ball crossed in, but it was over my head, and then next thing I knew it was in the goal."

"That will not happen again," he ordered.

"Yes, sir," we chimed.

"I'm not making any changes for the second half, so you girls go ahead and take the field."

London had the kickoff second half, and they drove the ball down the field, but I intercepted the pass headed for their precious number three and got a pass off to one of our midfielders.

"Can't you do anything right?" number three spat at her fellow striker.

I shared an all-knowing look with Nancy, the two of us giggling.

And then Marci had a breakaway. I cheered for her as she outran their defense, giving her a one-on-one with the goalie. She slid it into the bottom right corner, giving us our first score of the game. I celebrated with the team in the center of the field, giving her a high five.

"Be sure to contain," I said to Bianca and Nancy, as they set up for their kickoff.

They swarmed our defense again, but it didn't catch us by surprise, and when the cross came in, I managed to launch it back out.

The two London strikers argued their way back up to the half, as I pushed up the defense.

Sky slid the ball through their flat-back defense, giving Marci a breakaway. We played around with the ball in the offense for a while, but after a few minutes, their defense launched the ball over to our side of the field.

It was a footrace between number three and me. Of course the game couldn't end before there was some sort of footrace. I pumped my arms and legs, my lungs burning, as we sprinted toward the ball, neck and neck. My entire summer had been dedicated to speed, making myself the fastest player I could be. And this girl was giving me a run for my money.

As we both reached the ball, I stuck my foot out in front of hers, getting the ball back to Cassandra, and taking the two of us out. I rolled on the ground a couple of times, feeling the ground hit my hip bones, before slowly pushing myself up.

"Are you kidding me, ref?" number three demanded, as she pushed herself up.

"She touched the ball first," the ref said, with a nod.

"She took me out!"

With my hands on my hips, I walked back to the halfway line instead of jogging it out as I usually do.

We worked hard for the half, but as the ref blew the final whistle, we didn't punch in another goal, and neither did London. A tie. We shook hands with the other team before taking our sideline, feeling defeated.

"Nice tackle," Coach Tom said.

"Thanks," I said.

"Wicked bruise?" Jenica asked, as she plopped down next to me on the bleachers.

I dipped down my shorts and spandex to reveal my left hip, showing her the bruise that had already formed, and was still growing.

"Damn," Jenica muttered, shaking her head.

I resituated my shorts as we made our way across the fields to the bus to take us back to the hotel.

"Practice tomorrow at eleven!" Coach Tom called, as we made it to the bus. "It'll be a light practice for most."

Jenica and I exchanged glances as we found our seats on the bus.

"What do you think he meant when he said *for most*?" I asked, fear creeping through me.

"I think we know what he meant," Jenica said, confirming my fear.

Tomorrow was going to be hell.

PARIS, FRANCE
CHAPTER 27

After a long day in London with a punishing training session followed by a train ride to Paris, jet lag no longer kept us all from falling asleep instantly. And now we were in the City of Lights on the morning of our final game day.

"We have the morning to sightsee," I said, sitting crisscross on the hotel bed as we discussed our options.

"Coach Tom said that he made reservations for the team to go up in the Eiffel Tower," Jenica said, "so we're definitely doing that."

Nancy stood up. "Coffee first. And then I'm good for the Eiffel Tower."

No sign of Marci. "She's really not coming?"

Nancy shrugged. "She hasn't really said much since we got our ass kicked at practice yesterday. I doubt she's eager to miss curfew again."

"We're not missing curfew," I said, with a shake of my head. "I'm not in charge of directions this round."

We headed downstairs, getting our usual morning Beans on the way to the Eiffel Tower. The team took the Metro to get there, all of us stopping to stare in awe as we arrived. None of the photos did the Tower justice. Below there was an open area, with a couple of market shops and places to sit and marvel at the beauty.

I took a side detour to get some midmorning ice cream, much to Jenica's annoyance.

"I earned this," I said, as I took a lick. "You're missing out."

"I don't want ice cream for breakfast," Jenica huffed. "I just want to go up in the Tower."

We joined the long line that wrapped around the bottom, chatting amongst ourselves while eavesdropping on the conversations happening around us that were taking place in French.

"I only know once French word," Nancy said. "*Merde*."

"Which means?" I asked.

She giggled, clearly pleased with herself. "Shit."

Nancy began guessing what people were saying, which turned into the three of us making up life stories about the people around us. I took the man with the twirly mustache, creating a story for him that he was here to run away with the Bonnie to his Clyde. The time passed quickly as we played our game and giggled together, until it was our turn to go inside the elevator to the top.

The view from the top of the Tower was breathtaking. As Jenica was quick to point out, you could see a nudist pool from a certain angle inside. But more importantly, you could see all of Paris. And it was gorgeous.

I FaceTimed Zach. He answered, although he'd clearly been sleeping.

"What time is it for you?" I asked.

"About four a.m.?" he said, in a groggy voice. "Is that the Eiffel Tower?"

I showed him the view, Jenica shouting in the background about how jealous he should be.

"Go back to sleep," I said, with a wave. "I'll call you later."

He let out a yawn. "Deal."

"I'm so glad we did this," Nancy said.

"Absolutely," I agreed. "It's the number one tourist attraction for a reason."

We descended back down to ground level and took our obligatory Eiffel Tower photos.

"How does it feel to be in the City of Love without your love?" Nancy asked me.

I rolled my eyes as Jenica wrapped her arms around me.

"I'm your number one," Jenica said, before planting a kiss on my cheek. "Never forget it."

"Get off me."

She wiggled her eyebrows suggestively at me, before beckoning Nancy over. "Get in here, Nancy. You know you want to."

"I really don't think I do."

But she joined in the group hug anyway, Jenica wrapping us up tight.

"The City of Love with my loves," Jenica said. "It's perfect."

I had to admit, Jenica's mood was contagious. "I guess I love you guys too."

"I guess so too," Nancy said.

"That's the spirit!" Jenica shouted. "Now let's get someone to take our picture. I need to make Zach jealous."

Marci and I led the team to the field, the France team watching us.

We dropped our stuff on the bench and then began our pregame warm-ups, the team more fired up than ever. This was our last game together.

They called for captains and Marci called the coin. She called for tails and it was heads. France chose to kick off first half and then we took our respective sides of the field again, Coach Tom calling us over to the bench.

He gave us one last pregame speech and then the refs blew the whistle, signaling game time.

I took the field with my team, fist-bumping Jenica before we went our separate ways.

The opposing team's kickoff didn't start off as dynamically as China and London had. Several minutes passed, the ball bouncing around on France's half of the field. Then one of France's midfielders gained control of the ball and France moved down the field for the first time this game. Bianca was quick to shut them down, taking the ball and giving it back to our offense. By the end of the first quarter I'd touched the ball twice, the least action I'd had all season, competitive included.

"Their star forward is out," Coach Tom informed us, as we went to grab some water. "But she's warming up on the sideline as we speak."

As water break ended, France's coach substituted their current striker for their previously concussed one.

"I think this game is about to pick up," Nancy said, as they took their goal kick.

"I think you're right," I agreed, as France's defense took control of the ball.

Their goal was obvious: get the ball to their star forward.

It didn't take long for me to figure out why, because their right midfielder cut around Bianca and got a pass off to the striker. The striker streaked down the field, her footwork incredible and her speed phenomenal.

Nancy and I both chased her down. I pumped my arms and legs as fast as I could to try to intercept her, my lungs on fire. I intercepted her as she went to take her shot, the ball ricocheting off my foot and out of bounds. With my hands on my hips, I took some time to catch my breath as her team sat up for their throw-in.

"Holy shit," Cassandra said, raising her eyebrows at me.

"Tell me about it," I breathed, still gasping for air.

The girl did a flip throw, reaching the center of the goalie box. I jumped up and headed it out; Marci intercepted it and tore up the field.

My hands dug into my hips as I fought to catch my breath. "We've got to keep the ball away from her."

Less than two seconds after I said that, the ball reached the feet of France's left midfielder.

"Step up!" I ordered, a bit pissed off.

The midfielder tried to get around Nancy, but couldn't, and eventually ended up trying to ricochet it off Nancy and out of bounds. But Nancy saw that coming and intercepted the ball, sending it flying up the field.

"That's my girl!" I called, running over and giving her a high five.

As the pass came toward their star forward, I stepped up at the last second and intercepted it, dribbling it up a bit before sliding it off through a hole in France's defense and up to Amy, our current left midfielder.

France's forward narrowed her eyes at me, as I suddenly became her next target. Amy crossed the ball in and Jenica jumped up, her head connecting with the ball and hitting the back of the net. We were up 1–0. I ran across the field, taking Jenica up in my arms and twirling her around.

As France kicked off and began their drive the ref blew the whistle for halftime.

"She's good," Coach Tom said to me, as I reached for my water.

"She's insanely good," I corrected. "I can't keep up with her."

"If she gets a breakaway we're toast," Marci added.

"We have to keep her contained like we did during the second quarter there," Coach Tom advised. "Without her, they don't have anything on us." He walked away to talk to the midfielders.

Jenica slid next to me on the bench. "You have a blessed head," I said.

"I don't know how it happens," she admitted, laughing.

"It's beautiful though."

Halftime passed by way too quickly, and pretty soon we were on the field again, their star forward glaring me down. *What's her problem?* We had kickoff and we started off as we always did, Marci and Jenica taking the ball as far as they could before sending the ball out to Amy. The third quarter was uneventful, the ball bouncing around but never reaching France's forward or our strikers.

Things began to heat up in the fourth quarter, as the opposing team realized that they were down a goal and had to hurry up or they'd lose this game. France's right midfielder faked out Bianca, getting a pass off to France's forward. I began the race again, my legs and lungs on fire as I propelled myself toward her. I managed to cross in front of her as she went to take a shot off, turning so it ricocheted off my back. My legs were wobbling as I turned back around, Nancy fighting for control of the ball.

"Here!" I shouted, unwilling to let France get a shot off.

Nancy passed it off to me and I cleared it, sending it flying to France's half of the field.

France's forward let out a string of French words as she jogged back up with us.

"Merde," I muttered, as France's center midfielder gained control of the ball.

Britney fought the center midfielder for the ball, but it was chipped over all of our heads. There was no way I was beating this forward in a footrace, but I took off anyway, unwilling to go down like this. Their forward was caught flat-footed and I had a head start on the ball, much to my advantage. I planted my left foot, aiming to stick my right foot out to the ball to get it back to Cassandra so she could clear it. France's forward was right behind me and lost her footing, propelling right into my planted leg, or more importantly, my knee. I managed to get the pass off to Cassandra as I hit the ground, pain shooting through my left knee. I clutched my knee to my chest, letting out a whimper of pain and then sucking in through my teeth.

I'd been fortunate enough up to this point in my career to always walk off a spurt of pain. A ball to the face, an elbow to the diaphragm—I'd always gotten back up. But this was different. This *felt* different. I could vaguely hear Jenica's voice as I tried to come back to my senses.

Every ounce of me wanted to stand up, but the stabbing pain in my knee was blocking all of my other thoughts. All I could do was hold my knee to my chest, willing the pain to ease up enough for me to clear my head a bit. And then there was a trainer in my line of vision. Then another. The pair of them asked me questions about the pain, about how I was feeling.

"Where does it hurt?" Rebecca asked, the head trainer for the team.

Where? I forced myself to hone in on the pulsing in my knee. "The inside knee."

They examined what they could, before Rebecca asked me if I thought I could stand up.

"I think so," I said, my head still a bit foggy.

As Rebecca pulled me to my feet, the assistant trainer close behind, I felt myself nearly topple over as I put pressure on my right leg.

Pain. Pain. Pain.

Before I knew it, the assistant trainer had me in his arms, carrying me off the field.

Everyone cleared the bench and my knee was propped up, the

swelling already starting. Someone had run for ice from the concession stand and it was laid out across my knee.

The game resumed, and as much as I tried to watch it, all my mind could focus on was the different stages of my knee. The sharp pain of the ice compared to the sharp pain in my knee, the pain stages as Rebecca tried to pinpoint the source of the throbbing.

Everything hurt.

From what I was able to comprehend, the last few minutes were uneventful, our team keeping control of the ball up on France's side of the field, unable to score. They all shook hands after the game and then my team practically surrounded me, questioning me about my knee.

"Disperse," Rebecca ordered. "There's a wheelchair on the way."

A wheelchair? "For me?"

Rebecca nodded. "We're going to the emergency room now, so they can make sure nothing is dislocated or broken. And then we'll get you in for an MRI as soon as we get back to the States, Michael is on the phone now with the team training center."

Blinking back tears, I tried to comprehend everything that was happening. I was in a foreign country. There was something wrong with my knee. And I didn't know what to do. I wanted nothing more than to have my mom to break everything down for me. "Okay." Jenica took a seat next to me on the bench. "Here." She handed me her phone. "I called your mom."

As soon as I pressed the phone to my ear, it was like a floodgate opened up. I immediately broke down into sobs.

"Do you want me to fly out there?" Mom asked, her voice laced with worry. "I can fly home with you, honey. What do you need from me? What can I do to make this better?"

There was no sense in her flying out to be with me. "I'm scared, Mom."

"I know, honey. I'm going to meet you at LAX, as soon as you land. And we'll figure this out. I'm so sorry, Katie."

She talked me through getting loaded into a wheelchair. I took a taxi back, my knee propped up in Rebecca's lap on the way back to the hotel. Rebecca took over my phone call once we got in the cab, explaining to my mom the next steps to handling my knee injury. And that's when I took out my own phone and called the only other person I wanted to talk to.

"Katelyn?" Zach questioned. His voice sounded a bit groggy. "Are you there?"

I tried my best not to cry, not to sound too dramatic. But as soon as I went to say hello, tears came out instead.

"Katelyn?" he asked, his voice sounding alarmed now. "What's wrong? Are you okay? Where are you?"

It was hard to catch my breath after crying so long, hyperventilation starting to set in. "I got hurt."

He was silent a few moments. "Hurt?"

"My knee. They're saying it could be bad."

"Are you headed to the doctor? What's going on?"

I repeated the information that was told to me by Rebecca. "So I guess we're headed to the ER now."

He was silent again. "You scared the shit out of me. I've never heard you cry."

"I'm not usually a crier." In tough situations, I tend to get angry and my temper flares. But crying had never been something I'd struggled with before. And now I didn't know how to make it stop.

"It's okay to cry," Zach said. "Try not to imagine the worst-case scenario, okay? Once you're home, we can figure out what our next steps are. We can't treat it until we know what's wrong, right?"

His voice was soothing, and my hyperventilating began to calm. "It's like you've done this before."

"Hospital testing is a necessary evil. It's okay to be scared. It's okay not to feel strong. You've got a support system that can do that for you right now."

"Thank you," I breathed. "I should probably go. Thank you for waking up to calm me down."

"Always. Be safe, I'll see you when you get home."

The next couple of hours went by in a whirlwind. After an X-ray, it was determined that there was nothing broken. I was given a stabilizing knee brace and some crutches, along with a set of pain pills, and sent away.

We pulled up to the hotel, Rebecca signaling for the taxi driver to pull around to the front entrance.

Despite my arguments, I ended up being carried up to my hotel room by Michael. Jenica started singing "Hard-Knock Life" as Michael sat me down, Rebecca grabbing pillows to prop up my knee. The painkillers from the hospital hadn't worn off yet, leaving me a bit sleepy as I lay down.

"I could probably count on one hand the number of times I've seen you cry," Jenica said, after the trainers left. "It absolutely broke my heart."

"It broke my knee."

She shook her head in response. "I can't laugh at that."

"Me neither."

Jenica sat down on the edge of her bed, and I glanced down at my knee for the first time since the game. It was starting to bruise, the swelling prominent around the inside.

"Tell me what I can do to help," Jenica said.

I'd cried to the point where my eyes hurt to blink and my nose was too stuffed to breathe through. Despite the constant pain radiating down my leg, I was completely dried out.

"Take my mind off it," I said, my voice coming out a bit shaky.

Jenica flipped on the TV. "You know I always travel with my Apple TV. And I know exactly what movie you need right now."

"*Air Bud*?"

She pulled her Apple TV out of her bag. "The one and only."

We spent the rest of the evening binge-watching the best sports-playing dog the cinema has ever seen. And despite Rebecca coming in and out to provide constant care for my knee, nothing could take away from the amount of joy I got from watching Air Bud play a game of soccer.

As soon as we landed in L.A., I was immediately whisked off to the team training center. My mom was waiting for me at the airport, and she refused to let me out of her sight during the MRI and knee brace–fitting process. My heart felt heavy, and it was a relief to have my mom there to take some of the stress off.

The hardest part was being unable to get an immediate response after my MRI test. Since I was being treated at the team center, I had top priority, but I still had to wait a few days for results. Which meant that I would have to attend my team banquet without knowing my future.

ıılıllıılıllıılıı

The next evening I was back to sitting in a hotel room with Jenica, Marci, and Nancy, all of us jet-lagged and me still in a tremendous amount of pain.

"What are you guys wearing tonight?" Marci asked.

"My mom said it's a dress event," I said, as my phone buzzed with a text from Zach.

be safe. i'll be waiting for you at the airport tomorrow.

"Speaking of the banquet," Jenica said, checking the time, "we'd better start getting ready."

"I call bathroom first," I announced, standing up and grabbing my crutches. "As someone who is temporarily down for the count, you can't argue with me. Those are the rules."

The girls all groaned as I hobbled to the bathroom, closing the door behind me.

I straightened my hair and applied some makeup before giving up the bathroom to Marci. By the time I was done, my mom was back with a variety of dresses to choose from. And Jenica had taken it upon herself to pick out her favorite one.

I changed into a two-piece dress. The top was white lace with broad, tank-top shoulders. The bottoms were high-waisted and maroon. The top of the waistband met the bottom of my cropped shirt, leaving a peek of skin between. I slid my feet into my white Vans, much to the disgrace of my mom.

"I can change only so much," I defended. "Let me have this."

Despite being the first one to do my hair and makeup, I was still the last one ready, as it took me twice as long with my injured knee and bulky brace to get dressed.

We headed down to the hotel banquet room, where there was a buffet of food set up. Mom got me a plate of food and between the four of our families we took up an entire table.

The first half hour was spent chatting and eating. A lot of the team asked me about my diagnosis, and it felt like a rock in the pit of my stomach each time I had to answer.

I don't know. I don't know. I don't know.

As the feeling to explode grew stronger, Coach Tom took the stage, cutting off all avenues of conversation. And I couldn't have been more grateful.

"Welcome to the Limitless Apparel Showcase World Tour banquet!" Coach Tom announced. "Wow, that's still a mouthful. Tonight we're going to be recognizing everyone on the team, as well as awarding a couple of girls here with some very special opportunities."

I exchanged glances with Jenica.

"I'd like to start by recognizing each player," Coach Tom announced. "Each player will receive a team uniform, warm-ups, and a customized hoodie and T-shirt, all courtesy of Limitless. And a medal and a certificate. We'll start with Jenica Terry."

I clapped for her as she took the stage and accepted her goodies.

"Jenica was one of our lead scorers," Coach Tom explained, "scoring most of her goals with her head, which is quite the feat. She is a very gifted player and we were lucky to have her on the team."

Coach Tom went through the team. As he went from offense to defense, he skipped through Marci.

"And now," Coach Tom said, "and she probably thinks I forgot about her, but we have one of our team captains, Marci Adams."

We clapped as she took the stage, accepting her gifts.

"Marci was also one of the lead scorers on the team," Coach Tom explained. "She was a leader on and off the field, exemplifying courage and bravery. It was an honor to work with you."

She waited out a few pictures before returning to her seat, her eyes bright with tears.

"And then last, but certainly not least, we have Katelyn Jackson, our other team captain," Coach Tom announced.

Nobody prepares you for how incredibly awkward it was to use crutches. As I made my way to the front of the room, I was acutely aware of how ridiculous I looked.

"I'll take your gift bag to the table for you," the stagehand said.

"Thank you," I said.

"Katelyn is a brick wall back on defense," Coach Tom said. "She's willing to sacrifice herself, as you can see, for the sake of the game."

That earned a laugh from my team, only increasing how uncomfortable this entire experience was.

"Katelyn was not only an asset to the team, but the definition of a leader. She works hard off the field to achieve what she has so far, and I have no doubt that she'll only continue to grow."

I posed for a few pictures before heading back to my seat, the stagehand bringing my stuff over as promised.

"And then we have a few more awards," Coach Tom announced. "The first one goes to Jenica Terry."

Unsure what was happening, I raised my hands above my head to cheer.

"Jenica Terry has been offered a spot on the Under-17 Women's National Team," Coach Tom announced.

My jaw dropped as she let out an excited scream.

"Congratulations," Coach Tom said, handing her a folder.

She retook her seat before bursting into tears. I gave her a tight squeeze.

"Next we have Nancy Torino. Nancy has also been offered a spot on the Under-17 Women's National Team."

I cheered for her as she accepted her folder. She cried up in front of everyone, thanking Coach Tom profusely.

"There are three more," Coach Tom announced. "Next we have Sky Pollard."

More clapping.

"Sky's been offered a spot on the Under-17 Women's National Team."

She accepted her folder with a genuine smile before retaking her seat.

"And our last two are Marci Adams and Katelyn Jackson, if you'll come up here, please?"

Marci and I went up together. I had a feeling I already knew the announcement, hearing it three times before.

"Marci and Katelyn have been invited to the U.S. Women's National Team training camp," Coach Tom announced.

I felt frozen as Marci let out a squeal. He handed us both folders, and Marci took mine for me to carry back to our table.

"Congratulations, ladies."

I numbly made my way back to my seat, shock pumping through my body. Jenica wrapped me up in her arms, immediately talking my ear off. And my mom congratulated me, kissing me on the cheek.

I didn't really comprehend their reactions as I opened the folder, reading the information. I had until October to make myself U.S. Women's National Team–ready.

I'd missed the entire Midwest part of the tour. All that was left now were a couple of northern states, and then the Connor Jackson Live Tour would be coming to a close back in L.A.

All of the traveling I'd done just in the past week and a half was really wearing on me, especially with my new knee pain.

"Be careful," Mom said, as she stuck her arm out in front of me. "Let's wait for this area to clear out, so it's safer for you."

Even worse was trying to navigate the airport with crutches. The terminal felt never ending, my armpits aching and knee throbbing. My eyes continuously scanned for my boyfriend's familiar face, my heart racing as time passed. And then I locked eyes with Zach, a smile blossoming across his face. He was wearing his signature white T-shirt and black sweats, and he quickly crossed the space between us, taking me in his arms. I threw my arms around him, letting all of my worries and insecurities wash away as my crutches clattered to the floor.

"How're you doing?" he asked, pulling away to look into my eyes.

"I'm fine," I promised, before planting my lips on his.

I could hear the cameras around us, but I didn't care. I'd missed him way too much.

"Maybe we should take this somewhere more private?" Zach whispered into my ear.

As much as I knew he was right, I didn't want the moment to end. But he ended it for us, reaching down to grab my crutches.

"I don't want those."

He handed them to me. "You either use them or I pick you up bridal style and carry you through the airport."

I groaned, situating the crutches under my arms and starting across the airport.

"Why are so many people snapping our picture?" I asked, looking around for the first time as we made our way through the airport.

People were all around us, using their phones and cameras to snap pictures of Zach and me.

"Because you're a soccer superstar. I'm lucky to even be in your presence."

We reached baggage claim and I leaned against it, my underarms sore. "Maybe I'll have to take you up on that offer to carry me."

"Done," Zach said.

"It was a joke!"

"Too late, I've already agreed."

The baggage claim started, and a little girl came up to Zach with a Disneyland autograph book. It was clear she'd also come from L.A. and had dug up the book to add Zach's signature at the end.

I love fans, especially little kids. But once one kid asks for an autograph, it opens up a floodgate.

"Hi, Zach," the little girl said, with a smile.

"Hi," Zach crouched down to her level.

She extended out her autograph book and Sharpie. "Will you please sign your name after Daisy Duck?"

"Of course," he said, scribbling his name on the blank page.

"Thanks!"

"No problem."

She left, and more people approached us with objects for Zach to sign.

Once my bag came around, Zach pulled my bag off for me, his current fan a little disgruntled.

"I'm sorry, guys," Zach said to his small crowd of fans, "but we have to go."

The fans all groaned, and the girl in the front stomped her foot.

"Sorry," Zach apologized again, grabbing my carry-on for me.

My mom held out her hands. "Give me Katelyn's bags, I'll take them."

Zach obliged before reaching over and scooping me up in his arms. I buried my face in his neck, trying not to dwell on how embarrassing this was. We went out to the taxi, my mom loading the luggage as Zach placed me down in the backseat.

"Even though that was humiliating, that was much better than having to use crutches," I said to Zach, once he was situated in the car.

"I bet," Zach said. "I remember when Ross had to use them for, like, three days when we were little and he never stopped complaining."

"That's because it's a medieval torture device."

I propped my feet up in Zach's lap, feeling his phone buzz beneath them as I tried to get comfortable.

Zach's lips twisted into a frown and he swiped the notification away on his watch.

"Everything okay?" I asked.

"Jesse being the overprotective big brother, per usual."

Sounded like trouble in paradise. "Oh boy."

"What are we thinking for dinner?" Zach asked. "I want a lazy date night with you all to myself, dinner included."

"We should have Chinese takeout."

"Sounds good," Zach agreed.

We pulled up to the arena, just outside where the tour buses were located.

Zach carried me once again, and we went to his tour bus, as my mom was insistent that she needed an evening nap and wanted to be left alone in our bus.

"Jess?" Zach called, opening the door.

There was no answer.

He placed me down on his couch. I propped my knee up with an involuntary wince as it accidentally bent.

"Are you okay?" Zach asked, his hands immediately reaching out toward me.

I nodded.

"Want to watch some TV?" Zach asked, reaching around me to grab the remote and turning it on without waiting for an answer.

He lay down next to me, careful not to aggravate my injury. As I snuggled up close to him, he began playing with my hair, and an episode of *Little Mrs. Perfect* came on ... with guest star Connor Jackson.

"Why is my brother crashing our date right now?" I mumbled.

"Because your brother is currently blowing up America," Zach answered, with a laugh.

The tour bus door opened and Jesse came in.

"*Little Mrs. Perfect*?" he asked, taking a swig of his energy drink.

"Don't judge," Zach said.

"Too bad you're going to miss the episode."

Zach raised his eyebrows at Jesse. "What?"

Jesse held out his phone toward Zach. "You promised me that once you got back here today you'd call your doctor."

"He can wait," Zach grumbled.

"Call him," Jesse ordered. "Now."

I sat up, leaving room for Zach to get up.

"I'll pick up dinner while you do it," Jesse offered.

"I don't care about dinner," Zach grumbled, standing up and taking Jesse's phone as he headed toward the back of the tour bus.

"How's the knee?" Jesse asked, as the door in the back of the bus slammed shut.

"It's there," I said, with a half smile.

Jesse sat down next to me. "Zach took my phone but I already ordered the Chinese takeout. Aaron, Ross, and I are going to eat in the back, so you guys should be able to get some alone time up front here."

"That's not necessary—"

"You guys went over a week and a half without seeing each other," Jesse said, with a teasing smile. "You must be *dying*."

"Stop annoying my girlfriend," Zach said, as he came back into the room. He tossed Jesse his phone.

"How'd the phone call go?" Jesse asked.

"Fine," Zach said, handing Jesse back his phone.

"What's *fine* mean?" Jesse asked, tucking his phone away into his pocket.

Zach's jaw shifted, and I realized that I'd never seen him truly angry. "What do you think it means? He wanted to up the dosage of the medicine again."

"And you said?" Jesse prompted.

"I said no."

Jesse nodded. "I'm just asking; don't get all pissy with me."

I moved over, Zach settling in next to me again.

"I'm going to go and pick up the takeout," Jesse said, standing up. "Take a chill pill while I'm gone?"

Zach flipped him off as he left.

"Is everything okay?" I asked.

"About once a year, my neurologist reevaluates my medication. I guess this year I had a slight increase in the number of seizures, which isn't hard to do since I was hardly having one a year before and now I'm having one every couple of months. So he wants to change around my medicine, which I always hate doing."

He seemed genuinely upset, something I wasn't used to seeing with Zach. "Is there anything I can do to help?"

"I don't really want to talk about it right now. Maybe later?"

"Of course."

I repositioned myself so that I was leaning into him, Zach's hands playing with my hair as I half watched the show. Jesse was quick to come back with the takeout, and he handed me a fortune cookie. I cracked it open, unraveling the paper inside.

Good timber does not grow with ease; the stronger the wind, the stronger the trees.

"What do you think it means?" Zach asked, reading the fortune over my shoulder.

"I think it means that when times get tough, remember that there's something better to come out of it."

Zach hummed in agreement. "Deep."

"What does yours say?"

He showed me his fortune.

Do your work with your whole heart and you will succeed.

"And what do you think that means?" I asked, with a teasing smile.

Zach tossed his fortune over his shoulder. "I think it means that I should spend the night cuddling with you."

"I don't think that's what it meant."

"It's up for interpretation."

I tucked my fortune away, saving it for my memento box.

I spent the next morning backstage at the arena, my phone glued to my side as I waited to hear from the team doctor.

The dressing room door opened, and a furious-looking Connor came storming in, followed closely by my dad.

"Lana's manager isn't answering," Dad said. "I don't know what she's doing, Connor."

I raised an eyebrow in question. More Lana drama?

"She's doing a tell-all interview!" Connor shouted, as he turned around to face my dad. "It doesn't take a rocket-fucking-scientist to know that she's breaking the NDA."

"We have no reason to believe that she's breaking the NDA," Dad said, his voice much softer and calmer. "She's using your name for attention, which is something she's done before. That doesn't mean anything else is happening."

Connor took a seat on the couch across from me, his chest rapidly rising and falling. "I can't keep doing this."

I readjusted myself so I was looking at him, while still keeping my knee propped up. "What's going on?"

"Lana announced a tell-all special this week, where she dishes the secrets on her relationship with Connor Jackson," Connor said. "And every fucking time she does this, I can't sleep, I can't eat, I can't function until I know that she's not blowing it for me."

"I'm sorry, Connor."

I wanted to be able to offer something more, but I knew that Connor wasn't ready to address his relationship with Lana publicly yet. And he had to keep hoping that Lana wasn't either.

"You signed an NDA too," Dad reminded him. "So if she breaks hers . . ."

It was fair game.

Connor shook his head. "I may hate her, but I couldn't expose her. Even if she doesn't feel the same. I heard too much that night."

They both did.

Dad eased down onto the couch next to Connor. "Let's wait to hear from Lana's manager. And if she plans on actually doing a tell-all, then we'll address that as it comes."

"Maybe it's not such a bad thing?" I offered up.

Connor shook his head, a look of defeat on his face. "I don't want to do this right now."

Dad nodded. "I understand, son."

Connor stood up, swiftly leaving the room and slamming the door behind him.

An unsettled silence filled the room as both Dad and I stared after him.

"That wasn't how I planned the morning to go," Dad said. His gaze focused on me. "How're you feeling?"

"I took a pain pill about an hour ago, so my knee doesn't hurt too badly. I'm just trying to keep my mind off things."

"I'm sorry that you had such a rough ending to your tournament. I was able to watch some of the London one."

"Really?"

"Your mom, brother, and I watched it during lunch. From what I was able to see, you did really well."

I wasn't used to such an open conversation with my dad, let alone a compliment. "Wow, Dad. Thanks."

"I'd love to hear more about the tournament. Maybe later tonight?"

"Yeah! I'd love that too."

He stood up, his phone in hand. "In the meantime, I need to go and try to calm your brother down."

"Good luck with that."

As he left, my phone buzzed next to me. I quickly grabbed it: it was a Los Angeles area code.

"Hello?" I asked, my voice coming out a bit shaky.

"May I speak with Katelyn Jackson?" a female voice asked.

"Speaking."

She cleared her throat. "Hello, my name is Dr. Carmen Sanchez. I reviewed your MRI results, and I'd like a chance to go over them with you if you're available."

My heart was erratically pounding in my chest, and I took a moment to steady my voice. "I'm available."

"The good news is, from what I'm seeing now, I don't believe that surgery will be necessary."

It felt like a weight had been lifted from my chest. "Really?"

"You have torn your MCL, which we rarely do surgical intervention for. The ligament has enough blood supply to heal itself, if given the proper amount of rest and rehabilitation."

MCL tear, no surgery. I could handle that.

"From what else I can tell, it also looks like you've suffered from a partial LCL tear. A partial tear isn't something we'd normally do surgical intervention for—much like the MCL, it's able to heal itself with the proper care."

A bowling ball settled in my stomach. "What does that mean as far as soccer goes?"

"If all goes according to plan, I'd say that we can start integrating you back onto the field in the next six to eight weeks."

"Weeks?" I asked, my voice rising in pitch. "Are you sure it has to be that long?"

"Yes, Katelyn, I'm afraid so. We want to make sure that we give your knee ample time to heal so as not to cause further damage or problems down the road."

It was already late July. Eight weeks put me late into September, and the U.S. Women's National Team camp was in October.

I didn't know how to respond. "Okay then."

"I know this news isn't exactly ideal, but it's a much better situation than if we were talking surgery," Dr. Sanchez said. "Hopefully we can have you back on the field before September ends."

Getting into shape for camp was going to be nearly impossible if I couldn't hit the field before then.

"As for next steps, we need to get you into physical therapy," she continued. "I've written up a script for it. I know you're traveling right now, but as soon as you get back to L.A., I'd like to set you up with some appointments at the clinic."

Tears stung at the back of my eyes. "I understand."

"I'm going to call your mom now to go over the details and to see what we can work out," Dr. Sanchez said. "Do you have any questions for me?"

When do I wake up from this nightmare?

"No," I said, my voice thick. "Not right now. Thank you, Dr. Sanchez."

"Of course, Katelyn. We'll talk soon."

My body felt numb as I hung up the phone. All of my hard work. All of my training. It was all for nothing. I was going to lose everything.

DENVER, CO
CHAPTER 30

Footsteps came up behind me as I sat on the couch of the tour bus for yet another excruciatingly long journey. The whole reason I'd joined the tour the day before such a long drive was so I could spend it with Zach. Now I didn't want to see or talk to *anyone*.

I pulled a pillow over my face, ignoring the figure that came to a stop next to me.

"Want to mourn together?" Connor asked.

I peeked over the pillow to see him standing over me. He had deep, purple eye bags and looked to be as much of a wreck as I felt. He lay down on the couch next to me.

"What are we mourning?" I asked. "The loss of my future?"

"And the death of mine."

My phone buzzed next to me, and I clicked to ignore another incoming FaceTime request from Zach.

"Is that the boyfriend?" Connor asked.

"I've declined his calls three times today. You think he'd take the hint."

"Boys are dumb."

Amen to that. "You're a boy, Connor."

"And I'm dumb."

The bedroom area door opened, and I pulled my pillow back over my face as my mom walked in.

"Two pouting children in one place?" she asked. "Lucky me."

Neither one of us answered, and I could only guess that Connor had taken my same pillow-over-the-face approach.

"All right, I'm going to return to the back to answer some emails," Mom said. "If either one of my children would like to talk about this week's events, I'm always here to listen."

I waited until I heard the click of the back door closing before removing the pillow from my face. I looked over to see Connor doing the same. We remained there for the rest of the fifteen-hour drive, both of us ignoring phone calls and texts and staring at the ceiling in silence.

We Jacksons really do know how to actively ignore our problems.

The only move I'd made in the past twenty-four hours was going from lying on the tour bus couch to lying on Connor's dressing room couch at the arena.

Connor had now taken to lying on the floor.

A knock came on the dressing room door, and I immediately grabbed my face pillow, as did Connor.

"That trick's not going to work," Zach's voice said.

I ignored him.

"Katelyn," Zach said.

I figured me ignoring all of his texts and calls was enough to send the message, but apparently not. I continued to ignore him, hoping that he'd give up and leave me alone.

"Jenica somehow found my phone number," Zach said. "Because she called me and demanded to know if you were alive, since you've ghosted everyone."

Which I'd done for a reason. I still had to process the fact that everything was over for me. I didn't need other people trying to process it for me.

I wanted to be left alone to grieve what could never be.

"She's stubborn," Connor's voice said. "So good luck."

The pillow disappeared from my grip, Zach's face staring down at me. "Unfortunately you're in a relationship. Which means that you don't get to ice me out when the going gets tough."

I reached for my pillow back, and Zach raised it up over his head.

"Give it back," I demanded.

"Talk to me."

We stared each other down, and I could feel all of the anger I'd been repressing boiling to the surface. I pushed myself up vertical, swinging my legs over the edge of the couch.

"Leave me alone," I said. "And give me my pillow back."

"Talk to me first."

It was as though the words exploded out of me. "You don't get to decide that for me, Zach!"

Connor stood up. "I'm not down for a lover's spat right now. I've got my own shit to deal with." And he left.

Zach sat down next to me on the couch. "I'm not trying to decide anything for you. I want to make sure you're okay."

"I'm not. Is that what you wanted to hear?" I snapped. "I'm not okay and I don't want to talk about it."

"I understand, Kate. I'm sorry—"

"Don't tell me you understand! You don't have a clue as to how

I'm feeling, or what I'm going through right now, Zach. Don't tell me you understand when you've never been where I am."

He took a moment, his eyes wide.

But I wasn't done. Anger was pulsing through my veins, and it was as though I'd lost all control over the words spilling out. "I've played soccer since I was four years old. I've spent every free day training, working to be the best I could possibly be. And for that all to be taken away from me in a matter of seconds . . . You could never understand that feeling."

He laid his hand on mine. "You're right, Kate. I've never been through what you have. But I do know the feeling of having something you worked for taken away in seconds. I do know the feeling of having everything suddenly taken from you. And I'm sorry you're going through this, but I can help if you let me."

How dare he try to compare his experiences to mine.

"My brother made you famous via Twitter. Our situations are pretty different."

He paused, his eyebrows furrowing together in confusion. "You mean his weekly band shout-out? Where he dropped our band name, like, a year ago?"

"Yes, Zach. How else do you think you got on this tour? How do you think you got to where you are right now?"

"I don't know, Katelyn. Hard work? Dedication? I'm grateful to your brother for including us, but we weren't the only band whose name he dropped. Just like you've poured your heart and soul into soccer, I did the same with Skyline. And I'm sorry if you think I had it all handed to me, but I don't agree. At all."

"I'd call it a lucky break." Venom dripped from my words, silence hanging in the air as I glared at him.

Zach stood up, staring at me in confusion. "I don't know what you're trying to accomplish here, Katelyn. If you want to push me away, that's fine. I know how it is."

"Right, because you're Zachary Matthews. Overcoming medical obstacles is your brand."

He slowly nodded. "I think I should go."

"I think so too."

He reached into his pocket, dropping a piece of paper on the couch. "There's the list of things I collected for you while you were gone, so you could still have a piece of each tour stop. Guess that was a waste of my time too."

Tears pricked my eyes as he walked out of the room, letting the door slam shut behind him.

I had no idea why I'd lashed out at Zach. In the moment, it felt good. It felt right. But now? Now I felt empty. Confused.

The piece of paper was resting on the couch, and I leaned over to see what was written, misspellings and all.

new orleans - string of beads

orlando - mickey mouse keychain

jacksonville - this one was hard, don't judge me. a jar of sand from the beach.

buffalo - a little outside of buffalo but a niagra falls poncho.

pittsburgh - a cookie from prantl's bakery. I'm not sure you can save a cookie though.

cinncinati - a pamphlet from a haunted tour that the whole crew did in queens city.

indianapolis - Ross went out and did the searching because I wasn't feeling well, and for some reason he chose to go to the zoo/aquarium. so you're now the proud owner of a plush otter.

nashville - of course we went to the country music hall of fame. you got an ornament of the hall of fame building.

st. louis - we didn't have time to do anything here. I was lame and got a postcard.

minneapolis - a shopping bag from the mall of america.

milwaukee - I was writing a song, but Jesse and Aaron went to
the harley-davidson museum. they got a harley-davidson notebook,
and I wrote some of the lyrics inside.
chicago - a mini statue of that giant bean thing.

Zach had thought about me in each city. Not only thought about
me, but specifically gathered mini presents for me. And I'd repaid
him by blowing up in his face and telling him his success was based
on luck, not talent.

What was wrong with me?

SALT LAKE CITY, UT
CHAPTER 31

I needed to get out of this tour bus. I'd spent all night running through my fight with Zach, beating myself up over and over again. I didn't even watch the Denver show last night because I couldn't bear to see what effect my words might have had on his performance. And then I had to endure being on this tour bus for the eight-hour trip to the next stop, and I felt like I was going to jump out of my skin.

I needed out.

"Connor!" I shouted.

He was in the back room. I'd heard his guitar on and off all morning, meaning that he was probably working on a new song. Lana's tell-all interview was tonight. We could both use some time outside of our own heads.

He peeked out from the back room. "What?"

"Let's go do something."

A frown tugged on his lips. "Like what?"

"I don't know," I said. "We have a free morning, some time before sound check. And I think we could both use a distraction."

He came out into the main area, his arms folded across his chest. "I'm listening."

"We should go out into public."

He raised his eyebrows. "And get mobbed?"

"We'll disguise you."

"You're kind of famous too," he pointed out.

As if. "Okay, so we'll both go out in disguises," I conceded. "And we'll do normal people stuff."

"What do normal people do?" Connor asked, a smile spreading across his face.

"Go shopping?" I suggested.

"Go out to lunch?"

"Go to the park?"

"Feed ducks!"

That I wasn't expecting. "What?"

"They break up bread and they feed ducks!"

"Okay, I'm not sure about that one," I admitted. "But if you want to, we can feed ducks."

"I would love to do something as mundane and normal as feed ducks."

Actually, it sounded perfect. "Okay then, let's go get dressed and feed some ducks!"

"Meet in ten minutes."

I pointed to my braced knee. "I'll need fifteen."

"Deal."

He stepped into the bathroom and changed, and I picked out a pair of jean shorts and a white V-neck.

Connor came out looking seemingly normal, in a pair of khaki shorts and a black T-shirt. He had a hat pulled on backward, with a pair of sunglasses on.

"Is that your disguise?" I asked.

"The best I can do."

I went into the bathroom, pulling my hair into a braid as I changed.

"Do you really think this will work?" Connor shouted.

"No!" I called back, changing out of my hoodie and sweatpants.

As I came out of the bathroom, Connor handed me a hat. I pulled it on, along with a pair of sunglasses.

"The knee brace might give us away," Connor admitted.

"There's not much I can do about that," I huffed, as I grabbed my white Vans.

Eddie joined us as my brother called for a car to come and pick us up.

"Can we stop by the store?" I asked, once we were securely inside the car. "I'll give you extra money in cash."

"Sure," the driver agreed.

"What for?" Connor asked.

I extended my arms out to the empty car around us. "If you want to feed some stupid ducks, we're going to need a loaf of bread."

"Good point."

I pulled out my phone. No new texts, not that I expected there to be. I hadn't seen or spoken to Zach since our fight before the show yesterday.

"Selfie!" Connor announced, smushing his face up against mine and snapping a picture.

"What was that for?" I demanded.

"I'm going to make a collage of our day," he said, nonchalantly. "And then post it on my Instagram at the end of the day."

"You'll give up our disguises," I pointed out.

"We can always find new ones."

Eddie went into the grocery store, coming back out with a loaf of bread as requested.

The driver took us to the location Connor had put in, which was the closest lake he could find on Google Maps.

We headed down to the lake where all the ducks gathered, Connor swinging the loaf of bread around his finger while he whistled and me negotiating the uneven terrain with my crutches. I took a picture of Connor with the bread, at his request. Eddie hung back, trying to remain inconspicuous. But it was pretty difficult to do when he was six foot six. Connor quacked out loud, causing me to double over in laughter as a couple walking past us stared in confusion. As Connor's spirits lifted, I found mine lifting as well. And then Connor found his first group of ducks. I found a bench close by, taking a seat to relieve the pressure from my armpits.

"This is it!" Connor shouted. "Are you ready to capture this?"

I held up my phone as I snapped photos of him throwing the bread out toward the ducks.

What we didn't anticipate was for one of the ducks to charge at him.

"Shit!" Connor yelled, taking off running as the duck chased him.

I couldn't even capture the moment: my hands were shaking too hard as I laughed.

"Stupid duck!" Connor called out. "No more bread for you."

Taking the discarded loaf of bread, I broke up pieces and tossed them out to the rest of the ducks. As they feasted, I bent down and picked up a duck feather off the ground. I tucked it away into my backpack, my memento secured for Salt Lake City.

"Okay," Connor said, as he came jogging back toward me. "I lost the duck." He was out of breath, his hands sliding down onto his knees. "So . . . Zach hasn't been around."

I didn't want to address this, not now. "Yeah. I know."

"Did you push him away?"

I didn't respond, but I didn't really need to. Connor and I tend to do the same things under stress, one of them being pushing away everyone around us.

"I cut everyone off during the recording of my album," Connor said, "including you. And it's still one of my biggest regrets. I was scared that I wouldn't live up to my EP success, so I locked myself up in the recording studio day in and day out. I cranked out song after song, didn't talk to anyone outside of those four walls."

"I remember."

He leaned over, bumping his shoulder against mine. "Don't make the same mistakes, baby sis."

"I think I really screwed things up, Connor. I said things I didn't mean, I would've never said. I was so *angry*. And I still am."

"Don't push away the people who actually want to listen," Connor said. "Those people come few and far between."

"I can't take back what I said."

"No, you can't," he agreed. "But you can own it. And you can do better in the future."

"I don't know if what I said is forgivable."

He was silent a few moments, and I glanced toward him to try to read his facial expression. He was staring out at the lake with a pensive look on his face.

"What about you?" I asked. "Have you talked to Lana?"

"There's a good chance that Lana goes on national TV tonight and tells everyone that I'm not straight," Connor said, quietly. "And I'm not ready to address that publicly yet. I'm not ready to even address that privately. I don't have a label, I don't have a name for it. I just know that I'm attracted to all kinds of different people. I really hope that she lets me address this on my own terms."

Connor had mentioned his sexuality only once to me before. The morning after he and Lana got so drunk they'd spilled their secrets together, he woke me up, crying, sitting on my bed as he recounted what he'd told her.

"I know it's been a tough year all around, but I will always love you. No matter what."

"Thanks, Kate."

I kissed his cheek, wrapping my arms tightly around his shoulders.

"What happens now?" Connor asked.

I let him go with a sigh. "I guess we stop burying our heads in the sand."

"Are you sure we can't stay out here?" Connor asked, gesturing toward the lake.

"We don't need to leave yet."

And so we spent the rest of the morning trying to find peace within the serenity of the lake. To embrace the calm before the storm.

Nobody talks about how difficult it is to push a cart while using crutches.

I'd taken a taxi to the nearest Target and had been trying to gather supplies for my apology gift to Zach. But I'd quickly given up, instead placing a pick-up order and waiting around for the order to be filled. A poster board. A pack of markers. Colored construction paper. A stick of glue. And a lot of glitter glue. It was going to be the cheesiest thing I'd ever done. But I was hoping that it would be cheesy enough to work.

Thankfully, a Target employee helped me carry the bags out to my taxi. I went back to the tour bus, spreading my supplies out across the small table. According to the time on my phone, I had two and a half hours before the show ended. Thirty minutes before Lana's interview went live.

I was holding off on watching the interview until Connor was through with the show. And then we were going to find out what

Lana said. Together. Dad had a lawyer on call, ready to release a lawsuit if the NDA was broken. Not that it would matter; the damage would be done.

In the meantime, I wanted to catch Zach before the Lana interview recap. So I got to work on my handmade, jumbo-sized apology card. I didn't have an artistic bone in my body, so I didn't have high expectations for my apology card. But I knew that Zach wouldn't respond to me showing up at his dressing room, not after everything I'd said. I needed a gimmick to get me through the door, something to sway him enough to hear me out. And I was counting on this card to be my ticket in.

I spent the next hour and a half decorating the card. I tried to make it less kindergarten-craft and more whimsical and artsy, but it looked like a glitter glue explosion at the end.

On the outside, I'd written *I'M SORRY, ZACH* in big, block letters that I'd cut out of colored construction paper. I'd surrounded it with squiggly lines and arrows, keeping the apology the main focus of the front.

On the inside, I'd recounted some of the most memorable times we'd spent together. And in the center of it all I'd put a big, construction paper cutout of a heart.

I recounted our first lazy date night, complete with a construction paper cutout of a TV and two stick people lying in bed. I illustrated our segment on *Drama Llama* with a llama and a green light over the llama's head. I depicted our day in Atlanta with a polar bear and two stick figures holding Coke bottles. And I'd remembered me calling him after my knee injury with a cutout of a stick figure in a taxi and another one standing away, on a phone.

I put the card in my backpack, making my way from the tour bus to the backstage area at the arena. The encore was happening on stage, which meant that Skyline would be back in their dressing room soon. Finding Skyline's dressing room turned out to be a challenge, as I hadn't been backstage at this arena yet. Applause erupted as the song ended.

I leaned against the wall, taking a moment to catch my breath and rest my aching armpits. I dug into my backpack, pulling the card out as I waited.

Mackenzie was the first one backstage. She gave me a confused look but didn't question anything else as she disappeared into her dressing room. I could hear her backup dancers chatting before the door closed behind her.

Connor was next, and he stopped to stare at me.

"What are you doing?" he asked, staring at my card and then at me.

"Apologizing."

He shook his head. "You made a card?"

"I spent a lot of time making a card."

"Oh boy," he muttered. "This ought to be interesting."

And then I heard the boys coming down the hallway behind him.

Connor ducked off into his dressing room as the boys rounded the corner.

"Oh shit," Aaron said, as he saw me.

Jesse didn't say anything, disappearing into the dressing room without so much as a second glance. Ross glanced back over his shoulder, where I'm sure Zach was coming, before looking at me again.

"Keep walking," Aaron said to Ross, practically shoving him into the dressing room.

"Good luck," Ross whispered. "I'm still rooting for you guys, even though you sort of broke my brother's heart."

Ouch.

And then there was Zach. He came to a full stop, staring at me with an unreadable expression.

I lifted up the card, flashing the front at him. "Can we talk?"

"I'm a little busy right now," he said, in a clipped voice.

I felt like I'd been punched in the gut. Deservedly. But it didn't hurt any less. "I would really like it if we could talk."

"I wouldn't."

Tears pricked in my eyes. I blinked a few times, willing myself not to cry. "I understand."

He turned to head into his dressing room.

"I'll leave the card here," I said, leaning it up against the wall. "And if you have some time . . . I'm really sorry."

"Okay." He went inside, letting the door close behind him.

As much as I wanted to bang on his dressing room door and beg him to hear me out, I crutched away to Connor's dressing room. I knocked twice before letting myself in.

"So?" Connor asked. "How'd it go?"

"It didn't."

He nodded. "I figured."

Unable to be as dramatic as I wanted to be, due to my knee, I gingerly sat down on the couch as I wished I could throw myself down.

"Don't give up," Connor said, taking a seat next to me. "He's angry, as he deserves to be. Give him some time, and then try again."

"I really don't think that'll work," I said. "He doesn't want to see me."

"Give him time," Connor repeated. "Tomorrow is a new day."

Mom and Dad came into the room. "I watched a breakdown of the interview."

Connor sucked in through his teeth, a pained expression on his face. "Did she tell all?"

I wrapped my arm through Connor's for moral support.

"No," Dad said. "She talked about your fights, she talked about the good and the bad. But she didn't talk about . . . about anything else."

Connor's head fell back, the tension releasing from his shoulders. I wrapped my arms around him.

"You know what I think we need?" Mom asked, as she sat down in the corner of the room.

I raised an eyebrow in question.

"I think we could all use some good pizza and an old-fashioned family game night."

I exchanged smiles with Connor.

"I couldn't agree more," Dad said.

CHAPTER 32

I hobbled out of the shower, using the counter to support myself as I grabbed a towel to dry off. I hated getting dressed in a steamy bathroom, but I'd quickly learned that crutches on bare armpits were a devil's curse.

I crutched into my hotel room, my eyes zeroing in on the poster board on my bed. I made my way over, glancing down to see the card I'd made Zach two days ago. I ran my hands over the apology on the front, my heart tight in my chest. So much for that idea. I flipped the card open, a sticky note flying up before landing on the heart.

meet me on the rooftop.

The rooftop? Like of the hotel?

I grabbed my phone, making my way over to the elevator. And indeed, there was a button to go to the roof. I took the elevator up, slowly taking in my surroundings as I hobbled out. There was a railing that surrounded the top, an overgrown garden to the left. And to the right there was a seating area.

Zach was seated in one of the lounge chairs, his gaze following mine as I made my way over to him.

"I got your note," I said.

"I see that."

It was impossible to gracefully take a seat with crutches, so I sort of flopped down onto the opposing lounge chair.

"How's your knee?" Zach asked.

"I'm trying not to think about it too much," I admitted. "Or I just sort of . . . cry."

He nodded, silence lapsing between us.

I needed to apologize. Only I wasn't sure how to start.

"I read your card," Zach said.

"And?"

He shook his head. "Only you would make a card by hand and deliver it with wet glitter glue."

"I didn't know it was still wet."

He let out a small laugh. "You globbed it on there. I'm not sure it's dry even now."

"I wanted to apologize," I said. "I didn't know how to start. So I thought the card could break the ice. Clearly that wasn't the right answer."

"I liked the card."

Now that was a surprise. "You did?"

"I especially liked the polar bear drawing. It took me a minute to figure it out, I thought it was a Yeti at first."

This time I had to laugh. "I'm not gifted in the art department."

"I can see that."

Silence passed between us once again, and I found myself staring at Zach, trying to read his facial expression.

"I said some pretty awful things," I said, quietly.

He didn't say anything.

"I know that asking for forgiveness is a lot, and I don't expect us to go back to how things were. I was terrible toward you for no reason. And you deserve much better."

"I've said things I'm not proud of," Zach said. "What I was trying to tell you, back before you got upset, was that I've been in a similar situation. After my epilepsy diagnosis, I was very angry and bitter, and I said a lot of things to a lot of people that I regret."

"That doesn't make what I did okay," I said. "I attacked your band and your work ethic. But even worse, I went in for a personal attack on you. And I can't forgive myself for that, so I don't expect you to."

He shook his head. "You said what you said to get a reaction. I know the feeling: I did it last week to Jesse. I'm still angry about my diagnosis sometimes. I still lash out."

Zach switched so that he was sitting next to me, and my gaze dropped to the floor. "Zach, I—"

"My support system still stays, no matter how hard I've tried to push them away," Zach said. "So you're going to have to try harder to get rid of me again."

And then he was kissing me.

The tears spilled over onto my cheeks as I cupped his face in my hands. "I'm so sorry."

"And I forgive you."

And then he was kissing me again. I leaned forward as Zach deepened the kiss, my hands wrapping around his neck as his hands traveled down my chest.

"Hello!"

Zach quickly pulled away as my eyes snapped over toward the elevator.

Ross was standing there, a smile dancing on his lips. "Zach, band livestream in thirty."

"Fuck off, Ross."

He laughed in response. "Just a thought, but maybe you guys shouldn't suck each other's faces off on the roof."

"Bye, Ross!" Zach called out.

Ross waved over his shoulder as he headed back to the elevator.

"He's probably right," I said.

Zach leaned his forehead against mine, his eyes flickering shut. "When you left the tour, I was stuck spending all my time with my brothers. And these past few days reminded me of how torturous that is."

"You need to go get ready for your livestream."

He gave me another quick kiss. "Will you meet me after?"

"I'm not going anywhere."

After running backstage to get some ibuprofen from my mom, I was headed back to my seat to watch the sound checks. Now that Zach and I were back together, I wanted to be with him as much as I could. I could hear Connor's sound check happening, and I knew Skyline would be next. As I made my way down the hallway, a Nerf gun bullet came whizzing past me. I let out a surprised yelp, blocking my face.

Ross came charging down the hallway, Nerf gun in hand. "Surrender or die. Your choice."

"I surrender!"

His nose wrinkled in disgust. "That was too easy."

And then more bullets came from around the corner.

"You're a liability risk with your knee," Ross said. "I'm turning you over to the enemy." And then he took off running.

"Cease fire!" I called out. "I surrender!"

"Damn," Jesse said, coming out from behind the corner. "I'm out of ammo. I was trying to get Ross."

I pointed down the hallway. "He took off running and left me as bait."

"I'm not surprised."

Jesse pulled out his phone, pulling up a walkie-talkie app. "We need backup."

"For what?" I asked. "You're the only ones with Nerf guns and you have me cornered."

Zach came running around the corner, raising his gun and shooting me directly in the chest.

"Ow?"

Zach immediately dropped his gun. "You called for backup to shoot Katelyn?"

"Ross, actually," Jesse said. "You're trigger-happy."

Zach pulled a pack of ammo off his side, tossing it to Jesse. "I took Aaron out already. Let's go finish Ross."

Jesse loaded up his gun, firing off a shot at me.

"Ow again! What was that for?"

Jesse offered up a cheeky smile. "Just making sure it works." And then he took off running down the hallway.

Zach leaned over, puckering his lips for a kiss.

"Absolutely not!" I said. "You shot me with a Nerf gun."

He stole a kiss anyway.

"We can go somewhere more private," Zach suggested. "Let them fight it out."

"Where did you have in mind?"

In one swift motion, Zach picked me up, letting my crutches clatter to the floor.

"Right this way."

We stole away into Skyline's dressing room, Zach laying me down on the couch. I pulled his shirt so that he practically fell on top of me, my lips finding his. My right leg reached up to wrap around his waist, my left leg still pretty useless.

"You seem to have a habit of wrapping your legs around me," Zach said.

"If you don't like it, I can stop," I teased, with a smile.

"Oh no, please, continue," Zach said, before crashing his lips onto mine.

Our kiss deepened, and I ran my fingers through his hair, thoroughly enjoying the moment. I let Zach's hands explore as I pulled him in closer.

And then we were hit with Nerf gun bullets.

I glanced over to see Jesse, Ross, and Aaron standing at the door.

"Oh, shit," Zach muttered.

"Protect me?"

Zach dove behind the couch. "You're on your own for this one."

"Traitor!"

"We'll go easy on you," Jesse said, with a teasing smile.

"I don't believe you."

He cocked back his Nerf gun. "Good instinct."

Home again.

I thought I'd be excited to be back home in my own bed, but dread settled in the pit of my stomach as my mom dropped my suitcase in my room. This was it. The Connor Jackson Live Tour was coming to an end. I wasn't ready to let it go.

"We should get to the arena before the show starts," Mom said.

The car was waiting outside.

"Richard!" I called out, as he stepped out of the car.

He shook his head. "Injuries are not part of the plan, Ms. Jackson."

"I missed you, Richard."

"It hasn't been the same without you, Ms. Jackson."

I climbed into the backseat, Richard taking us around the back of the arena. It was close to show time, and the crew was gathering in the halls for one final send-off. I leaned against the wall, waiting for everyone to gather around.

"Before we go on, I have something to say," Connor said, once everyone was there. "It's been a privilege working with every single one of you, and I'm sincerely going to miss you guys once the tour ends."

Mackenzie's eyes were bright with tears as she absorbed Connor's words, one of his arms slung around her shoulders.

"It's been an honor working with you, man," Jesse said, with a nod. "We've learned a lot from you, and we've had one hell of a time."

"You're a great guy," Mackenzie added, with a small smile. "I'm lucky to have gotten to know you on a personal level. Even if it did take you nearly half the tour to come out of your shell."

"I'm really going to miss you guys on my next tour," Connor said. "I would've loved to experience Europe with you guys." Connor's European tour was set to take off early next year. And while I'd actually ended up enjoying the Connor Jackson Live Tour, I wouldn't be joining him on the next one. My mom was going to stay home with me so that I could continue playing soccer, whether that was with the U.S. Women's National Team or not.

"Hey, man," Zach said, "we wouldn't be on tour without you. So we owe it all to you." Skyline cheered to that.

"You also wouldn't be dating my sister without this tour," Connor added, his eyes sparkling. Jesse, Ross, and Aaron all laughed while Zach and I blushed.

"All in all it's been a great ride," Connor finished. "So let's go out there tonight and finish this thing."

Everyone cheered to that, and then Mackenzie was called to stage to start the last show of the Connor Jackson Live Tour. It was a bittersweet moment. Skyline and Connor headed back to their dressing rooms and I went out to the audience to watch the show for the very last time from the front row. Jenica was already in her seat and wrapped me up in a tight hug as I joined her.

"Never ghost me again," she ordered.

"I'm sorry. I promise."

Mackenzie's set went flawlessly, and I knew she'd do great on her solo tour. She hadn't announced the tour dates yet, but she was bound to sell out. The usual thirty minutes between sets passed, but Skyline didn't appear on stage. I checked my phone, but there were no delay warnings from anyone backstage. Thirty-five minutes passed, and then I started to worry. What if something had gone wrong? Then a single spotlight hit the stage, illuminating Ross on the drums. The crowd went wild. The next spotlight illuminated Aaron, but the cheers weren't quite as loud. I cheered a little louder to help even out the volume. The third spotlight hit Jesse, and the volume shook the arena. Jesse smirked. The final spotlight came on, illuminating Zach. The volume was deafening, louder than any of the other cheers, including those for Jesse.

"My name is Zach, and we are Skyline."

I liked the new introduction, even if it was only for one night.

For the first time on the entire tour, their set went off without a hitch. It felt wrong almost, but the beaming smile on Zach's face at the end was contagious.

"Thank you for having us," Aaron said, with a wave. "My name is Aaron, and we are Skyline."

"You're one lucky girl, Katelyn Jackson," Jenica said. "I would die for a boyfriend that cute." She spent the next half hour, during the transition between Skyline and Connor, gushing about how cute Zach was.

Connor's set was flawless, and then there came a surprise. After "Possibilities," as Connor went to do his usual chat session with the audience, Skyline came out onto the stage. The audience went nuts.

"Hello," Jesse said.

Connor busted out laughing, as did the rest of the audience.

"Hello," Connor said, once he regained his composure.

"We have a present for you," Jesse informed him.

"Is that so?" Connor asked, amused.

Mackenzie came onto the stage, carrying a cake.

"Can we get Katelyn on stage, please?" Zach asked.

A chorus of *aw*'s came from the crowd, and I felt my face flush red as two of the security guards helped pull me out of the front row and onto the stage, crutches and all.

"These two people are awesome," Ross informed the audience. "And we'd like to take this moment to appreciate everything that Connor and Katelyn Jackson have done for us."

Tears built in the back of my eyes as Zach put an arm around me, kissing me on the cheek.

That caused quite the reaction from the crowd.

"We baked you a cake," Mackenzie said. "And there are two stools for you to sit in while we serenade you."

Connor laughed, taking the cake from Mackenzie. Zach guided me to my seat, taking my crutches as I took a seat.

Cue the crowd reaction.

"We also wrote you a song," Jesse said. "Titled 'The End.'"

Stagehands came out and delivered microphones to Mackenzie and the members of Skyline. I exchanged glances with Connor, who was just as surprised.

The song recounted our experiences on tour, starting with the first full-show rehearsal all the way up to last night's show. As someone who hadn't been much of a crier before these past few weeks, the floodgates opened as I realized that this was it.

This was truly The End.

As the song finished, Connor thanked everyone. I locked eyes with Zach, and even though every part of me was against public displays of affection, I pulled him close to me and gave him a big kiss to thank him for the song.

It was perfect.

The tour wrap-up party started almost directly after the show.

Everyone was going to meet up at the hotel the crew was staying in, as not everyone was from the Los Angeles area. Connor had rented out the meeting room, and the room had been decorated to celebrate the end of the summer.

To celebrate the end of the tour.

Jenica and I went back to my house to get ready. As someone who wasn't really a dress person, I'd had a difficult time finding another dress to wear. Luckily, Jenica had thought ahead, bringing me one of her favorites.

The dress was white and strapless. The top was rhinestoned in gold, and it was tight throughout the hips, and then flared out.

Jenica did my hair and makeup and then I slipped the dress on. My knee brace sort of ruined the aesthetic, but she assured me that it was still perfect. She handed me a pair of gold sandals. "To complete the look."

I stared at myself in the mirror and did a slow twirl.

"You are going to be the talk of the century," Jenica said. "Crutches and all."

"Your turn," I said, tearing my eyes away from my reflection and flashing her a smile. "We are going to rock this party."

Jenica's dress was short and black. It had three-quarter length, lace sleeves. It was simple yet elegant. She paired it with a pair of black, chunky heels.

Once she was satisfied, Richard took us to the hotel.

The party was already in full swing by the time we got there, Zach almost immediately finding me. He was wearing a polo shirt and pair of khakis, simple yet still adorable.

Eventually Jenica left me for a guy she met, which I knew would happen. She was incredibly sociable, and she loved meeting people, especially cute guys.

"You look beautiful tonight," Zach said, his eyes boring into mine. "In case I haven't told you already."

"Thanks," I said, with a blush.

I gave him a kiss.

"Jesse is making an announcement," Zach said. "I'd better go before he kills me."

I raised an eyebrow in question as he made his way over to his brothers.

"Can I have your attention?" Jesse asked.

The room quieted, everyone's attention landing on the boys.

"Is this *the* announcement?" Connor asked.

Jesse nodded, and a smile spread across Connor's face.

"As you guys know, we're headlining our own tour in the fall," Jesse said. "But what you guys don't know is that yesterday we officially signed to Lightshine Records."

My jaw dropped. That was the record label Connor was signed to.

Zach flashed me a smile.

"And in two weeks' time, we'll be moving out to L.A."

Moving to L.A.?

"Surprise," Zach said to me.

I pulled him in for another kiss, my heart soaring. "I can't believe it."

"Hopefully you didn't think this was just a summer fling," Zach said, with a slight laugh. "Because I plan on sticking around for a while."

"Aren't you glad I made you come along now?" Connor teased, as he came over to congratulate Zach.

I looked around the room.

There was Mackenzie, the surprisingly good friend. Someone whom I'd misjudged at the start, but who turned out to be a genuinely good person.

There was Ross, the goofball. He was the funniest of his brothers, and I'd come to learn that he was also the sweetest.

There was Aaron, the mysterious one. He didn't talk much, but once you put him with Ross, they were quite the troublemakers.

And Jesse, the badass with a soft side for Zach. He'd become a good friend over the tour.

And then, of course, there was Zach. My shy, sweet, talented, lovable boyfriend. My best friend—aside from Jenica, of course.

Zach tilted my head, his eyes staring into mine as he tried to figure out what I was thinking.

"Yes," I said, without breaking eye contact.

"Yes?" Zach asked, with a smile.

"I'm glad I tagged along for the ride."

THE END

ACKNOWLEDGMENTS

I cannot believe this journey has come to an end. Writing my debut novel was a roller coaster filled with many sleepless nights, emotional breakdowns, but most importantly, many happy tears. I am so happy to share Katelyn Jackson's story with the world, and I hope you all love her just as much as I do.

A massive thank you to I-Yana Tucker for being an amazing talent manager. Thank you for helping me through my editing woes, for listening to me when I really thought I wasn't going to come through to the other side, and for always being available to chat.

And a shout-out to the entire Wattpad Books team for believing in me, for taking a chance on me and my story. Thank you to my editing team, Deanna McFadden and Jen Hale. Thank you to Deanna for taking my monster, unedited novel from Wattpad and helping me turn it into something that I'm proud of. And thank you to Jen for polishing the story and helping me put the finishing touches on it.

Thank you to my parents, who are amazing in every way. You guys have always supported me in everything I've done, and your support for my writing has meant the world to me. Thank you to my dad for telling every single person he knows that his daughter is an author, way before I was ever published. And thank you to my mom for acting as my agent, reading contracts with me, and calling every news outlet to run my story.

Thank you to my brother, who carries my business cards around in his wallet and actively asks me to restock him. You've always roped everyone you know into supporting my writing, whether it was your football team for a Twitter campaign or your boss who refers to you as "Rachel's brother." I couldn't ask for a better partner in crime.

Thank you to my nana, who has encouraged me to read since I was three. You fed my book appetite all throughout my childhood and have always encouraged me to follow my dreams. My biggest cheerleader, my best friend, my confidant.

Thank you to my grandma, who gave me my very first laptop. It wasn't equipped with Wi-Fi, and I only used the laptop to write stories. While those stories will never see the light of day, you've read every single story I've ever posted online and even created a Wattpad account to support me. I'm so lucky to have you.

Thank you to my papa for sparking my creativity as a young child. One of the stories in this novel was inspired by you, as you used to tell us stories of Francisco the Flying Elephant, who somehow only you could see. You laughed at my stories every time I "missed the bus," always there to pick me up.

Thank you to Kendall Picone (@kendallpicone on Instagram) for letting me interview her about living with epilepsy. I wanted to keep Zach's experience authentic and real, and Kendall took the time to answer every question I had and to give feedback.

Thank you to my cousin, Toni. My best friend. You kept me sane when I was spiraling; you're the voice of reason in every situation I blew out of proportion. Without you, *Drama Llama* wouldn't exist. I couldn't do this life without you.

Thank you to Ali Novak and Jordan Lynde, who helped push me through periods of writer's block. Thank you for reading my scenes, for pushing me to be the best writer I can be. Thank you to Ali for letting me vent for hours at a time via phone. And thank you to Jordan for responding to my text spams when I didn't think I could finish.

Thank you to my Cohena family. You girls always know how to make me laugh, how to pick me up, and how to shower me with love. And how to make me stay focused, even when I tried hard to procrastinate.

Thank you to Amy for sitting with me on FaceTime while I plotted out every single tour stop in this book. My late-night editing Snapchats, my spam texts about what's "trendy." You always know how to make me laugh when I'm on the verge of losing my mind.

Thank you to Victoria for your never-ending support and love. Your encouraging text messages, your thoughtful gifts. You've quickly become my best friend.

Thank you to my aunts, uncles, and cousins, who have read my stories on Wattpad, shared my news stories, and sent me words of encouragement and love. I was deep in edits during the holidays this past year, and your support helped get me through the overhaul.

And most importantly, thank you to my Wattpad readers, who knew Zach and Katelyn before anyone else. Thank you for believing in my characters, for giving me a platform. I am forever grateful for the little orange website that changed my life.

ABOUT THE AUTHOR

Rachel Meinke was born and raised in the Sunshine State. She started writing at the ripe young age of thirteen years old and started posting her early stories on Wattpad at fifteen. Since posting on Wattpad, Rachel has accumulated over 240,000 followers and over 300 million reads. *Along for the Ride* is her first novel. When Rachel isn't writing, you can find her jaunting around Disney, watching endless Marvel movies, or eating excessive amounts of Chick-fil-A. You can also find her posting on Twitter about her Broadway soundtrack obsession of the month, sharing photos of her family adventures on Instagram, and talking about books on YouTube. Find her everywhere @knightsrachel.

Want more? Why not try . . .

JESSICA CUNSOLO

She's With Me

Can Amelia hide her dark past from bad boy Aiden?

Want more? Why not try . . .

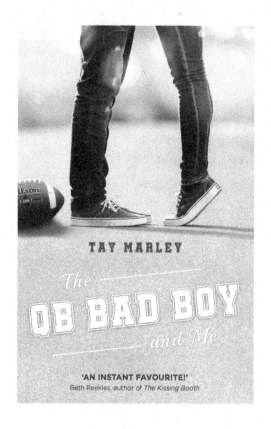

Sparks fly between star cheerleader
Dallas and bad boy Drayton. As opposites
attract, is their love destined for disaster?

Want more? Why not try . . .

From the outside, Everest has it all, but there's only one girl who can see him for who he truly is

Want more? Why not try . . .

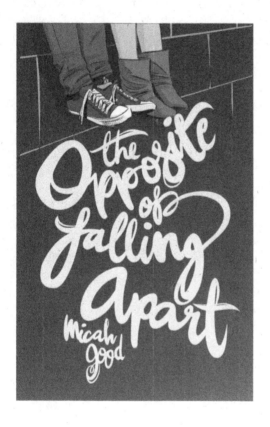

Can Jonas and Brennan help each other
to stop living in the past and start
dreaming about the future?

Want more? Why not try . . .

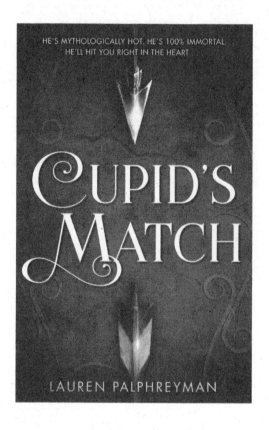

Cupid isn't a myth – he's Lila Black's perfect match.
As arrows fly and feelings become stronger, can Cupid
and Lila resist each other's magnetic pull?

Want more? Why not try . . .

Sometimes the last thing you're looking
for is. the one thing you need the most . . .

wattpad

Where stories live.

Discover millions of stories created by diverse writers from around the globe.

Download the app or visit www.wattpad.com today.

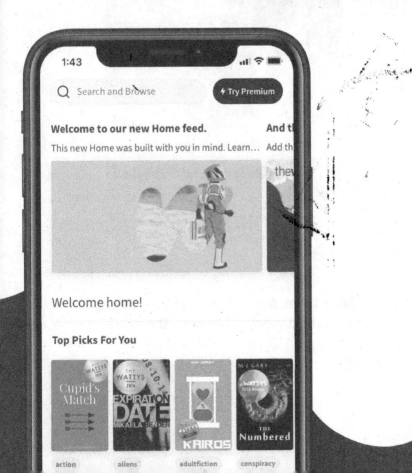